Bradd Chambers

UNDERCONSTRUCTION

Bradd Chambers

Bradd Chambers

Other publications from Bradd Chambers:

'Someone Else's Life'
Released June 2017
Available now on Amazon

'Our Jilly'
Released November 2017
Available now on Amazon

'In Too Deep'
Released February 2019
Available now on Amazon

'Daddy's Little Girl'
Released January 2020
Available now on Amazon

Bradd Chambers

Readers are loving books by Bradd Chambers.

Praise for *'Someone Else's Life:'*

" With this dark, gritty debut, Bradd Chambers marks himself out as one to watch in crime writing."
Brian McGilloway.

'Enthralling,' *'Awesome'* and *'Would make a great movie.'* *'A book for every thriller novel lover.'*
MCXV Reviewer.

"A great first novel by Bradd Chambers, very well written with an enticing storyline and I was shocked when I found out the killer. Was certainly kept guessing until the end. Excellent read."
5* Reviewer.

'Fantastic debut. Excellent plot with believable characters. Look forward to more from this author as I literally couldn't put this one down.'
5* Reviewer

Bradd Chambers

Praise for *'Our Jilly:'*

"Brilliant book. I was hooked from the first page, truly would be a fantastic gift for the Sherlock in your life."
5* Reviewer.

" This is the second book I have read by this author and was not disappointed! Could not put the book down and read it all in a day, [I'm] looking forward to reading more from this author and would 100% recommend this book to anyone looking for [a] great read!"
5* Reviewer.

"Another 5-star book from this stand-alone author, and again I would highly recommend. As a fan of murder mystery, I still thoroughly enjoyed this book despite the reveal of the murderer from the offset. You will turn each page craving justice for Jilly wondering will the murderer get away with it!"
5* Reviewer.

Bradd Chambers

Praise for *'In Too Deep:'*

"This is the first book I've read by Bradd but won't be the last. It was well written with solid believable characters. It tackles issues such as suicide and mental health issues in a very real way. I read this book in just one sitting as I was enthralled with the main characters and couldn't put it down. I would thoroughly recommend this book to everyone."
Goodreads Reviewer.

"Thoroughly enjoyed this book. I was gripped from the first chapter and just could not put it down. The plot was clever and every twist had me hooked. The book has a large focus on mental health and suicide, particularly in Londonderry, with the main character running a charity and running campaigns to help raise money and awareness to help [the] prevent[ion] of suicide. Massive praise for Bradd for writing about such a difficult subject and for helping to raise awareness himself. Please read this book! Highly recommended."
Goodreads Reviewer.

Bradd Chambers

Praise for *'Daddy's Little Girl.'*

"Very well written characters and the story definitely gave me the creeps more than once."
Goodreads Reviewer.

"A solid police work with deeply flawed characters, it's a fast-paced plot that builds to a tension filled chilling climax."
Amazon Reviewer.

"If you like your mysteries creepy and dark, this might interest you. I wasn't sure whether to love the writing or hate the cruelty. Highly recommend it."
5* Reviewer.

"A chilling read, covering loss in many forms and how it affects people's perceptions and behaviour. A breath-taking psychological read."
Amazon Reviewer.

Bradd Chambers

For my wee goddaughter,
Miyah.

Bradd Chambers

Prologue:

Pulling my handbrake up, I let out a deep sigh. Thankful for the downpour as the chances of running into someone will be slim, but aware that visibility will be even harder now. I should've come an hour ago, when it was dry, instead of driving about half the Waterside in procrastination. How was I to know what time would be the perfect time? The time with less, or better yet no, onlookers. Not that they'd be looking at me... Too consumed by their own grief. But I need to keep a low profile.

I watch the rain batter the windows and lazily flick the wipers on. The smooth left to right motion followed by the soft squeak makes my eye twitch irritably. Surrounded by grass, flower displays and erected headstones displaying eternal short descriptions of the remains buried there. A relic to the person who once lived and breathed. I wonder if half of them even deserve to be remembered.

Where do I even begin? I've never even been here before... It's huge. I guess I should be thankful that I've not had to go to Derry City Cemetery, the one over in the Cityside and the biggest in the town. I'd need a map to find my way out of there. I've never gone near it, never had to, but memories of staring, mesmerised at its grandeur from the backseat of my parents' car whilst they migrated around the tiny roundabout at the Top of the Hill creep back into my memory.

Why couldn't he be buried in the one beside the Glendermott Presbyterian Church? That can't have more than a dozen rows. Last time I was there, for a wedding five or six years ago, there were talks of extending it. I guess he'd never been a church goer, and what he publicly said about religion in his later years probably cemented those cemetery gates shut for him. His remains would've crawled out of the hole six foot under and lay to rot in a surrounding field of cow shit instead anyway. He'd have preferred that. Better off here... But where?

Bringing out my phone and blowing out apprehensively, I click on the Google app. 'How do you find someone's grave?' I search. Worth a try, right? A few websites come up boasting and advertising about how they're the best at chasing your ancestry before I click on one that looks legit. I enter his name and search Londonderry. *'No results found.'* Fuck. After a few more frustrated attempts, I pocket my phone once more. Maybe they don't have it on the internet in case someone would defile it? Lifting my hood up, I step out into the cool air, the rain now reduced to a light drizzle, but one that will leave you soaked right through. I best be quick.

Turning a full circle, I question where's best to start. Spotting a white within all the black gravestones, I decide that is as good a place as any. As I get closer, I see the elements have made it more of a creamy colour and struggle to see the writing through the bird shit. This Ernest McBride has been dead for over thirty years. Looking from left to right, I decide to follow the incline up as the stones look a bit newer here. I meander down a random row and see that I must be on the right track, these ones are all from the late 2000s. Pushing my face deeper into my coat, the zip rubs aggressively against my chin. Looking at my new shoes going darker with the damp; I take five long strides before trying the next row on my left. 2013, much better.

I continue my journey before I halt suddenly. Two lights make their way towards me in the form of a Subaru. Shit. I face the ground once more and take the next row on my left. I count to six and turn with my back to the car, pretending to be observing a small charcoal grave. This little girl didn't even make it past her fourth birthday. How sad. The sodden teddy bear battles with the wind as it presses its right side against the stone, threatening to fall over. I'm just about finished half reading the short bible verse engraved at the bottom when, out of the corner of my eye, I see the car creep past, but the driver's attention is straight in front. When they reach the T-junction at the bottom of the hill, they indicate left and crawl past my car. It's a tight enough squeeze. They're almost at the end of that road too, before they unexpectedly park up. I don't recognise the car or number plate, and from over there I'd be hard to distinguish anyway. I continue down the path and keep my back to them.

Now I'm at the very edge of the cemetery, with five or six rows left. I must be getting close. I'll snake my way through each row with a customary glance at each name before – Oh, poor Stevie. My old driving instructor. I didn't know he'd passed. Two years ago, awk bless him. A memory of him parking up outside my house and lighting a fag whilst demanding for me to book my theory test through his clenched teeth pops up. He was a lovely man. I pay my respects to him before continuing, my neck getting sore from checking every grave from left to right. Two rows later, he presents himself. I gaze around me at the car, but the driver is nowhere to be found. Probably perched in front of a gravestone yards away. Minding their own business. Turning back to his grave, I read the short paragraph with distain.

'Aaron Parker,
Devoted daddy and loving husband.
Taken too soon.
Sleep well Papa Bear.
Your dream will be a reality one day.'

I sneer, upturn my nose and trod off in the direction of my car. Realising I felt more for my driving instructor than I did for him. What a waste of time. The hollowness in my chest hasn't dispersed like the counsellor said it might. If anything, I feel more... Empty? As I reach my car, the back of the other visitor's head pops up from behind rows of gravestones. I panic, rushing the last few steps and pull the door handle, cursing when I realise it's locked. Scrambling around my coat for the keys, keeping my back to the driver, I drop myself into the seat and push the car into gear even before the key is twisted.

Whizzing back up the hill towards the entrance, I don't even bother to give the row his remnants rest in a second glance as I turn the wipers back on as the rain worsens and comes down in sheets.

Chapter One:

2019

———

"Ma, will you tell her to keep to her side the wee bitch?"

Nuala glances into the rear-view mirror just in time to catch Michelle sticking her thumbs in her ears, the other four fingers of each hand wagging and her tongue stuck out to annoy her sister.

"Michelle!"

Seeing she's being glared at, she returns her hands to beneath each armpit and pouts, turning her attention to the window. Shaking her head at her immaturity, Nuala resumes her gaze to the road ahead. You'd never believe she's turning 17 next month. Ever the baby of the family, they'd all spoiled her for too long. Now she can get a job and will be learning to drive. Maybe that will give her the kick up the arse she needs? She'd calmed down a good bit after starting big school, but since leaving in June, and Danielle's return from uni for the summer, it's like they've been transported back ten years. With one massive missing piece, of course.

Just as he springs to mind, she checks to make sure no car is following her too close behind and rests a foot on the brakes, slowing the car down to just below 40 as they approach their old house. Her old house. The house she grew up in with Ma and Da and her brother, Kealen. Living on the busy Glenshane Road always irritated her mother, but she found the whoosh of cars flying past in both directions at all hours of the morning soothing as she rested her head to go to sleep. Better than counting sheep.

She narrows her eyes in disgust as she sees the exterior wall of what used to be their kitchen sporting an underground organisation's name and slogan. That wasn't there last week. An impressive bit of graffiti regardless. Wasted talent, she thinks, trying to put a positive spin on it as she spots a car approaching in her rear-view mirror and speeds up again.

"Ma, what's a fenian?" Michelle obviously had the same idea as her, observing the skeleton of their old home and the sectarian slur.

"Michelle!" Danielle gasps.

"Never you mind, and don't let me hear you saying that word again. Especially in sch... Tech," Nuala coughs.

"Why? Is it bad?"

"Oh, grow up, Michelle," Danielle rolls her eyes, resuming her attention to her phone.

"What?"

"Just leave it, Michelle," Nuala spits.

Michelle frowns, her mouth open in astonishment, before exhaling frustratedly and lagging her head back until it hits off the headrest.

Nuala and their father had done well to raise their children neutral. Something extremely hard to do, in Derry especially, what with the history and ongoing peace process. Of course, they knew of the different religions, but didn't feel any animosity towards either community. Living on the outskirts helped, and although it was against their father's wishes, they had gotten into catholic grammar schools. The city not having a diverse choice of mixed schools anyway, Nuala had heard bad things from her nieces and nephews who attended the few that were available, so decided the catholic grammars were the lesser of two evils.

Two members of separate religions themselves, having to have a civil ceremony in a hotel for their wedding, Nuala and their father didn't bring their children up under either practice. So, when they returned from those schools in the first few days, they were astounded to find they had to say prayers and sing hymns. Their father was a devout atheist and so informed them they didn't have to do anything they weren't comfortable with. Nuala's proud of the way their children were raised, unlike toddlers in some of the council estates and other areas of the city where the slurs were probably one of their first words, raised by ignorant and unyielding parents set in their ways.

Feeling at fault somehow for, what she hopes to be, Michelle's innocent question, she informs her youngest daughter that it's a hateful and derogatory term for a catholic.

"Are they talking about us? Sure, we aren't catholics and Da was fighting to change all the hate."

The girls' father was a politician who was breaking the mould. Bang in the centre of both wings, he took all views in his stride and was determined to overshadow the two opposing leading parties. One right-wing, the Ulster Jacks, more commonly and casually known as Jacks for short, their name derived from the Union Jack. The other left-wing party called Ardóimid, Irish for *'we will rise.'* Both with lasting reputations and rumours that couldn't be ignored, but both communities voting for them regardless to keep the opposing party from power. He campaigned for his independent party which took religion out of the equation. Young people were starting to vote for him, getting them interested in politics was the main problem. Of course, he had death threats from both sides and even a stone through the living room window one evening at the beginning of his political career, but it wouldn't stop him, despite Nuala and their children's protests.

Until, three years ago, he'd gone missing. With absolutely no trace as to where he went, and due to his growing popularity within the city, the search had been lengthy and costly, but to no avail. Nuala is convinced it was one of those same organisations he was trying so hard to keep in the past that took him out of their hair. Not liking that he was a threat to their party. Experience in covering their trail and keeping their nose, and hands, clean. The police too scared to investigate past the preliminaries when they were mentioned. The police in Northern Ireland have had bad reputations from way back in the height of the Troubles. Even today if there's some form of riot, they have to sit tight and take petrol bomb after petrol bomb whilst they shelter in their fire-resistant land rovers, unable to retaliate in case they're accused of police brutality.

That would open a brand-new can of worms. As will continuing to dig further into these organisation's actions to find out what happened to Nuala's poor husband. They never admitted it, but she knows that's why. The last thing they, and the country, need is another civil war on their hands.

They say the trouble is over, and it is to an extent, but there's still spats on both sides of the River Foyle, which splits the city down the middle. Episodes of violence across the city every now and then further highlights that these people are still at large and dangerous.

"I know, pet. But sure, it'll all be rubble in a few weeks anyway," Nuala purses her lips as a tractor pulls out onto the main road, making her stamp on the brakes and bringing her down from 60 to 30.

The irony isn't lost on Nuala as she becomes annoyed at potentially being stuck behind this arsehole in single lane traffic until she climbs the Glenshane Mountain in a dozen miles. The main road between Derry and Belfast, Northern Ireland's two biggest cities, has been a headache in the making for over a decade, and the reason they've had to move out of their house. A new dual carriageway is in the works, promising a faster commute, but to the loss of many people's homes and businesses on the Glenshane Road. They've known for years that they'd have to up and leave, but they sure as hell didn't go quietly. Aaron, her husband, fought and fought, trying every avenue and three or four solicitors, but after he went missing, Nuala could hold them off no longer. The fact that they wanted to stay in case Aaron showed up again and would know where to find them wasn't a justifiable argument in the government's eyes. So, Nuala had had to settle with a compensation of the price of the house if they were to sell, plus an extra third on top of that

But that wasn't enough. In her eyes, it was priceless. After all, it was Nuala's father's house, and his father's before that, who helped build it from scratch. Her mother offered it to her and her little family after her husband, Nuala's father, died, saying it was too big for her to fart around in on her own. Since Kealen showed no sign of moving back from Australia with his wains, it would've gone to waste.

Relieved to see the tractor veering left into an old country lane, Nuala pushes the car into fourth gear and gives it the welly as she crawls back to 60, just to be met with a 40 speed limit sign ahead, shortly followed with a men at work sign behind it. The sooner all this is done, the better, she thinks, growing agitated and checking the time on the clock on the dashboard. Even though there are talks it could take another few years.

They're on their way to Belfast City Airport to drop Danielle off for her second year at university, the bulging suitcase with half her wardrobe fit to burst in the passenger seat beside Nuala. Newcastle, she chose, despite Nuala's nagging that Coleraine was both closer and cheaper. What with only being less than an hour up the road and yet to be hit with the £9k student fees that the mainland adhered to.

Nuala just hopes she'll return after her studies, unlike Ritchie, her eldest son who had shipped off to Cardiff and got a job there even before his graduation. Now she's lucky if he's back at Christmas or an odd weekend during the year. They'd went to see him a few times, of course, but the Welsh accent gave her a migraine, she doesn't know how he can stick it. But after having a fortnight-long argument a few months back with Michelle about having to continue her education and not having her laze about the house watching Netflix all day every day come September, they finally settled on the North West Regional College, or the Tech as the young ones call it, in the city. It seems she has no plans to fly the nest just yet.

Spoilt rotten, Nuala thinks as she looks back at her, mirroring her sister with both their attentions engrossed on their phones. They hadn't had it easy, none of them had. Between Aaron's disappearance and the intense search for months afterwards. Then, finally having to admit defeat that he was dead and try to move on, whilst battling with the government to keep their home. Now, they rent a lovely house in Altnagelvin, unable to find a good enough one to buy just yet and not wanting to settle for one they'd grow to resent and regret. For the first time in a few years, life is good.

Chapter Two:

The boisterous cheers of the lads follow the smash of the glass as the barmaid reaches down to retrieve the broken pieces, beetroot faced. Even more embarrassed that she must bypass their table to get to the kitchen, where she receives a few more wolf whistles and misogynistic jeers. As the door through to the kitchen swings shut behind her, Chris turns his head back to the table of friends and pints. It's been a while since he's been out with the boys, work taking its toll on him. Wanting to spend the weekends getting overtime rather than enjoy himself. Too physically exhausted to even cook when he finally crawls through his front door, the Dominos app telling him his pizza is out for delivery, never mind get a shower and go out on the piss.

"Your round," Dave winks at him as he smacks his lips and slams his empty glass down on the table.

Rolling his eyes, Chris slugs from the table over to the bar, where the barman gives him a disgruntled look, obviously aware of how himself and his party treated his colleague.

"Give us five pints of Bud there, would ye hi?"

Nodding with pursed lips, he pulls a few shiny pint glasses out of the cupboard and lines them up in front of the tap. Chris can feel his brain swirling in his head as he steals another glance at the boys talking excitedly about the Liverpool match tomorrow night behind him. It *had* been too long. Sure he hadn't even seen Travis since the Christmas night out, where they all adorned slimy jumpers brandishing laddish slogans like *'tickle my xmas balls'* and *'if found return to pub.'* He had got a right slagging when he'd landed with a snowman with makeshift eyes that goggled about when he walked. The only one left in Primark in his size as it seemed the entire city had the same idea as him. That had been a good night, just like tonight has been. He needs to make time for them more often.

"24 quid lad."

Tapping his card off the contactless machine, he's just trying to engineer how he's going to lift all five pints at once when a girl leans over the bar beside him. Her blonde hair falls to just above her perky bum, which is fully on show in that short pink dress.

"Three double vodka and cokes and a blue WKD, please."

He knows that voice. Turning towards her, he's annoyed to see her looking the other way, hiding behind her hair. Intentional? Everything about her is familiar. Scanning her up and down as she brings a hand to her face, he nods towards her heart tattoo on her ankle, double chin on full show as he tries to place it.

"Steph?"

She looks back towards her table by the window, ignoring him, and he gazes around her. It has to be Steph. There's Abbie and Georgia and Katie down at that table, eyes on their phones and wielding them in each other's faces as they laugh along at some meme or video.

"Steph?" he tries again.

Jutting out her chin, she turns towards him, before widening her eyes in fake shock.

"Chris!" she elongates the 's' at the end of his name, going in for a hug that's more like a pat on the back, "didn't see you there. How's things?"

"Good, aye. Workin' away," he manages to just about supress his burp, "same shit, different day. What about ye?"

"Aye, we're all just out for a girls' night. Jimmy's got the wain for the night, so we're helping Georgia let her hair down for a change. She deserves it," she spins towards Georgia who's laughing away with a glass in her hand.

He stares at her gorgeous blonde locks and gets a whiff of her shampoo as she whips her head back towards him. He'd always admired her looks. But, oh, shit...

"What about you, who are you out with?"

He takes a step back to block her view, making a perfectly shaped eyebrow raise.

"Just some of the boys from back in the day, ye know? Dave... Travis... Jase..."

Her suspicions growing, she jolts a head over his shoulder before he can stop her and her brow creases. It doesn't help that Jimmy bursts into a cackle just at that time.

"So, what've ye been up to? Uni and all or wha?"

"What?" she resumes her attention to him, before apologising to the barman who has finished up with their drinks. Pulling out her purse, she hands over a few notes. "Aye, grand. Workloads a bit shite like, but sure what do I expect studying psychology?"

Chris snorts.

"Aye you're right, don't know how ye could be at that. I'd have fallen asleep in one of the classes."

"Lectures," she corrects him with a fake smile, "right, well get you back to *the lads,*" she air quotes, "I'm sure I'll see you again."

"Jesus what's taking ya so long, lad? Dyin' a drooth here."

Chris closes his eyes in embarrassment. He hopes that isn't Jimmy. He glances over his shoulder and is relieved to see that it's Jase.

"Awk, Jesus. Alright, Steph? Didn't see ye there, how ye keepin'?"

Chris leans back to let Jase step into the conversation, both physically and theoretically, whilst trying his best not to cringe. Jase always had an unreciprocated fancy towards Steph. Steph looks at him now and he can tell she's equally as disgusted with him now as she was back in their teen years.

"Grand, aye, Jason. And yourself?" she says while turning her back to him and lifting her drinks.

"The very best after seeing your sexy self," Jase laughs before frowning at her departure.

"Anyway, nice speaking to you, Chris."

"Er... Right, hi. Good luck."

He resumes his attention to Jase, who lifts three pints at a time, his dirty fingers splashing around in one of the glasses.

"That one's yours ye dirty bastard," he nods towards his blackened fingers from the garage as they make their way back over to the table, "and wait till ye see this drama."

"What drama?" Dave takes his pint from Chris's hands and gulps down a few mouthfuls, "you cheesin' with Steph again ya dirty heure, was her best friend not enough?"

Everyone laughs except Chris, his eyes fixed over towards the girls' table as they all link heads, before Georgia jerks her head around towards them with as much subtlety as a bull in a china shop.

"Jimmy, where's the wee man tonight?" Chris spits through gritted teeth.

Jimmy looks up from his pint and hiccups.

"My ma has him. Why?"

"Aw fuck, here we go boys," Travis squirms in his seat as they see Georgia marching towards them.

Jimmy, still with his back to the scene, is none the wiser until she looms over him, arms crossed. Looking up from her shadow, the blood drains from his once beaming face. Now, he looks like he's going to lose a few kneecaps.

"Alright, Geor-"

"Where the *hell* is William?"

"He's grand, he's with my ma. Calm do-"

"You barely ever spend time with your own son, Jimmy... And when you get a chance, you're out with all your friends getting steamin'?"

"Look, Georgie, I spent all evening with him."

"All evening?" she screeches, "I dropped him round after work about half 6, it's not even 11 yet, Jimmy?"

"Well, sure he's in his bed and all now anyway."

The boys around him inhale awkwardly. Bad move.

"So, you think it's okay to just come out drinking when he's in his bed? Jimmy, I look after our son every day, how often do you even try to see him? It's always me that has to ask you to fuckin' babysit your own son when I want a night to myself."

"Well, you still can have a night to yourself. We're only stoppin' here for one then we're heading down Waterloo Place and doin' a bar crawl."

"Whilst your ma is looking after my son. And you'll be hungover in the morning, so I take it you're not going to get up at 5am to watch cartoons with him?"

"With any luck I'll only be getting home by then," Jimmy laughs and lifts his drink to his lips, looking around at his friends expectedly with a wink.

No one laughs. No one smirks. No one even looks up from their laps.

"Nice one, Jimmy. Still the pathetic little boy you always were."

Georgia turns to leave but Jimmy grabs her wrist.

"Georgie, wait, will ya? Talk to me."

"No!" she spins back around as Jimmy stands, waving his hands at her in an attempt to calm her down, the other tables are looking. "What else is there to talk about, Jimmy? Nothing in your life has changed, has it? I got fat, had to push a baby with your massive fuckin' head out of me and now I look after him whilst tryin' to hold down a job. I couldn't go to uni in England or Scotland or whatever I had in front of me. And all for one stupid one-time fling with you, which I don't even fuckin' remember, shows how good you were."

Jimmy leads a hysteric Georgia out to the stairs for a slither of privacy, although her wails echo around the bar. At once, the other three girls have fished their drinks and migrated over.

"Squeeze up," Steph brings a chair over from a vacant surrounding table to beside Chris, "that was a bit of a shit show, wasn't it?"

The girls have clearly come over to divide the boys' attention from the ongoing argument that can still be heard petering through from the stairs.

"Aye, you're right," Chris laughs, "wouldn't wanna be Jimmy's balls at the minute."

The group decide to leave them to it and chat and laugh about old times. They had gone to different schools, but had met through mutual friends, house parties and nights out. They talk about the time Jase got so drunk he passed out and pissed himself on Abbie's sofa, everyone laughing along apart from the two in question. They discuss their other friends, who's riding who and who has gone where for uni or where they ended up working.

Out of their bigger friendship group, the only people to have stayed in Derry are the nine in this bar. Everyone else went to uni in Belfast or the mainland, Katie's twin Decky even moved to Australia when he decided chemical engineering just wasn't for him. Dave is just finishing a story about the time he caught Abbie getting down and dirty with his cousin Bobby when Chris recollects what night he's talking about.

"That's the first night I met Danielle," he mutters, more to himself than to the table.

Steph turns her head in his direction, but if anyone else heard him they haven't acknowledged it. As Dave bursts into laughter and points to Travis, about to delve into another embarrassing story, Steph whispers in his ear.

"Do you still think about her?"

Chris moves his mouth to the side, thinking how honest to be with his ex-girlfriend's best friend.

"Everyday."

Chapter Three:

2016

———

Squinting against the light shining through her window, Danielle yawns. She forgot to close her blinds when she got home last night. She doesn't remember a lot, but the curtains lying useless either side of her window tells her as much. She shifts around to get more comfortable and finds Chris lying beside her, topless and snoring. She has an urge to cuddle into him and try to drift back to sleep, but something stops her. A niggling feeling in her head. Did they have a fight? God knows they've been having plenty the past few months.

Deciding she won't be able to get back to sleep just yet, what with the morning light, and the fact she needs to pee, she exhales frustratedly before stepping out of the bed and thrusting the curtains over the window. The sliding noise makes Chris snort and stir, so Danielle pads out of the room and down the hall towards the bathroom before he wakes. Sitting on the toilet, she rests her elbows on her knees and her pounding head in her hands, urging flashbacks of last night to both go away as well as reveal themselves. Is she in the wrong? Even if she isn't, Chris sure as hell won't admit it. Stubborn ballbag.

She remembers something about Katie's living room. Bitching to Dave about how annoying Chris is, maybe? But, why would she go off into a rant like that? And to Chris's best mate of all people? Not that Dave is a certified gossip, but that's sure going to get back to Chris's ears. Did he do something? Something about... Oh, shit. What happened? She flushes the toilet and falls over to the sink, giving herself a look of disgust once she sees her dishevelled hair and smudged makeup from hours of crying, no doubt. Stepping out of the bathroom, she closes the door behind her and that's when the memory floods back.

She was standing in Katie's kitchen. They all were. Pinning shots of Cactus Jacks and playing beer pong. Jase's idea, as usual. Even if they're heading out to town, Jase will still land to pre-drinks with 20 red cups and a packet of ping-pong balls from the pound shop around the corner from his work. The boy is too obsessed with American teen programmes and parties. Does he not know that at any other house party in Derry, you bring a carryout and stand in the kitchen talking. Maybe boke on the backdoor step and ride someone in the host's little brother or sister's bed. Hope you remember your underwear to hide the evidence. But no, Jase always has to make it into a party like those in *Scream*.

Anyway, Chris had just scored a shot against Katie, who was fuming that she had to sink a cup of frothy warm beer. He had kissed Danielle on the head and muttered something about having to piss, she had barely made out a word he said over the new Rihanna song blasting over the cheap speakers Jimmy had brought. She stared after him as Steph shouted *'tune'* and grabbed her wrist, dragging her up onto the worktop to dance along with her.

Several songs later, and to derail herself from Steph and Travis's looming argument about who changed what song over, she hopped down from the counter and skirted past the beer pong table and into the hall. As she reached the stairs, she looked up to see a queue of five or six people resting themselves against the walls of the ascending steps, threatening to knock off Katie's parents' wedding canvas. Where was he? She tried the living room door, but it wouldn't budge. Panic rising within her, she had thrust all her weight against it again to fall through embarrassingly. Inside, she found the widescreen TV turned on to the MTV channel, a few discarded glasses, and Georgia and Jimmy both slumped against the window.

"Alright, Danni?"

"Oh... Er... Sorry," Danielle eyeballed Georgia in shock before stepping back and closing the door.

She shakes her head now, looking out of her window at the top of her stairs where she can see the Glenshane Road and the rush of traffic perfectly. What the hell was Georgia thinking? Snogging Jimmy... That was a recipe for disaster. But it was what happened after that had been the problem. She had trodden back through the house to the kitchen to a jeer from the lads, and the back of Chris's head hugging Dave as Katie gave them the fingers before plucking a ball out of another cup and lifting it to her lips.

Annoyed, Danielle trotted over to the corner and filled up her own cup. Standing with her back to the sink, she pretended to be engrossed in a discussion Shauna and Emer were having about their looming history exam. She doesn't even study history. It took several moments before Chris rocked up, hooking a hand around her waist.

"Could ye give us out my fags, D? They're in your purse, aren't they?"

She ignored him, laughing along with Shauna and Emer slagging off Mrs Wilson.

"D? Danielle?"

That's when she turned towards him as if in slow motion, her lips pursed.

"My fags?"

"Aw, so you pay attention to me now you want your fags?"

"What're ye chattin' about?"

"Where did you go there now?" she smirked at him, turning her back on the twins to exclude them from the conversation. She didn't want anyone else knowing if she expected the worst.

"I told ye. I was goin' for a pish."

"Well, when I looked up the stairs you weren't there."

"What? Ye have x-ray eyes now that can see through doors or wha?" he laughed.

"Stop being ridiculous, Chris."

"Then what're ye on about?"

"There was a big queue, and you weren't a part of it."

"Well, I was clearly in the toilet then, wasn't I? Jesus, ye saw the queue."

"And who were you in there with?"

Chris looked beside himself. Blinking rapidly and stuttering over his words.

"Can't answer that, can you?"

"What the fuck is wrong with ye? What d'ye mean *'who was I in there with?'* Are ye havin' a laugh?"

"Well it took you long enough to piss, Chris."

"Aye, 'cause the queue was fuckin' massive. And then I came down here and ye weren't here, so I joined in on beer pong again. Is that a fuckin' crime or what?"

"Stop making a scene," she hissed at him as several people around them stopped talking and turned their head in their direction.

"Naw, I'm not makin' a scene," he glared at the people staring, who returned their heads to their drinks, "it's you who is makin' a scene, c'mere."

He grabbed her wrist and wrenched her forward with him, towards the utility room at the back of the house. Danielle looks down at her wrist now, in the cold light of day. There's no mark, but she can still feel the burn of her skin under his fingers.

"Get off me," she had screamed, pulling away from him with such force she had fallen to the side, knocking Laura's drink over them both as she banged against her.

But Chris wouldn't stop. Apologising to Laura, he had pushed her through and closed the utility room door.

"What the fuck is wrong with ye?"

"You attacked me."

"I *attacked* ye?"

They had both looked down at her wrist, falling limply within her other hand.

"Grow the fuck up, Danielle. I was away for a piss, and then I came back and ye were gone. Nothin' fuckin' happened. With anyone. You saw the queue for the toilet. Why do ye always have to make somethin' outta nothin'? And stop actin' like a fuckin' victim now, goin' on like that. Wise up, will ye? Sayin' things like that... You're an attention seeker."

And with that, he opened the utility room door, the sound of the party in full swing greeting him, before slamming it behind him, leaving her in silence with her own tears for company.

The rest of the night was a blur. She went back in after being consoled by Katie and Steph, who threw Chris aggressive stares as they brought her back in and refilled her drink. She was completely plastered, boking down Katie's toilet and having bits plucked out of her hair by Steph as they danced on the tables to Drake's *One Dance*. She just about remembers being hauled into a taxi. In fact, that's one of the last things she *does* remember. But why did Chris end up back here if they'd had such a bad falling out? Deciding to leave him to his hungover state, waking him would only lead to another argument, she trots down the stairs to find her mother sitting at the kitchen table, a cup of coffee in one hand and the other pressed over her face in worry.

"Ma... You okay?"

She slides her hand down her face and gazes over at Danielle with tears in her eyes.

"It's your da... He never came home last night."

Chapter Four:

2019

———

"Hurry up now, will ye? I'm dyin' to get home."

Sighing aggressively, it takes all of Seamus's willpower not to tell Trev where he can stick his home. He's been on this plot of land since 5am this morning and it's pushing dinnertime now. His stomach, and mood, still not settled from the shock of seeing the KFC down the road converted into some sort of gospel hall. He'd had to get a sandwich at the garage instead, and of course it had bastardin' mayo in it. This, along with the demands of Trev, who has done nothing but stand by the road with a hard hat on, barking orders from behind the huge sheet of paper in both hands, hasn't helped his anger issues. The only way it could get worse is if it were raining.

He must keep his temper though. This is the first proper job he's had in months. Finally able to bring a bit of bacon home for Sally and the wains. It was rough going there for a while. What with being on the dole and the embarrassment of going in to sign on every Tuesday. Nodding to people he would know to see. The same disgruntled face of the woman he always seemed to get landed with when he pledged that yes, he was, in fact, actively looking for work. Her raised brow and pursed lips as she handed him over his envelope with a curt nod that was the unspoken sign for: *'I'll see you again next week.'*

After doing a paint job for Mrs McGlinchey down the street, he heard, or rather eavesdropped through the open window, from her son, Greg, who had popped in for his lunch, that the council were looking for other workmen to help with the development of the new road between Belfast and Derry. When the son had stepped out again to go back to work, he nearly walked straight into Seamus on the doorstep, who begged for him to put in a good word for him with his boss, Trev. Now, it's two months later and it seems like they're no closer to finishing this road. And the winter months are coming. With the wind and rain and sleet and snow, his temper will worsen, surely. He's even been checking the job search websites when perched in the portaloo on his breaks.

He's just after knocking down the fourth wall of the lonely garage out the back of the, now demolished, house when he sees Greg waving his arms at him from his rear-view mirror. What the hell does he want? Pulling up the handbrake, he sticks a head out of the door and scrunches up his eyes at him, but he still can't hear what he's shouting about or see what he's pointing at. Growling and hopping out of the vehicle, he trudges through the muck and wreckage he's just recently created and comes to within spitting distance of Greg.

"Wha?"

Greg's face is sheet white, and before he can continue, he doubles over and vomits. Exhaling in disgust, Seamus turns to head back, intent on finishing off clearing the mess so he can go home before Greg splutters after him again.

"You on the pish last night, or wha?"

"A body," Greg spits chunks of Christ knows what out of his mouth as a layer of vomit or drool slides down his chin and onto his hi-vis, "I found a body."

"Awk... Your arse," Seamus stutters unconfidently, "where are you lookin'?"

Pointing over towards the rubble he had been clearing in a neighbouring dozer, Greg looks up to

Trev's booming voice, demanding to know why all work had stopped on this side of the plan. Walking cautiously towards the wreckage Seamus himself had tumbled not ten minutes ago, he glances about through the bricks and grass to see what Greg could conceive to be a body.

And that's when he sees them. Four long skeletal-like fingers leaking out from a filthy navy suit jacket. Creeping over, he kicks a few more bits of ruins away before gasping, his hand flying to his mouth too late as the disgusting sandwich he had barely managed earlier escapes from his throat. Turning away, he empties his stomach at the side of the scene. When there is nothing else left to come up, he wipes his chin and glares over again. A black leather shoe sticks out behind some plasterboard, with the suit trousers still managing to hide the majority of themselves beneath the debris. A, once crisp, white shirt darkened by the dirt follows, with a smudged red tie leading up to a skull with blackened teeth smiling up at him, the skin so translucent it looks like a light breeze would blow it off. It has to be fake, right? Some kind of Halloween prop the family forgot to take with them or throw out, kept in the garage every other month of the year... But something deep in Seamus's twisting gut tells him that it isn't. That it's real.

"What the-"

Swaying beside him is a sickly pale Trev, his eyes bulging at the site.

"You know whose house this was, don't you?" Greg stands behind them, out of sight but his words still strike them as they all stare at the skeleton, almost laughable and cartoonish dressed in a smart man's suit. "This was that politician who went missing's house. His body was never found... That's him... That's fuckin' him."

Chapter Five:

Drumming his hands on the steering wheel impatiently, DI McNally still can't get over the security standards and procedures adhered to by the Police Service of Northern Ireland, or the PSNI for short, he needs to get used to saying that again. Massive stone walls with fireproof metal gates shelter the police from the people of the city who they ultimately put their lives at risk to protect. The irony and obscenity of it all still tickles him, as the large gates open to let him sneak through, Chloe giving him a courteous nod as he passes her booth.

Parking up the station's car, he grabs his phone and his keys from the glove department and slams the door shut, making his way up towards the main building stretched in front of him. Strand Road Police Station isn't the biggest station he's ever worked for, but it sure as hell beats the dive he worked at in Rong Valley. Still, he shouldn't be ungrateful. If it hadn't been for the Yates case that rocked the sleepy town a number of years ago, he might not have made it as far as DI.

He'd been promoted to sergeant in Peterborough after a few gruelling years chasing drug lords as a DC, but made the move down to Rong Valley when they offered him better money. That was the only good thing about the job. Apart from working with his, then, superior, DI Dawson, of course, who taught him everything he knows. He needs to remember to send him a text, actually. Living it up with his wife, Helen, in Spain. Not even buying a place, which, with his police pension, they could definitely afford comfortably. Opting, instead, to rent Airbnbs across the country and moving from city to town to city. Last he spoke to him, must've been two weeks ago now, when his old DI had texted him good luck before his first day in Derry, he was in Marbella with plans to visit Gibraltar the very next day.

Nodding politely towards the lady on reception whose name he always forgets, he goes through and climbs the stairs to the incident room before crossing to his office. Smiling smugly at his newly carved plaque on the door before he closes it behind him, he's intent on fishing out his things and leaving for the day. He'd only been a DI for two years, but when the chance of transferring to his homeland for the first time since he left for university presented itself; he would've been a fool to turn it down, especially with his parents' deteriorating health.

Originally from Portrush, a small seaside resort town on the north coast, Derry is less than an hour drive from his family home, and he promised his sister, Lindsay, that he would help pull his weight with the care of their parents after being out of the country for longer than two decades. Not only that, but Northern Ireland is still thriving with crime and policework, unlike Rong Valley, where the two biggest stories were committed by the same family, albeit ten years apart.

"Sir?"

McNally looks up from his desk, where he was just putting the finishing touches to paperwork, to find DS Ferguson's head peering through the gap in the door.

"Come in, Ferguson."

Closing the door after him, Ferguson crosses to his desk.

"This doesn't look promising," McNally nods to the bulging file in Ferguson's arms, where sheets stick out at all angles.

Thoughts of an early night in front of the TV and a few glasses of wine are out the window.

"It isn't, I'm afraid, sir."

Placing the file down on the relatively empty desk, DS Ferguson blows out whilst flicking his overgrown fringe out of his face.

"Builders working on the dual carriageway on the Glenshane Road have called in a body found on one of their sites."

McNally's eyes expand in surprise.

"I'm listening..."

"SOCOs are still at the scene, but statements have been accounted for and the body has been removed. Currently with the pathologists, but judging by where the body was found and the length of time since death... I'd bet my mortgage that the body is that of Aaron Parker, leader and founder of the Everyone Unite Party."

He taps the file in front of them both. McNally nods his head, not needing to initially look down or inspect the file. Although in England three years ago when Parker went missing, he followed the story religiously. The misper case shocked Northern Ireland as Parker was making waves with his dominance in politics for the Foyle constituency. Foul play was suspected, but couldn't be established. Members of both opposing parties and underground organisations were questioned thoroughly, but kept tight lipped. To this day, his disappearance was a mystery... Until now.

"Do we know cause of death?"

"Pathologists believe it to be a head injury. Hard to establish now after all these years and the fact that he was dug out of a building site. His body being there for so long left him vulnerable to the elements and wildlife. They said they'd fast track it through, though."

"Grand, well... Let's scope it out, and then it looks like we've a family to speak to. Would you like to join me?"

Chapter Six:

"Michelle! Your dinner's getting cold," Nuala screeches, the vein in her head fit to burst. "I'm not calling you again, if you're not down here in five seconds then I'm giving it to the dog."

"Alright, alright," Michelle appears at the top of the stairs, one earphone hanging limply across her chest, the other blasting the new Lewis Capaldi song in her ear, "keep your knags on. And Pepper died years ago, you can't keep using that threat."

Rolling her eyes, Nuala turns and retreats into the dining room, her recently vacated chicken hardening on her plate. She'd had to take up the cooking in the years before Aaron's disappearance as he wasn't in the house that often. She'd burnt toast before... Still does now if she's rushing around in the mornings. She'd got much better, but after her long day in work today, being used as a human coat rack for discarded and unwanted items by people leaving the changing rooms, she just wasn't fit to stand and slave over the hobs. She'd done well to ignore the niggling voice at the back of her head taunting her to just fetch a takeaway on the way home, and whooped when she'd wrestled out some sweet potato fries from the bottom of the freezer. Healthier than chips, right? It wouldn't do her, or Michelle, any good to keep scoffing fatty food. They'd both gone up a few dress sizes since Aaron's disappearance.

Michelle slugs through to join her, but before she goes to sit down opposite her, she suddenly stands bolt upright, even taking her eyes from her phone, which is Nuala's initial inclination that something's wrong.

"Who's that?"

She's gazing in front of her, through the window. Twisting around, Nuala sees two men making their way down her drive towards the front door. Both smartly dressed, one in his early to mid-forties, the other a few years older. Both with grave expressions on their faces. Someone from the council, perhaps? Coming to tell her that they made a mistake and they can all move back into the house again? Ridiculous, she knows, but she can only dream. The doorbell goes and she waits the mandatory three seconds before getting up, the wooden seat screeching against the floor, and *'shoos'* Michelle away as she makes for the door. Once opened, she smiles up at the two men, who don't return the gesture.

"Nuala Parker?"

She nods.

"How can I help you?"

The two exchange glances, before the shorter and younger looking one steps forward.

"I'm Detective Inspector Liam McNally. This is Detective Sergeant Cian Ferguson. Do you mind if we come in?"

She stares at them dumfounded. Oh, fuck. What's happened? Are Ritchie and Danielle okay?

"Aye, aye... Er... Yeah, please..."

She stands back and points in front, before following the detectives into the living room. As she turns to close the door, she sees Michelle still standing, eavesdropping, at the dining room door.

"Upstairs," she barks, her face showing she isn't joking.

Slamming a bare foot on the floor in frustration, Michelle whines, before thundering up the stairs. Nuala doesn't close the living room door until she hears the slam of Michelle's. Turning, she sees the two detectives seated in the armchairs. She falls into the, usually, comfortable sofa. Now, it's like she's slowly getting swallowed up by quicksand. She knows she should be bustling about making tea and coffee. Bringing home-baked treats and resting on the arm of the chair whilst her husband does all the talking. Isn't that what happens on the TV? But she's the head of the household... And the thought of delaying what they have to say further makes her want to scream at them to tell her what they know.

"Is... Is it... My children?" she finally squeaks after being unable to hold it in any longer.

"Are we right in thinking, Mrs Parker," the inspector ignores her, "that you were the owner of 210 Glenshane Road before you sold the property six months ago for the development of the new dual carriageway?"

"Aye... I was."

Where are they going with this? Is this about the graffiti?

"Mrs Parker... There's no easy way to say this, but a body has been dug up from behind your garage a few hours ago. Nothing has been confirmed, but we have reason to believe that it is the remains of your husband, Aaron."

Nuala can only stare at them. Has her heart stopped? Aaron? Behind the garage? The garage that contained nothing but shite that they had gathered over the years. No, they're wrong. It can't be. He couldn't have been there, all this time. Just yards from them. They're mistaken. They're taking the piss. But something in both of the men's expressions tell her that they aren't. She tries to speak, but her mouth is too dry. She tries to lick her lips, but her tongue won't work. She looks down at her hands, seconds before clenched tight with worry, now hanging limply to her side. She begins to look back up at the officers, but she's falling forward. Her eyes glazing over. She's gone before she can feel the impact of her body on the carpet.

Chapter Seven:

She should have brought a glass. All those weeks of her ma scowling at her to bring all the mountains of glasses half-filled with water down to be washed. Why out of all times had she listened to her only days ago? Now Michelle can't hear a thing. Just muffled sounds of the men's gruff voices as she tries desperately to hear anything from downstairs. Her hair pulled to the side so her ear is pressed against the cold wooden floor. Growling frustratedly, she sneaks over to her bedroom door and winces as it creaks open a slither. She expects the living room door to fly open and her ma to scream up at her to get back to her room. Like she did so many times before when she would sneak out of bed to wind up Danielle. But everything is silent.

She stares at the bannister, as if it will reveal to her the secrets she's missing. Why would two peelers be at their door? She hasn't stolen anything in months, and she doubts they'd come to tout on her smoking up the walls. Surely, they'd have more important things to be doing. She jumps as she hears the bang, and she senses movement downstairs. Stepping one foot out onto the landing precariously, she strains to hear what's going on below.

"Mrs Parker? Mrs Parker! Ferguson, get her some water."

That's all the confirmation she needs. Throwing her door closed behind her, she jumps down the stairs just as the older looking man steps out and looks up at her.

"The kitchen's through there," she jabs a pointed finger towards the door on her right, but doesn't stop. Skidding into the room, she sees her mum lying face down on the carpet. "What the fuck have you done?"

She squares up to the other man, who isn't much taller than her.

"Please, Miss Parker, can you sit down. Your mother has fainted."

Ignoring him, she skids on her knees towards her mum, who is moaning incomprehensibly.

"It's alright, Ma. I'm here, what's wrong with ye, eh?"

Pulling her up into a sitting position, Michelle's shocked to see her nose is bleeding. Fishing out a hankie from her pocket, she presses it onto her ma's nose, who winces in pain. The scene remains like that for several more seconds, until who she guesses to be Ferguson returns to the room with a wine glass of tepid water. Michelle's mum takes it gratefully in her shaking hand, swallowing large gulps. Michelle and the other peeler, McNally she thinks he's called, both take an arm each and lever her back onto the sofa, Michelle perching beside her, holding both of her hands encouragingly.

"Now, Mrs Parker... I know you're shocked, but we need to talk to you as fast as we can to kick off proceedings."

"Kick off what proceedings?" Michelle directs the question towards the peelers, despite still looking at her mum's hollow face.

No one answers her.

"What proceedings?" she huffs, becoming more perturbed.

The detectives don't take their eyes off her mum. Finally, after what seems like hours, her mum squeezes her hands and looks up at her.

"It's your da... Sweetheart, they've found him."

Michelle's heart sticks in her throat. She gasps and is just about to break into a smile when she sees the hurt in her mum's eyes.

"It's not good news, honey... He's dead."

Chapter Eight:

When the last slice of pepperoni pizza remains, McNally nods towards DC Fleming, who had been eyeballing it, and stands to clear his throat. The excited gossip disperses, leaving only the occasional loud chew and sip of a coke can.

"Right, guys," McNally steps over to the giant board which takes up the majority of the back wall in the incident room. The only thing on it is a large picture of Aaron Parker's professional political shot, one used in papers and social media when he went missing, as well as his campaign posters on lampposts throughout the city. "Now that we're all fed and watered, can I start by asking if anyone here worked this case three years ago?"

Half a dozen hands shoot up, including Ferguson's.

"Okay, Ferguson, would you like to lead on this one?"

Smacking his lips and drying his hands on a greasy napkin, Ferguson stands and fidgets with his collar.

"Well, DI Quigley took charge of the investigation when Parker's wife, Nuala, called it in. It was the 19th of June 2016. Parker had been out the night before at some political charity do in the Waterfoot Hotel. He never made it home. CCTV from outside the hotel sees him leaving on foot, but no other camera in a two-mile radius of either the hotel or his home picks him up. That includes busy roads like the Crescent Link or Limavady Road, depending on which direction he went in. His phone was switched off whilst still in the immediate area of the hotel, and was found by the hotel's gardener two weeks later in a surrounding bush.

"We interviewed all guests at the hotel, both for the function and those just staying, but no one even saw him leave. CCTV sees him leaving at five minutes after midnight, two minutes after his phone stopped giving off signals. The rest of the party started dribbling out shortly before 1am, but he was, presumably, long gone."

"Did he have any known enemies?"

McNally knows the answer to this question, but doesn't want to sound incompetent by deliberately leaving it out in front of his new team.

The room fills with dry sniggers, even Ferguson snorts.

"'*Enemies*' isn't how *he* would put it, sir. Sure you can't get that far in politics without... Er... Ruffling a few feathers, should we say?"

"But he never really got any threats, did he?" Fleming says, the sides of his lips still stained with tomato sauce.

"Aye, he did. Sure, the Jacks threw a stone through his living room window a few months before he went missing, the ol' doll tol' us," chips in O'Connor.

McNally nods, he hadn't heard that in England.

"Awk that was years before, and sure we spoke to the underground organisation over in the Waterside and they said they had no idea what we were talking about," Fleming bites the top of his pen.

"Of course they would, ye dick," O'Connor rolls his eyes, "they're hardly going to plead guilty to the whole thing."

"So," McNally stands before there's a full altercation between O'Connor and Fleming, "were Ardóimid questioned?"

"Yes, sir, of course," Ferguson resumes his seat, "but, again, feigned innocence."

"And were there any known... Problems," McNally closes one eye as if he flinched, choosing his words carefully, "between either party and Parker?"

"Well, we know that Parker publicly criticised Darrell Boyle, current leader of the Ardóimid party, for wanting a United Ireland, despite previously being health minister," Ferguson sighs, "but Boyle has never admitted being part of the underground organisation. Parker always talked about how detrimental he would be to the NHS if things were to escalate. But, then again, he was against privatising the NHS, which is what Billy Taylor's Ulster Jacks party are campaigning for. And we all know that man has no problem with the rumours that he's high up in the underground scene."

Everyone in the room nods reminiscently, even McNally. Billy Taylor is someone they've been trying to catch red handed for years, but it always seems to only be his cronies they bang up. Their loyalties to him as hard as nails, with potential lighter sentences or immunities ignored when they're dangled in front of them to spill who the brains behind the operations were. He's the reason for so many of his men being housed up in Magilligan Prison, but they're not in short supply. Every time the PSNI seem to lock one down, another three pop up.

"Well, that's just a single part of his manifesto," McNally shakes his head, "were *all* avenues checked?"

"Not to sound disrespectful, sir," Ferguson looks around the room, giving McNally the impression that he drew the short straw and has to supply this message, "but you never met DI Quigley. He was a hard nut, nothing got past him. We interviewed everyone we could think of, it still bothers him that this case was one he couldn't crack."

"And where is he now?" McNally had heard about the famous DI Quigley, silently thanking him for leaving his job behind for McNally.

"He's up in Belfast, sir."

"Has he heard about this?"

Ferguson looks around the room, but all faces look back at him blankly.

"Well, we'll speak to him first thing in the morning. Hopefully by then we'll have a few more answers from forensics. In the meantime, get you all home to your families. Looks like we have a long day ahead of us tomorrow."

Chapter Nine:

She barely hears her ringtone over the screeching of the guitarist in the corner, and the giggles of her peers. Bringing it out of her bag, Danielle suppresses a sigh when she sees that it's her mother calling. She means well, she knows she does, but she's so clingy. She's constantly ringing or texting to ask where she is and what she's doing. Understandable, she knows, given current family dynamics, but she makes it relatively impossible for her daughter to enjoy herself, even with the Irish Sea separating them. She presses the hold button once to silence the ringing. Then, when the missed call bulletin shows up, she clicks *'automatic message.'* Choosing *'can't talk now, will ring you back later,'* she feels bad and gives her half a dozen kisses.

Her mother's lonely, even with Michelle in the house. All her sister does is sit on her phone in her room or watch Netflix in the living room. At least

Danielle tries to engage with their mother when she's home. Going out to Tescos with her. Getting her hooked on the latest craze TV shows. She even started walking the Peace Bridge with her. Only in the summer mind you... And if it was dry.

She resumes her attention to her friends, who are talking about how fit the guitarist is, when her phone bursts to life in her hand once more. Looking down, she exhales frustratedly, flicks on the permanent silencer, and lobs it at the bottom of her bag, before kicking it to beneath the table with her feet. Man, she's annoying. She looks up to the raised brows of her classmates.

"Sorry, my ma. She's a dose. If I don't tell her where I am right away, she has a shite attack."

A few look at her confused, before resuming their conversation. She still has to remember to speak slower when she's over here, and not to use phrases like *'dose'* and *'shite attack.'* Catherine's an exception. She showed up to first year halls and Catherine was the first person she met in the kitchen. She's also studying geography, so they share the majority of their lectures together, apart from when they've chosen separate modules. They became friends instantly, and there's very few times she has to slow down or reword a sentence for her to understand.

"Hi, did you see we have Thursday afternoons off?" Danielle says when the conversation draws to a close with a sip of their pints.

She's sure she's said this already, but wants to be included again. They decided to pop into the bar after their lecture, Danielle's idea of course, and she was shocked that everyone had agreed. These people are more of Catherine's cup of tea than hers, all they really speak about is uni. Catherine has invited them over to a few house parties and they never really bother to mingle.

"Yeah, I'm well happy," Hilary nods, "the libraries are usually dead then anyway, everyone's always at the student night at Bijoux the night before and too hungover to do any work, so that suits me."

Danielle nods unenthusiastically. She was just about to say that that means they *could,* in fact, go out on Wednesday nights, but it looks like these guys have different plans. She's just glad she gets on with the rest of her flat, if she had to be stuck with these bunch of boring bastards for the next two years, she'd be asking for all her money back. The group start to discuss the looming class trip whilst Danielle stares at Catherine engrossed on her phone, trying to telepathically tell her to look up. She wears a confused look on her face, before finally meeting her glare. Danielle widens her eyes and jolts her head discreetly towards the bar. Catherine frowns, before standing and smiling at Jemma as she shuffles over to let her out of the booth. When Catherine and Danielle are collected at the bar and have ordered their drinks from the impatient looking barman, that's when Danielle erupts.

"Theseins do my head in, is it too late to move groups?"

Catherine chuckles.

"We've already agreed to do the class project together, and we're also roommates on this trip. Anyway, why is your sister messaging me?"

"My *what?*"

"Yeah, Michelle isn't it? She came up on my requested notifications on Facebook Messenger."

Danielle snaps the phone out of her flatmate's hand, ignoring her whiney *'hey.'*

'Hi Catherine you probs don't know me but can you tell Danielle to ring mum rite away its really important!!'

Jesus Christ, what now? Danielle thinks as she slinks over to the table to dig out her phone. She waves it in Catherine's direction, who chortles something about having to pay, before stepping outside. Five missed calls? Something must be wrong.

"Ma, why the hell is Michelle messaging Catherine? What's wr-"

"Danielle, I'm only after booking you on the next flight home, it's leaving in just over an hour. Make sure you're on that flight. I swear-"

"Jesus, Ma. I have uni this week. And I've only been here a few days... What's wrong? What's going on?"

Silence over the line, and she has to stick a finger in her ear to ignore the jeers from lads clinking their glasses together in a neighbouring outdoor table. She steps away and frowns. Is that crying she can hear?

"Ma... Are you okay?"

"No, Danni... I'm not. They've found your father's body."

Chapter Ten:

Doing the weird hop-jump you do when pulling on your jeans, Chris fumbles with the buttons. Why had she taken all four out? Must've been in her haste to get them off. He reaches for his t-shirt hanging limply on her dressing table chair and glances over at her, bending down to pick up her socks. Fuck, she's sexy. Looking up at him, she smiles awkwardly, before sliding on a hoody brandishing University of Ulster's logo. As he sits down to tie his shoes, she coughs and plays with a teddy on her sideboard.

"Don't worry, Steph," Chris says as he stands, "I'm still not gonna tell anyone."

Steph makes a show of acting like that wasn't what she was going to say, before Chris leans in for a kiss, surprising her.

"My parents are at some wedding on Saturday night... If ye want to come over then?"

Steph raises her shoulders in a shrug, but

can't contain her smirk. She leads him to the front door and slams it in his face with a giggle as he turns at the bottom step to kiss her again. She presses her finger against the pane of glass and mouths *'maybe,'* before running towards her room, where he can faintly hear her ringtone blaring. Smiling, Chris takes one last look at her retreating bum before hopping down the path. As much as he would love to tell Dave, or even write into the group chat that he managed to get Stephanie Davidson into the sack, he knows it's not worth it. For one, he doesn't trust his friends, not even Dave. Someone will tell someone who will tell someone else and it'll be around everywhere, and then Danielle will definitely find out. He doesn't want that headache, for himself, but especially not for Steph. She's still best friends with Danielle. He has the excuse that they broke up over two years ago.

He's not even sure how it happened. When Georgia and Jimmy returned that night in Granny Annie's, Jimmy grabbed his jacket from the back of his seat and said goodbye to the lads before he sulked off home to his son. Georgia pulled up a chair triumphantly, but her smirk was quickly wiped off her face when Dave asked what the reason was for Jimmy having to go home. They had a heated debate before Jase suggested Sambucas. What followed was like an unexpected reunion. They hobbled down Waterloo

Street, bar hopping and running into more and more people they recognised until they finally managed to squeeze into the Metro nightclub.

From there, there were more shots, Refresher Bombs this time, and dancing. They were all laughing and having a good time... That is, until Steph saw her ex-boyfriend, Gerard, and gave him the finger. His new woman rugby tackled her to the ground and the bouncers somehow managed to disentangle limbs, hair and nails to pull the two girls apart, just before they kicked them both out. Since the girls were nowhere to be seen, in the toilets or smoking garden, Chris went to make sure Steph was alright. He found her outside still hurling abuse at her ex, who was retreating with his new girlfriend towards the bottom of Shipquay Street whilst she walked up the walls, around the corner of the Millennium Forum. He hurried to catch up with her, draping an arm around her shoulder. They walked up by the historic cannons overlooking Foyleside Shopping Centre and both sat down delicately, managing to avoid the broken glass.

"What a – a – a – a wanker," Steph spat between her sobs.

"Aye, I know. He is, he is," Chris managed, head lulled in front of him, sleep, or the drink, threatening to overpower him and knock him out completely.

"I mean, did you see - the state of her? She was wearing wedges, for Christ's sakes. And a - blue top with navy leggings, has she never heard of blavy?" Steph hiccupped.

"He's a stupid cunt," Chris opened one eye and looked over at her, although she was more of a blurred mess at that moment, "lettin' someone like ye go. I used to think ye were too good for him. Far too good for him. Ye can do so much better, ye co-"

He never finished his sentence as Steph pushed into kiss him. Ten minutes later, Steph stood and did up her denim jacket, wiping at her bloody knees from being on top. Chris zipped himself back up, tucked himself in and took her hand before waving down a taxi, still easily done as none of the bars had closed yet. When they got to her house, she thanked him and kissed him on the cheek.

They didn't speak about it for a few days, until she asked him round to hers to discuss what happened. They agreed to never talk about it, but their animal instincts took over and they ended up doing it again. Now, that's the third time Chris had been over in a week, and he hopes it will continue. It's just too good. Bringing out his phone, he sees that Steph's ringing him. Smirking confidently, he answers.

"Wantin' more already?"

"What? No! Chris, get back now. This is a

mess, this is a whole fuckin' mess. I'm just off the phone with Danielle, oh fuck. Oh fuck, oh fuck, oh fuck!"

Chapter Eleven:

"Another one won't hurt."

Ferguson looks like he disagrees, but nods regardless.

"You've twisted my arm. Just another pint then, early start tomorrow."

McNally laughs and slaps him on the back, nearly making him spit out the drink he'd just lifted to his lips. He orders another two pints and looks up at the TV. It's another few minutes until the 10 o'clock news and luckily no one has sniffed out the recent revelations and plastered it over social media just yet. He should be thankful. The shit storm is coming, he's just waiting for the wind to pick up. Leaning his elbows on the bar top, he makes small talk with the barman. Jordan, twenty-something, has went from job-to-job the past few years with no real motive. Not someone he'd usually become friends with, but desperate times when you've moved to a brand-new city. If it wasn't for Ferguson agreeing to go for a few cold ones after work, he'd have been stuck in his house with nothing but the TV for company. He hadn't even got around to setting up the internet yet.

He's grateful, he thinks, as he turns around with a pint in each hand to see Ferguson lounged back in his chair, looking up at a mop of brown curly hair. Marching over, McNally can't help but admire the slit of leg peering out from her black pencil skirt. Since the nasty break-up with Kirstyn, he hadn't even thought much about the opposite sex, putting all his energy into work. But, hey, nothing wrong with window shopping, right? Taking his original seat, he smiles up into the beautiful woman's face. Her makeup is natural and light and her sparkling green eyes look down on him before she breaks into a smile, showing elegant white teeth.

"Sorry, boss. This is Niamh, Jane's sister."

He hovers from his chair to take her proffered hand, subtly inspecting to see if there's a ring on the other hanging limply by her side. There isn't.

"Nice to meet you, Niamh. I'm Liam. I'm Ferguson's..."

How does he put this? He hates to sound pompous.

"He's my new boss," Ferguson smiles, taking over.

"Well, I guessed that," Niamh laughs, her thick Derry accent taking McNally aback for a second, "you called him boss before, and no one else calls Cian here Ferguson, now do they?"

McNally smiles.

"Are you joining us?"

"I'm actually just coming back from the toilet, me and a few of the girls from the salon just came in for a bite to eat and a few wee cocktails after work, but thanks. Anyway, Cian, what big crime had ye missin' my sister's lovely gammon dinner tonight?"

The link between the two clicks in McNally's head. He isn't sure if Ferguson ever told him his wife's name. Jane, he'll have to remember that one.

"Police business, as I'm sure you well know, nosy hole. Like I'd tell a hairdresser of all people."

"A *beautician,* ya cheeky bastard," Niamh wags a finger at him, "and sure it's all well and good when you need to get the word out. I'm always the first person you come to then."

She winks at McNally and he can't help but chuckle, despite himself.

"Well, anyway, I'll let you boys get back to it. Make you think that you're doing a bit of work."

She slaps Ferguson playfully on the back of the head, making him growl, before placing a hand daintily on McNally's shoulder.

"Nice to meet you, pet. I hear you're new. I-"

"Niamh!"

"What? Us girls talk, we're sisters, for buck sake, Cian. Anyway, if you ever need someone to show you the ropes, let me know. Can be lonely on your own."

"Oh, like you know what it's like to be lonely."

"Shut up you," she turns back towards her brother-in-law with a smile, "you're giving me a bad first impression. But seriously, could be a double date sort of thing."

"Not a hope," Ferguson lifts a boot and gives her a jab with it, "now away with ye."

Niamh cackles and waves at the two as she retreats down to the restaurant area. McNally doesn't realise that his head is following her departure, pint against his lips, until he resumes his attention back in front. Towards Ferguson's look of disapproval.

"What?"

"No disrespect, sir. But don't go there."

"Go where?"

Ferguson raises an eyebrow as he takes another slug of his beer.

"Believe me, she's trouble."

"She looks it," McNally barely stifles a snicker.

"Honestly, a maneater if ever I've seen one. She was after me before I met Jane."

"Now I know you're talking shite, who'd be after you?"

The two laugh and clink glasses, before the 10 o'clock news theme blasts from the TV above the bar. They wait with bated breath to see if any snake had managed to slither its way into their story.

Chapter Twelve:

Cathal O'Flaherty watches Niamh from Suzie's Salon as she returns to her seat by the window. She sees him glaring over as she tucks herself in and gives a friendly wave. He nods politely at her. She's not the story tonight. She'd been good for a source once or twice, but not tonight. Tonight is big, he can smell it. No one rings the office requesting to meet at this time of night with a suggestion of a story in exchange for a pricey sum if it isn't important.

Cathal had just been putting the finishing touches on his story about the controlled explosion in the Bogside when the phone had rung. With only himself and his editor, Jodie, in the office, he knew where he was in the pecking order. He thought it was a prank call to start, with nothing but heavy breathing down the phone. He was just about to put it down when he heard shuffling and a ruffled woman's voice in the background, encouraging the caller to *'say something.'* Journalistic instincts taking over, Cathal had glanced to Jodie in her office, the door closed but her fingers scrambling across the keyboard, no doubt knee-deep in an important email.

"Have you a story for me?"

The breathing was cut short. A slap was heard before a voice finally broke through the headset. A clipped *'aye.'*

"Well it must be a good one if you're this nervous about it..."

"You... You won't regret it, son."

Protruding his bottom lip, Cathal plucked a blue biro from the breast pocket of his shirt.

"Go on..."

"Not over the phone."

"Okay..."

Silence.

"Do you want to meet me somewhere?"

"Somewhere we won't be overheard."

Blinking confusedly, Cathal had begun to bite the top of his pen lid.

"Okay... How about the Icon?" he glances at his watch. Close to seven o'clock. By the time he edits this story and submits it for print... "Half seven?"

"No... Too early. Too many people."

"When, then?"

"10 o'clock."

He'd have to wait about the office for a few hours, he's sure there were things that needed done. But this better be good. Worth it.

"That'll do, who will I look out for?"

"I'll be wearing a black hat... Red coat."

"Okay, see you then."

He brought the office phone away and was about to return it to the receiver when he heard the tinny sound of the voice still talking, but by the time he'd brought it back to his ear, it had stopped.

"Sorry?"

The voice breathed out deeply, like this was a huge effort.

"Do you pay for your stories?"

Cathal had leaned back in his chair.

"Not usually... In certain circumstances..."

"This one you'll want, trust me."

"Okay... How much do you want?"

"How much do you have?"

Cathal had laughed.

"What's funny?"

"That's an odd question to ask."

"You'll want this story boy, oh believe me."

Narrowing his eyes, Cathal took another glance at his editor, who had slowed down on the typing, her chin resting on her hands as her eyes strode from left to right, reading her screen.

"I don't know how much I can offer... I'll have to ask my editor. It depends on the story, I sup-"

"Well meet me tonight. Bring half then, before I tell you the story, and then give me the rest when you think you know how much it's worth. No less than fifteen hundred, though."

Cathal's mouth fell open, about to haggle with the mystery caller, but the line went dead. Hanging up, he knocked on Jodie's door and he explained the situation.

"Sounds like a waste of time," she returned her attention to her screen.

"I think it sounds legit... You didn't hear him. He sounded... Worried... Weird..."

"Probably a bunch of scumbags trying to chance their arm. Are you really going to meet him?"

"I want to."

Jodie raised an eyebrow and blew a raspberry.

"I wouldn't."

"How much can we give out?"

"For a non-story? For you to be mugged? Absolutely fuck all, to be honest, Cathal. The newspaper industry isn't what it used to be, y'know?"

"Well, on average, if you were contacted like this?"

Sighing, as if he were an inconvenience to her, Jodie stood up and marched to the filing cabinet.

Opening the bottom drawer, she took out the Londonderry Letter's cheque book.

"I'll put £1,000 on this, for now."

"He said he wants fifteen hundred."

"Well, if it's as good as you feel it is then he can get the other 500 after. And don't you be giving this out willy-nilly. If the story is shite or made up, refuse payment. Check your facts. I'm counting on you."

And now here he is, isolated at a table towards the back of the room in the Icon bar and restaurant, where he'd met so many sources before. But something about this feels odd. He isn't in control, like he is in every other interview. He has no idea how tonight is going to go. A flash of red coming in through the door makes him look up. It's him. He looks around before spotting Cathal seated with his notepad and Dictaphone resting on the table. Slouching over, he pushes his cap back and removes his sunglasses.

"Get rid of those," he hisses as he takes a seat, nodding towards Cathal's instruments.

Pocketing them, Cathal observes him. He wouldn't be close to 50 yet, with deep rings under his eyes and a sickly skin tone. Something has happened. Something bad, but what? He guesses he's going to find out.

"You brought the money?"

Cathal fishes out the cheque.

"I wanted cash!"

"Well this is the best I can do for you; I'll need your name if it's going to be any use."

"I'll write it in later."

"I don't think that's going to w-"

"Do you want the story or not?" he spits.

Leaning back, Cathal nods for him to proceed.

"I'm to remain anonymous in all this, alright?"

"I don't know your name anyway."

"Aye... But your lot... You can dig anything up."

Cathal thinks for a moment, before nodding.

"The missing politician, Aaron Parker... I know where he is."

Cathal stops juvenilely swinging on his chair and sits forward, shock etched across his face. He doesn't know what he was expecting... But not this.

"I'm listening..."

Chapter Thirteen:

2016

———

Voices from downstairs carried up through the floorboards pull him from his dreams. Moaning, sickness swirling in his stomach, Chris rolls over and expects to be met with the coldness of his wall. But his arm hangs limply off the bed. Opening one eye precariously, he's confused to find himself in Danielle's bedroom. How the hell did he find himself back here? Especially after that corker of an argument. Guilt batters against his chest as he remembers calling her an attention seeker and even pointing at her in distain as he sang the *'jealousy'* lyrics when him and the lads drunkenly belted out *Mr Brightside* in the wee hours of the morning.

Sitting up and scratching his head, he wonders who is downstairs. The voices sound urgent. He can just about make out Danielle's mum's

quivering tremor before it's replaced with a hardened
monotone. Searching the room for his discarded
clothes, he pulls them on, hoping the company won't
be disgusted with the wrinkles, and trots downstairs,
thoughts of a bacon bap at the forefront of his mind.
As he reaches the doorway through to the kitchen,
he's instantly enveloped in a sea of brown hair and
pink fluffy pyjamas. His chest gets soaked right
through his shirt as Danielle presses her face into
him. Whatever has happened, it has taken
precedence over the silly argument last night.
Looking up, he sees Danielle's mum at the island, a
hand over her face, with Michelle propped beside
her, biting her lip. Across from them sit two men, one
dressed in an itchy-looking woollen jumper and
cords, another in a suit and tie.

"This is Danielle's boyfriend, Chris," Nuala
nods towards him, "Chris, this is Detective... Sorry,
I've forgotten your name."

"Detective Inspector Joe Quigley," the man in
the suit stoops off the stool and offers his hand,
which Chris accepts after untangling his own hand
from Danielle's hair, "and this is DC Dermott Curry."

Chris nods his head in the direction of the
older officer, who smiles at him concerned. What's
going on? Police? Could this be because of what
happened last night? Danielle accusing him of
attacking her. This is over the top, even for her. But

surely if it was, she wouldn't have just greeted him like that. And Nuala wouldn't have been so friendly... No, something else is up. But what?

"We're actually wondering if you could shed some light on the matter, Chris?" Quigley sighs, as if he read his mind, as he retakes his seat.

"Me?" Chris is shocked, looking down to a departing Danielle who unpeels herself from him and joins her mother by the island, "it depends on what's been going on, I suppose."

"Your girlfriend here doesn't have any recollection of getting home last night," DI Quigley nods towards Danielle, who buries her face in her pyjama top to supress the howls. "Care to help?"

Chris blows out in apprehension, before taking the final stool at the island. "I'm afraid I'm just as in the dark as she is. Too many shots," he snorts nervously, "took me a second to realise where I was when I woke up actually."

"You were both at your friend's house, Katie Woods, is that correct?"

"Well... D's friend's, aye."

"Do you remember when you left?"

Chris shakes his head before his mouth falls open. Digging around in his pocket, he brings out his phone. It's dead.

"Could I lend a charger, Nuala? If I could get my phone charged, I could check to see if I rang a taxi."

Nuala nods towards the sockets by the fridge, where a white lead snakes its way behind the microwave. Plugging in his phone, Chris waits for the *'low battery'* symbol to be replaced with his home screen.

"What's all this about, anyway?"

The two cops look at Nuala, who nods her head sullenly.

"We're trying to find out the whereabouts of Mr Aaron Parker, actually. He didn't come home last night."

Chris stares at the officers in shock, before having to run to the downstairs toilet to vomit.

Chapter Fourteen:

2019

_____

It feels weird pulling up the drive. The drive they thought they would never pull up again. They'd said their goodbyes three months ago, following the moving lorry out onto the main road and glancing back at their house in the rear-view mirror. Now, bypassing all the strategically placed construction vehicles obscuring the large forensics tent from the road and greedy eyes of the public, there isn't as much action as Nuala thought there would be. She was expecting blues and twos. Dozens of police buzzing around the area. But there seem to be only a small handful of people clad in their white jumpsuits, masks and goggles, filtering in and out of the tent, where the light illuminates the shadows inside like on a crime TV show. Only this isn't TV. This is their lives.

Switching the car off and sighing, Nuala turns to look at her girls in the back seat, not fighting for once. Allies in grief. Her left hand is cupped, and she smiles towards Ritchie in the front seat. It's been months since she seen him. They met up in April, during the school holidays. Herself and Michelle had gone over to Newcastle to surprise Danielle and get the flight the next day home with her for Easter. Ritchie had said he was off work for a few days, and was contemplating coming home anyway, so made the 7-hour trip by train up north to be reunited with the family for the first time since Christmas. They had dined at the Dog and Parrot, Danielle's favourite, and had a good catch up. When something as devastating as what happened with Aaron occurs in a family, it brings you closer. And it's not often they get a chance to spend time altogether. They will have to rely on each other's resilience over the next few days.

"Right," Nuala sniffs, "I'm going to find out what's going on. Please stay in the car," she squeezes Ritchie's hand before stepping out. "You're in charge."

She had just collected both Ritchie and Danielle from Belfast International Airport after paying an extortionate amount to get them home on the next departing flights before zooming up the road to collect them, barely having time to let Michelle clamber into the back seat. Now, as she hobbles over the mess that was once her house, her heart hurts. For herself and the kids. For the house. For Aaron.

"Hi, you can't be here!"

She looks up from examining what once was her front doorstep to a figure hopscotching towards her, avoiding the debris.

"This is my house."

The figure stops short of connecting with her and stares.

"You're Mrs Parker?"

"I am."

He sighs and tells her to wait there, before doddering back the way he came. After a few moments, with Nuala constantly glancing back towards her car to make sure her wains hadn't abandoned ship, another body approaches her after battling its way out of the tent. Pulling down her hood and removing her goggles and mask, a pretty woman with shoulder length ginger hair holds out a gloved hand.

"Karen McGuire, head scenes of crime officer," she returns her hand to her side once she sees Nuala isn't going to take it. "I understand this was your house?"

"Yes, it is," Nuala can't bring herself to say *'was.'*

"I know you have a lot of questions, but unfortunately, we're only doing our job. DI McNally was here hours ago. I'm sure he's been in touch?"

Nuala musters a nod.

"Well, I can only tell you the body has been removed. We're conducting more forensics at the moment. Seeing if there's anything we're missing."

"You're not going to find any more bodies." Karen frowns.

"I'm not suggesting we will... Unless..."

Why did Nuala say that? She shakes her head.

"Sorry... It's just so hard... I don't even understand how Aaron... How he ended up here."

Karen nods, still suspicious.

"Was he planted here? When we left? Or was he..."

She can't ask if he was here the whole time. And even if she could, does she want to know the answer?

"That's what we're in the middle of investigating. But don't worry. We've got the best in the business out here. We'll know soon. And I'm sure you'll be appointed a FLO in due course."

"A FLO..."

"Aye, a family liaison officer?"

Nuala knows what a FLO is. They had one when Aaron went missing. But she hadn't considered contacting him.

"Dermott..."

Karen raises a brow before clearing her throat as Nuala stares into space.

"Anyway, there are no officers here at the moment who can help you, I'm afraid... So, if you don't mind... I know this is a difficult time, but..."

"You want me to go?"

Karen smiles her confirmation and utters a small *'sorry'* when Nuala retreats to the car. Falling back into the driver's seat, Nuala *'shushes'* the wains as they all start bombarding her with questions. Turning on the ignition, she reverses out of the drive and makes a start for home. Their new home. Whether they like it or not.

Chapter Fifteen:

He might've only had a few beers, but with only two measly slices of pizza for dinner, he's already feeling tipsy. Pulling open the fridge and grabbing last night's casserole dish with leftover pasta bake, he'd never been able to measure out realistic amounts, McNally plops a generous portion on a plate before bustling it into the microwave. Filling a pint glass with water, he slugs half of it whilst he waits for his dinner to reheat. A jingle in his pocket tells him someone is calling. It's gone 11, who could be ringing this late? Thoughts of his mum or dad in trouble disperse as he sees Dawson's name on the home screen. Bringing the phone to his ear, a smile on his face, McNally answers.

"Alright, boss?"

"Stop calling me that, McNally."

"Well stop calling me McNally then, Donald."

Dawson chuckles over the phone as the microwave beeps.

"I don't like it when you call me Donald. Sounds like I'm in trouble."

"Sounds bloody weird to me," McNally snorts as he presses his phone against his shoulder and lifts out the piping hot plate with a tea towel.

As he escorts it to the small table in front of his single leather armchair, he groans when he realises he's forgotten a fork.

"What's on the menu tonight, anyway, *Liam*," Dawson shouts over the clattering of cutlery.

"Left over pasta bake," McNally says as he flops back into the chair, ignoring Dawson's retches.

"You need a good woman to wait on you hand and foot when you get home from a long day, not clogging your arteries with that pre-made shite."

"It's homemade shite actually," McNally teases, blowing on a stray bit of chicken and popping it in his mouth, "and we can't all be tended to like you with Helen. It is 2019, you know?"

"No matter what year it is, my Helen would do anything for anyone," Dawson clicks his teeth, "bit late to be only getting a bite now, isn't it? Must be near midnight back there."

"And bit late for an ol' man like yourself to be up past his bedtime, it's definitely past midnight over there."

"Oh, ha-ha. Just back from the bar there, actually."

"Where even are you now?"

"In a beautiful little city called Lucena."

"Never heard of it."

"You need to get out of the house more, but honestly, what has you eating dinner at this time?"

McNally catches his old boss up with the evening's events as he scoops pasta onto his fork.

"Wow... Wouldn't like to be landed with that within my first two weeks through the door. What you gonna do?"

"Well, I have to wait to hear back from forensics tomorrow to make sure that it definitely is Parker. Then I want to speak to this Quigley fella. With a turnaround rate like his... Something must be up."

"You think he's bent?"

"I don't know... I wouldn't mark it off just yet... They all seem to idolise him in the station. But who is to say he didn't take a bribe from one of the big organisations? Or blackmailed. Either way, I have pretty big shoes to fill."

"True... Though you should be used to that, you had to do the same in Rong Valley."

"Oh, yeah. Good thing it wasn't a hat because I'd never be able to fit into it after being on your big head."

The two laugh. It's like old times.

"Anyway, what about that girl? Niamh, wasn't it?"

"Aye, she's lovely."

"Go for it, lad. You're not getting any younger."

"Piss off," McNally tries to inject a sense of humour to his defence, although he knows he's right, "should probably stay away from shitting on my own doorstep, right enough."

"Speaking of... How is the new pad? Bachelor heaven?"

McNally gazes around his empty living room, only a stone throw away from the bar he had just left. He had found this on PropertyPal relatively quickly, and was able to move in right away. The only way of decoration is the dead flowers in the pint glass in the corner of the room the station had given him on his first day. The darkened pedals curling on the floor.

"Needs a lick of paint."

His phone buzzes in his hand, and he brings it away to see a text with a link to the Londonderry Letter's website from Ferguson. This can't be good.

"Look, boss, I'll need to call you back. Thanks for ringing. We'll get a proper catch up next time."

"Stop calling me boss. You're the boss now. And keep at it. Proud of you, son."

McNally smiles.

"Thanks, speak soon."

Hanging up and clicking on the link, McNally moans as he clunks his fork back on the plate.

'Has local politician Aaron Parker's remains been found in the rubble of his old home?'

Chapter Sixteen:

Finally, after hours of tossing and turning, Danielle hears the creak of the stairs. Someone's up. Falling out of bed, she drapes herself in her dressing gown and shuffles into her slippers before trudging down to the kitchen, where she can hear the kettle boiling. As she opens the door, she sees Ritchie's back as he stretches for a mug. He turns and they stare at each other for a second. They haven't seen eye to eye ever since Danielle started seeing Chris, who was once one of his friends. In the end, they just stopped talking about it... And then, with him going to uni, they stopped talking altogether. Even now, when she's no longer with Chris, they have yet to build their bridges. They play happy families in front of Michelle, and Ma especially, but they still find it awkward when they're alone together.

"Want a cup?" Ritchie brings down her pink cat mug, a birthday present from Michelle years ago.

She nods and takes a seat at the kitchen table, discarding her slippers beneath it and starts to flick through some of the post for something to do. Aware that it's all bills that have been lying there since before she left for Newcastle at the weekend. He clunks her mug down in front of her and she bites her lip to stop herself from telling him he'd made it too milky as usual. They aren't arguing. It's progress. She won't spoil it. Ritchie steps into the conservatory and pulls at the doors through into the modest back garden that their mum had done well to upcycle.

"Ma's work, I guess?" he shouts through.

Danielle rolls her eyes and smirks, standing and joining him on the grass, the dew moistening her bare feet.

"Of course, you know her when she has a project..."

When the girls had moved in three months ago, it had been a barren wasteland. The grass was like a jungle, nearly meeting the tiny broken patio. But a summer of TLC from their mother has made it look like something from a gardening magazine. The grass neatly trimmed with shrubs blooming. An aqua coloured trellis housing pink hanging baskets and LED solar lights on the far left-hand side. She half-expects a butterfly to flutter past and perch on the outdoor furniture on cue.

"Nice place..."

Ritchie was as adamant in not moving as their parents, despite having not actually lived in the house for the past three years. He had ultimately fallen out with their mum for several weeks once he heard that she'd finally given in and had accepted the payment. He'd said she should've fought more, but by that time she was deflated. She wanted a fresh home with new memories to make. Not be reminded of ghosts around every corner. With their old front door literally knocked down, and their father's body currently lying on a slab, they now know he'll never show up again. Their years of protesting against moving for that reason worthless. But were their months of searching also in vain?

"We did with it what we could," Danielle tries to break her own daydream.

"Well, you're not slumming it until you make the big buy, that's for sure."

Danielle smiles and nods towards him, taking a sip and trying not to wince. This is good. They're talking... They barely said a word to each other before their mother collected them from the airport last night. They stood at the bus stop like two strangers. Someone walking past would never have guessed they were siblings. No greetings. No grief-induced tearful embraces. Nothing.

"How's your uni house?"

"Pfft," Danielle shakes her head, "there was no heating when we arrived, they've still to send someone round to look at the boiler. And whoever was in my room before hadn't even bothered to clean it properly. When I went to flip the mattress, I found all sorts underneath the bed. Knickers, socks, food cartons, condoms..."

Ritchie's head jerks up.

"Unused, thankfully."

They both smile before bursting into laughter.

"What are yousins laughing about?"

They turn to see Michelle standing at the conservatory door, wrapping her hoody around her tighter as the cold morning air hits her. The older siblings wipe their eyes and look at their younger sister with toothy grins.

"You'll find out when you're older," Ritchie says, taking a slurp of his tea.

"Can I have some toast?"

"What did your last slave die of?"

Michelle pouts, but Ritchie sighs and steps back inside, fishing out some bread from the cupboard, on his fourth try, and drops it into the toaster. Danielle and Michelle join him at the table, Michelle bringing her feet up onto the chair so she can rest her chin on her knees. The room becomes silent, nothing but the hum of the fridge and a squawk from a bird from the open door can be heard.

"How's Ma been?"

Ritchie looks up to Danielle, who had directed the question to Michelle, who shrugs.

"She fainted last night."

"What? When?"

"When the police told her about Da."

"That Quigley guy?"

"No, someone else. McNally, I think he was called."

"What happened Quigley?"

"How am I supposed to know?" Michelle strains, glaring at her sister.

"Right, you two. Settle down. Last thing Ma needs right now is you at each other's throats. It's going to be a hard enough few days, alright?"

The three fall silent again, before the toast pops. Michelle turns on the TV on the wall as Ritchie butters it for her.

"Gone watch that in the living room, would you? My head's splitting," Danielle spits, before adding a sombre *'please'* when Ritchie glares at her.

Sighing, Michelle scoops up her toast and plods off into the next room, leaving Ritchie and Danielle with the booming voice of Piers Morgan before Ritchie shuts it off. They sit in silence for a few more seconds, looking around the room or out of the window, until they finally make eye contact.

"How have you been?" Ritchie gulps.

Danielle shrugs.

"Hard to take in."

"I know, me too."

Silence once more.

"Look..."

Ritchie leans back in his chair, taking his sister in.

"I'm sorry," she looks down at her hands.

"For what?"

"For everything... I should've listened to you. You were right... Chris is a dick."

"I never said that. I just always seen how he was with girls. On nights out, like... I didn't want my sister to be just another of his conquests."

"I know... But you telling me all that... It was weird... It made me want him more. Forbidden fruit, and all... But it also made me very wary. I didn't trust him, which I know I should've if it was ever going to work."

She looks up and he sees she's got tears in her eyes.

"What happened?"

"It wasn't working for a while. I was oversensitive and jealous. He flew off the handle instead of consoling me... Then, I think it was close to

113

over... But then Da went missing. He couldn't have left then; he'd have been the worst in the world... So, we just sort of... Paused it... Then, when things started to get back to normal, or as close to normal as it ever was going to be... We realised we shouldn't be together. Not then, anyway..."

"And now?"

"What?"

"Do you think you could be with him now?"

She shrugs again.

"Do you still love him?"

Danielle bites her lip and looks up at her brother, and that's all the evidence she can give before the doorbell goes.

****

Parking down by the Belfray Hotel, I pull my hood up and cross the road before trudging the half mile uphill to the house. It's late, really late, and I'm only met by three cars making their way towards Belfast, my back to them. The lights give way to their presence before I hear them, and I pull the right side of my hood over my face further and look at the ground as they whizz past. Begging for none of them to stop and ask me what I'm doing. No one I know would be travelling around here at this time on a weekday night, but I can't be too careful. I can't be seen.

I dodge past all the cones and men at work signs, judging every step so I don't end up in some hole. That would be subtle. All I need. Having to answer questions on why I'm stuck down there and what my intentions were at this time of night. As I round the corner to the old house, I gasp. They've already started work. I didn't think it would've been so soon. They still have a good bit of the road behind me to work through yet. Part of the garden is under construction, no doubt to level it out for the new road and get rid of the hill leading up to the house. Through the darkness, the mass of machinery which will be used to bulldoze the house stretches out into the sky above me like dinosaur silhouettes in a film I definitely watched when I was younger. I don't have much more time. My ears perk, alert, as I hear voices coming from the house. Who the hell could that be?

Stepping into the trees surrounding the left-hand side of the house, where it runs down to the pavement I just recently vacated, I nuzzle onto the ground, army crawling through the low hanging branches until I bypass all the roadworks machinery by the road and climb the steady hill and see the house head on. Carefully lifting a branch out of the way, I wait for my eyes to adjust to the moonlight beaming down on the garden. After a few seconds, I see three figures by the wall furthest from me. One looks like he's keeping dick, as he continually looks around at his accomplices and spits something that I can't hear from way over here. What I do hear are rattles and then hisses.

Cocking my head further out into the open, I now know what the sound is. Spray cans. Paint, presumably, as I see the graffiti on the darkened side of the wall, hidden from the moonlight by the jutting out of the entranceway's shadow. One of them is spraying over sectarian slurs in black, but it doesn't look like they're do-gooders, as another is spraying out the 'London' in 'Londonderry,' and obstructing reading the name of the, presumably, opposing party's organisation below. Charming. How long will they be? What a weird place to congregate. I assume they must've spotted the original graffiti from the roadside and decided to return to correct it. Are they dangerous? Or just a pile of youths? Chavs from surrounding council estates angered by the hateful comments sprayed so openly on the main road linking two of Northern Ireland's biggest cities.

My thoughts are caught short as I almost exclaim aloud. A piercing cough just came from my right, at the bottom of the garden where it meets the roadside. A towering figure with a large coat and baseball cap, barely identifiable beside the machinery. How long has he been there? The cough echoes through the garden, making the three figures curse before spreading out and bolting it in the opposite directions, throwing the spray cans at their departing feet with two loud clangs. Towards the open fields that will eventually lead them to the Tamnaherin direction, their meetup point, I can guarantee. I expect the figure to barrel after them, pursue a chase. But instead, it stands watching them retreat.

After a few moments of me holding my breath, the figure begins climbing up the garden to the house, staring at the new graffiti, before shaking its head and sliding towards me. I start to panic, inching backwards unnecessarily because I know there's no way it can see me. But before it reaches my hiding place, it turns at the side of the house retreating to the back before disappearing altogether. I count to 100 before slowly making my way back the way I came. I don't know what's going on here, but I don't want to stick around to find out. Too spooked by the ominous figure. I'll have to return another night.

Chapter Seventeen:

The door is opened by a boy and girl in their late teens or early twenties. It doesn't take a genetics specialist to see that they're the eldest wains of Aaron and Nuala Parker. The boy has Aaron's strong jawline, and the girl has her mother's eyes, the same eyes protruding from the face of the youngest girl, Michelle, last night behind her dishevelled hair. McNally coughs and tries to stand to his tallest.

"Hello there, is your mother home?"

They nod and stand back to let him through, where he has to slide between them. He instinctively goes through to the living room whilst the girl goes upstairs, presumably to fetch her mum. Meanwhile, the boy leans on the threshold of the living room door. He spots the TV on in the corner, some mindless talent show on the screen, but no volume. When he stations himself by the coffee table, he sees

Michelle nestled on the sofa, her eyes glaring at him, her phone open on her lap.

"Hello, again. Er... You okay?"

She doesn't respond. What a stupid question. He hears footsteps from right above his head, and soon enough the stairs creak and down comes the second daughter and Nuala, who has bleary eyes and a pink jumper haphazardly threw on over her pyjamas.

"Michelle, make Mr McNally a cup of tea, will you please?"

Groaning, Michelle stands and retreats into the kitchen before McNally has a chance to thank her. He takes the seat he had yesterday, whilst the other three sit on the edge of the sofa, grouped together like a close-knit family should be. Both older children either side of their mother, almost as if by doing so they can protect her from the news. This will make what he has to say both easier... And harder.

"So... We've heard back from forensics this morning..."

No one blinks or says a word. He clears his throat. Best to just come out and say it.

"We've established that the body found in your old garden behind the garage... I'm sorry, but it *is* that of Aaron Parker. Your husband and father... We were able to identify him by his dental records. I'm so very sorry."

The girl, Danielle, starts crying and clings to Nuala, who stares at the coffee table with sunken eyes. The boy, Ritchie, places both palms flat on the back of his neck and bends forward.

"So, where do we go from here?" Nuala finally manages, swallowing her grief.

"Well, we've heard from our forensic entomologist that the body has been there for quite some time. It wasn't moved there once you up and left. However, as I'm sure you can guess, it's going to be hard to determine if that's where he was killed-"

"Killed?"

They look up to see Michelle hovering in the doorway, her eyes brimming with tears. McNally coughs and looks at Nuala again.

"Should we maybe do this in private?"

Nuala shakes her head.

"No, they have a right to know. He was their daddy."

"It's just... It could be quite... Upsetting."

"Then put it into simpler, more empathetic language please, Detective," Ritchie sits forward, grabbing Michelle's hand and pulling her onto the sofa beside him.

"If you're sure?"

After a few seconds Nuala nods.

"Okay, well... Yes, we are opening a murder inquiry. Aaron's skull was fractured, but the rest of the body seems to be intact. At this moment, we're treating this as the cause of death..."

He coughs again, looking at the sorry foursome collected together. Michelle still looks forward, silent tears rolling down her eyes. Ritchie sits consoling her, with another arm around his mother's lower back. Nuala continually bites her lip whilst Danielle sobs into her chest. This is hard. Where the hell is that FLO?

"I am so sorry for your loss. Believe me when I say we are reopening this investigation and want to bring whoever did this to your husband and father to justice. Now we have a body, we can see if there's any evidence. And with retrospect, comes a great deal. As well as fresh eyes on the case."

"Fresh eyes?" Nuala finally looks at him.

"Yes, DI Quigley has taken up a post with the PSNI in Belfast, so I'm the new lead investigator on the case. As well as this, I have several detectives helping me from an outsider's perspective, as well as half a dozen who worked the original case. We're all working together."

"How did the media find out so fast?" Ritchie asks, "they knew before us."

McNally was anticipating this question, but they're still no closer to finding an answer.

"That was just speculation. They didn't know for sure because we didn't... Officially. As for how they found out, I can't say. The Letter are incredibly protective of their sources, and I'm sure you can guess with us opening a murder enquiry they want to protect them even more. We can only guess at the moment."

"And what about Dermott?" Nuala says.

"I'm sorry?"

"Dermott Curry, he was our FLO."

McNally chews the inside of his mouth. He'd heard nothing about Curry.

"Let me just ring DS Ferguson, but you have been appointed one already."

"I want Dermott. He knows us, he knows the case. I tried to ring him last night, but I must have lost his number when I got my new phone. Speak to DS Ferguson, he knows us and knows the case too. He'll know we'll want Dermott back."

Nodding, McNally stands, excusing himself, and steps outside into the garden. Being sure to avoid the window, he calls Ferguson.

"Sir?"

"Ferguson, where's the FLO?"

"He's not there? Well, he should still be on his way. Traffic's bad, massive crash on the-"

"Well, tell him to hurry! And also, they're asking about a Curry? Dermott? He was the FLO last time?"

"Oh, aye. Derm retired, though."

"Fuck! Right, well I want a statement from him with everything he knows. The family seem to know and trust him and want him back, so even if he could come for moral support?"

"Right away, sir."

"Anything else to update?"

"Well, Fleming is currently trying to make contact with one of our underground investigators who is acting as a mole within Ardóimid. With the news breaking late last night and this morning, we're hoping it'll open up a new line of inquiry with them."

"Good work, Ferguson. And the Jacks?"

"Still trying to find a way in, sir. You know Billy, he's airtight."

"Right, well let me know about any progress."

Hanging up, he brings his phone to his mouth and stares out at the traffic on the way up the Church Brae. Where to go from here?

Chapter Eighteen:

"Congratulations, newbie."

Cathal fights the urge to roll his eyes and thanks Ethan, who pats him on the back on the way to his own desk. Despite being with the Londonderry Letter since he underwent work experience here almost two years ago, he is still called the *'newbie'* by his co-workers. His age doesn't help, as the only one closest to his age is Alex, who is in her mid-thirties. Looking down at the front page spread with his by-line, he knows this is a moment he'll remember for the rest of his career.

"Hi, Cathal," Jodie storms out of her office, Cathal bracing himself for the telling off. "I've just had the police on the phone complaining about your story."

His mouth falls open and everyone around him goes quiet. No more typing, telephone voices or plans for the weekend.

"They... I... They did?"

"Aye, good bloody job."

And with that, she slaps him on the head with this morning's rolled up paper. His colleagues around him start laughing and cheering and he looks from his editor to them and back again, shock still on his face.

"So... I'm not in trouble?"

"No, of course not. They're ragin' we got the scoop. You didn't write anything libellous and you aren't corrupting a trial, are ye? This was cold hard facts, with an exclusive interview. They have nothing to go on. News is something someone somewhere-"

"Doesn't want you to publish," Cathal nods, remembering the old saying he learnt at the local tech.

"The rest is advertising," the whole room chips in before a big whoop.

"I think Cathal here deserves a round of applause, don't you?" Jodie places down her coffee mug to join in, "he went with his gut with an anonymous call. Something I wouldn't have done. And we've got there even before the BBC. Good job. Now, find me more!"

The natural sounds of the office return to normal as Cathal folds the paper, making sure his by-line is facing upwards as he loads his computer. His first front page scoop. The feeling is incomparable.

Opening his emails, his smile starts to drop when he sees a message from an unknown sender. It looks like a made-up email address. Probably some phishing expedition. It has an attachment and a short message, which is what makes him sit up and take notice, rather than delete the whole email.

'I'd stop writing stories if I were you.'

Guffawing, Cathal clicks on the attachment which downloads as a picture file. Double clicking, his eyes widen and he almost jumps back from the screen. Why has this person sent him a picture of his younger sister's Facebook profile picture?

Chapter Nineteen:

Parking up, McNally is just about to step out of the car when his phone blares. Checking the caller ID, he sees it's Joe Quigley returning his call. Deciding to take this in the comfort and privacy of his own car, he leans back and clears his throat.

"DI McNally."

"Well, how's my old job looking?"

He hears laughter over the phone. What a smart, cocky little bastard.

"Joe Quigley, thank you for getting back to me so soon."

"I had a missed call. I pressed return. Hardly newsworthy."

McNally raises a brow. What a weird man.

"Anyway, McNulty, how can I help you?"

"It's *McNally*, Quigley."

"Oooh, McNally, sorry," he chortles.

This guy was definitely the school bully. Presumably also how he got so far in his career.

"Well, Quigley. I'm sure you've heard the news this morning?"

"No, I haven't. I don't go on social media or watch the news on my days off. Hard to turn off, you know? Prefer to enjoy them in peace with my family."

"Right... Well, I'll just dive straight into it then, shall I?"

"Please."

"We've found Aaron Parker's body in a shallow grave behind his garage."

Silence over the line for several seconds.

"Hello?"

"I'm still here, McNally," he chirps irritably.

"Right... So, shocked?"

"Aye... Understandably... I mean, the family are innocent?"

McNally shuffles around in his seat, clicking his seatbelt off to get more comfortable.

"We don't know that."

"Their alibis are solid. The mother and youngest daughter were in the house all night. The older daughter was at a party with her boyfriend, they didn't get home until almost 2am. The son was over in the mainland studying. The body had to be moved there-"

"No, we have heard back from forensics that the body has been there for quite some time, undisturbed before the construction workers uprooted it."

More silence.

"I'm now leading this investigation, so would love it if you could give me anything. Any inside information or any personal thoughts..."

Quigley still doesn't respond. McNally decides he'll wait it out, pushing his head back onto the headrest. This is like interviewing a suspect, the silent treatment sometimes works. But Quigley will have years of experience, he won't bite. He'll know exactly what he's doing.

"I... I'm just in complete shock."

Oh, maybe he thought too soon.

"I know, it must be-"

"I mean, it's one of the reasons why I moved away. It just angered me that I couldn't solve the case. Walking down the same corridors and seeing the same faces. It constantly reminded me of my failure."

"I understand, Quigley," McNally nods, it's weird to see this humbling side to him, "but at the end of the day, we have to put our own successes to one side and do what's best for the family."

"How did he die?"

"Forensics believe it to be a head injury. We should have more conclusive results this morning."

"Mad... It's just mad. Well, I don't think I can help you. Everything I've got is in the file. And as for personal attributes, you have Ferguson. He'll keep you right. I really have to go; I need to run and collect the young boy from nursery. Goodbye, McNally."

Three beeps indicate he has hung up. McNally returns the phone to his pocket and shakes his head. Something isn't right. He just knows it. Why is he being so secretive? His demeaner completely changed once the subject of Parker was brought up. Is it a guilty conscience, for the sake of the family, or is it his own ego that's bruised? Or better yet, is it a reminder that he was blackmailed, or bribed? One thing is for sure, he knows that won't be the last time he has a run in with DCI Quigley.

Chapter Twenty:

The blurred outline of a shadow slowly creeps towards the frosted glass of the front door. A few clicks later and it swings open, revealing a smiling Dermott with his arms outstretched.

"Derm," Ferguson goes in for a hug.

"Alright, ol' boy, what's the craic?"

Pulling away, Ferguson steps inside the house, waving to Grainne in the kitchen baking her station famous goods and shuffles through to the living room.

"You're not really watching *Loose Women*, are you?" Ferguson nods towards the TV in the corner, "retirement can't be that bad."

"Piss off," Dermott frowns, switching it off with the remote, "I was upstairs in the office ye cheeky bastard."

The old friends laugh whilst they take their seats.

"So, you've seen the news?"

"Aye, awful isn't it? I was going to contact Nuala, but thought against it for a few days. Until the dust settles, y'know?"

"Well, Derm... That's actually why I'm here."

"Oh?"

"Aye, Nuala's been asking for you."

"For me?"

"Before we even had a chance to get a FLO to her house, she was begging for you. Shouting about how you know the case and you know them personally. She said she wants you back, despite us saying you've retired."

"I'll do it."

Ferguson rests back on the chair. He was anticipating this, but he still needs to cover all angles.

"Derm... You've been retired for years."

"And I'm bored out of my fucking tree. Please, let me do this. Speak to the super and get me on it. They'll not want to build relations with a new FLO. I can just slot back into place. Like all this time never happened... And at least you know you can trust me."

This does all make sense, Ferguson thinks.

"But what about Grainne, Derm? You retired for her. To save your marriage."

"It was a reason, aye... But she knows how much my work meant to me. What it still means to me now. How much I became a part of the families that I touched… How many people I still communicate with, despite being retired. I want to do this, Ferguson. Please?"

Ferguson opens his mouth to speak, but the living room door bursts open.

"I hope you've not come with a full belly, Cian. I've made some scones, you'll have a few won't you?"

Bending over the coffee table, Grainne slides a tray of assorted goodies in front of him. From scones to caramel squares. He even spies a few Party Rings amongst the madness.

"Thanks Grainne, you're too kind."

"Not at all, sure it's been a while since you've last been over. Out making the world a better place. Hope you still have time to look after that wife of yours. How is Jane?"

"Aye, grand. Still working away."

"And still no sign of wains?"

Ferguson scoffs as he accidentally inhales half a cupcake with the shock. She slaps him on the back, and he coughs it back up, landing sodden and uncurling on the carpet.

"Sorry, so sorry," he lifts it and wraps it in the paper, "sure we're far too old for that now."

"There's means and ways," she nods towards Dermott, who avoids her eye, "and here, what about them finally finding Aaron Parker?"

"Aye, I'm on the case."

"Oh, I wish you could tell me what's going on, but I know better than to ask. How's the family?"

"They're in shock, as you'd expect."

"Aye, of course, of course. And is it true that he was found in the garden? Or can you tell me that?"

"Behind the garage, aye. Construction workers dug him up."

"Awful, sure Jesus... That's just sick."

Trotting out, still shaking her head and mumbling, Grainne leaves the men with their tea and treats. Ferguson glances over at Dermott with raised brows.

"What?"

"Wains? At my age?"

"Awk, don't start. Sure, she's been at me about adopting and all sorts."

Both Grainne and Dermott are in their early 60s, there's hardly a chance they could conceive naturally at this stage.

"Did you two not want wains?"

It suddenly becomes apparent that in all the years that Ferguson has known Dermott that this subject has never been breached. As is the way of officers, not a lot of your personal life slips through the cracks. Not at the station anyway. Dermott shuffles around defensively, taking his contempt out on a Jammie Dodger, the flakes hitting the carpet.

"It's not that we didn't... I mean, we talked about it. But you know... Everything we see in this line of work... I couldn't have imagined if something similar could've happened to one of ours... And how I'd feel. I'd be crushed... Then, we started arguing because I kept saying I wasn't ready. That went on for months, almost a year, before I finally caved. I thought, fuck it, if it happens... It happens. And it never did."

"Oh, Derm... I'm sorry."

"You're grand, turns out I can't anyway."

"You mean..."

"Aye, got checked. Very slim chance, apparently."

"And is that why she's started bringing up adoption?"

"No... Er... To be honest, I never told her until I retired."

"Dermott!"

"I know, I know... But I just couldn't bear the thought of anything happening to them. And if they ever came to harm because of me, y'know... Me being in the police? I'd never forgive myself. And I was scared that if she knew then she would leave me..."

Ferguson shakes his head. Dermott had been a close friend for the better part of 30 years, both inside and outside of work. They'd worked many cases and he constantly saw him as nothing but the big-hearted creature he always has been. Making him the perfect FLO when he started to get older and his bones didn't work like they used to, as he would always complain about. His compassion was incomparable for families going through a hard time... It's no wonder he still keeps in touch now. He was more than a link between the family and the police... He was a friend. But this new revelation... It's tainted his image. How could he have lied to Grainne all these years?

"Anyway, please, get me on this case, won't you?"

Dermott is downplaying the arguments the two would have about him landing back at all hours and being absent from the dinner table even if he's sitting chewing. His mind somewhere else. She'd nearly had a stroke when she'd found out he was shot at almost a decade ago. His retirement was the best thing he could do to save their marriage.

"What about Grainne?"

Dermott frowns and shakes his head as if he'd suggested a tiny obstacle in the road.

"I'll deal with her, just you get me sorted."

"I feel like I'm going to regret this, but... Okay."

"You promise?"

"I'll try everything I can, but I can't make any promises."

Chapter Twenty-One:

By the time the doorbell goes again, the Parkers are up and dressed, with the majority of their untouched breakfasts scraped into the bin. Dermott is ushered into the living room after they've all disbanded from their tearful greetings and hugs. Collected on the sofas with mugs of tea rested on the coffee table, all eyes are on him.

"Thank you so much for coming over, I understand you're retired," Nuala holds a sodden tissue to her face, "I'm sorry."

"It was a no brainer. As soon as I heard, I'd wanted to make contact, so coming and refilling my place is not something to apologise for. I wanted to do it."

The family thank him again, tears in all their eyes. Dermott had become like an uncle to the kids, and a good friend to Nuala. He was more than a confidant.

"I'm just so sorry that this isn't what you wanted, ideally..."

It's the only thing he can think to say. For months after, when the search was ongoing, and it became apparent Aaron wasn't going to just walk in off the street like nothing happened, the best case scenario they all thought of was that he was having an affair and jetted off without telling them. Of course, his passport was resting in his bedside drawer. His bank account unscathed. All of his clothes, now shipped to charity shops, lying idly in his wardrobe.

"Have you heard anything? From the police?" Ritchie asks.

"Just as much as you have, I'm afraid," Dermott leans forward and squeezes Ritchie's bare knee, protruding out from his ripped jeans, "but as soon as I know something, I will be informing you all right away, you know that already."

The family all nod. Dermott had been pivotal in their grieving process as soon as he walked in the door with DI Quigley that first day Aaron hadn't come home.

"So... A head injury?" Michelle wrinkles her nose to stop the tears.

Dermott nods.

"And who are they speaking to? I hope they're looking into those underground organisations. They're at the heart of this, I know they are."

Nuala calms herself down from upsetting her kids as Dermott raises a hand, palm forward, and smiles at her. He knows all this. He's heard it before.

"I've been told investigations are underway. With it reappearing in the media, it might do you a favour. A blessing in disguise. Whoever it was might become sloppy. Give something away. It's brought the incident to light again, when they thought they could hide forever. Every avenue is being investigated, trust me."

"If DI Quigley couldn't find out what happened, what makes you think DI McNally will be able to?" Danielle stares into space, too afraid to look at Dermott.

"We don't, we just have to believe and trust in the justice system. But we have new eyes, and a body... Evidence. A lot of things we didn't have before."

"But it happened over three years ago," Ritchie shakes his head, "CCTV won't have been kept that long. And if you ask ordinary Joe Bloggs off the street what he was doing three years ago, there's no hope of him remembering."

"Stranger things have happened, and trials have lasted longer. Sure, there are loads of cases where people are asked to recall what happened or what they were doing decades before. If it means something to someone, they won't forget."

The family take this in as the doorbell goes again. Ritchie, the closest to the living room door, stands to answer it. Muffled greetings are exchanged before the living room door swings open and in steps Steph. Danielle bursts into fresh tears and rushes over to be consoled by her best friend. They cling to each other, crying and whining uncontrollably, no one having a clue what they're saying. They're not even sure what they're saying themselves. When things have settled down, Steph continues to apologise, her hands entwined with Danielle's. They're just catching her up with what has happened so far when Dermott's phone goes. He apologises and excuses himself, all eyes following him out of the room as he closes the living room door. It's Ferguson. He steps through into the dining room and looks out of the window overlooking the front garden.

"Ol' boy. Any updates?"

"We've just heard something back from the mole in the Ardóimid's organisation. It doesn't look good."

Chapter Twenty-Two:

Why won't she answer her phone? Panicking, Cathal does laps of the small space out the back kept primarily for interviews. Clumsily banging against the rickety table and sidestepping the chairs, he urges Orla to pick up the phone.

"Come on, come on, come on!"

On his fourth try, he gets through.

"Jesus Christ, Cathal, *what?*"

Cathal sighs out in relief. If she's annoyed at him for hounding her, nothing bad has happened to her... Yet.

"Where are you?"

"I'm in work, you dick. What's your problem?"

Cathal nods, taking the seat usually reserved for sources. His heartbeat starts to resume to normal.

"Look, just... Keep safe, okay? Don't be talking to any strangers."

He doesn't want to scare Orla by telling her

about the email he received. She may be 17, but after the life they've had of being abandoned by their parents at young ages, Cathal forced to grow up before his time to make sure they didn't end up in separate children's homes, he still tries to protect her at all costs.

"I'm a big girl now, Cath... I think I know how to look after myself. And I'm in the middle of Foyleside, what could happen?"

Don't tempt fate, Cathal almost exclaims out loud, but does well just telling her to be safe before saying he'll see her tonight. Walking past Jodie's office, intent on returning to his seat, he decides to knock on the door. Taking the proffered chair on the other side of the desk, he tells his editor what's happened, who listens contently.

"Right..." she nods her head, biting her bottom lip as he finishes, "so, this could either be a practical joke, or we'll have to take it very seriously. This is a highly irregular high-profile case. It could be other journalists, ragin' that you got there first. Or whoever is behind this... Could it be your source?"

Cathal shrugs.

"Did he request any more money?"

"No, he was happy with the fifteen hundred, and why would he tell me to stop writing stories if he was the one approached me?"

"True... Very true. Well, the only thing I can suggest at the moment is to take things very carefully. I'm sure the police won't be too happy if we try and contact them now after all that's been said... But maybe best to take your by-line out of the paper for future stories around this case, aye?"

"You're still going to let me cover it?" Cathal smiles, previous worries abandoned.

"Of course, you started it. Why would I ship it over to someone else? That is, of course, if you're not comfortable-"

"No, no. I want it. I'm just unhappy that my by-line won't be there."

Jodie nods and smiles.

"It's still your article, future employers will understand if they request to see your portfolio. Probably best keeping you safe now, and your sister... That's the main thing?"

Cathal nods before thanking her and returning to his desk. Feeling a bit better, he clicks to archive the message just in case, before trolling social media to see if he can find anything more about this body. Starting with the family. The mum and son aren't on any platforms, not that he would consider contacting them through that forum anyway. Turns out he's the same age as the first sister, Danielle, but bizarrely they share no mutual friends on Facebook. That's completely unheard of in a town as small as

Derry. Someone always knows someone who knows you. Her Facebook is relatively private, with nothing but her profile picture, name and hometown on show.

Searching for the youngest sister, Michelle, he smirks as he sees she's the complete opposite. Her entire life on show for the world to see. Silly videos of herself and selfies plastered across the page. Desperate for likes and striving to be virtually famous like all these idiots who make a living out of having no talent. Earning six figure sums from recording ten second videos of themselves swearing by some product or another. Michelle has everything on her profile set to public. Over 1,000 friends. And one of them, he's gleeful to see, is his sister.

Chapter Twenty-Three:

2016

———

"Oh, you need to grow up, there are more important things going on right now!"

And with that, Nuala slams the door to the living room, leaving Danielle to digest what she had just said. It had been a long day. People were still out searching now; they even had the Foyle Search and Rescue out patrolling the River Foyle. The charity created for people who enter the river, whether accidentally or not. The family had told DI Quigley that it was a waste of time and resources, there's no way their da would jump the bridge, the most common form of suicide in the city. But stranger things have happened... Her mother and Danielle had just had a huge fight, each not wanting to be the one to break the news to Ritchie. Nuala not wanting to because she needed to go back out and join the search. Danielle, because they hadn't spoken in nearly a year, despite him being home for Christmas and Easter.

Guilt swirls in Danielle's hungover stomach now. She knows her ma is right, but after so long it's just going to be too hard. He needs to hear it from someone else, he probably wouldn't even answer the phone to her anyway. Her mother's voice carried out from the kitchen tells her she has given up and bitten the bullet. She listens attentively to her delicately telling him his father has gone missing before she jumps with the sound of the doorbell. That wouldn't be him... Unless he's lost his key? It's probably the police back. Would they have news?

Crossing the hall, she opens the door to girlish cries. In flies Katie, Georgia, Abbie and Steph, hugging her and dragging her back into the living room, everyone talking at once. Asking different questions and consoling her that everything will be alright and he's safe. A plastic bag emptied onto the coffee table with crisps and sweets and chocolate. Like they'd just come over for a film, or a sleepover. Like they've done dozens of times before. But this time, she knows that something's wrong... That something's just not right.

"We've heard nothing from him," Danielle holds back her tears as they finally drop onto the sofa and silence falls, "he's made no contact. They've tried the hotel, he's not there. They're currently checking through CCTV and contacting people who were at the party. But nothing has come up. They even have people searching the Foyle," she squeals the last sentence, burying her face in her hands.

The girls instantly envelope her once more. Grabbing tissues, offering tea, rubbing her back. After formalities are finished, they put on a chick flick for some form of normality, background noise more than anything, and sit in their own thoughts, battling for something to come out to make everything better. Of course, they all come up short.

"Where's Chris?" Georgia manages.

Danielle shrugs.

"He left a few hours ago to join the search, but I've heard nothing from him since."

"Are you two... Okay?" Steph blushes.

"I don't know, we haven't spoken about last night. But I woke up to him beside me in bed this morning."

The girls look alarmed.

"Jesus, after that argument I'm really surprised..." Abbie looks away embarrassed.

"Me too, even though I don't remember most of it," Danielle laughs.

The others giggle along. This is what she needed. To try and forget about this. Not sit in on her own waiting for him to come back... *If* he'll come back. Earlier, Nuala had rendered Michelle too young to stay by herself, not a problem when she gets back a half hour earlier than Danielle from school, and was escorted into the back seat of the car and was told to stay put. There she stayed, even now when Nuala had just come home to see if he'd returned and argued with Danielle over who should call Ritchie. The front door slamming declares that she has returned to the search, a sinking feeling in Danielle's heart stops her from getting up and looking out the window at her retreat. The chick flick goes to an ad break, the latest MTV show teases its launch. She remembers seeing this ad... Last night. That reminds her.

"George, what the hell were you and Jimmy up to in the living room last night?"

Katie's head snaps towards Georgia's direction, who turns pink with embarrassment.

"Er... Nothing that you walked in on."

"Meaning?" Abbie gasps.

"We were just having a kiss... But it might've lead to something else," she bites her bottom lip and closes her eyes against the hurls of abusive lashes the girls throw out, Steph even manages to dart a pillow her way.

"You slag!"

"Jimmy? Georgia, ugh!"

"That's mingin'"

"I'm gonny boke."

Despite herself, Danielle manages to burst into laughter and the rest join her, like they're unsure what they can and can't laugh at. Sensitive to her condition.

"And was he any good?" Steph winks.

"Ugh, I don't even want to know," Abbie retches.

"I only remember bits and pieces, so it's almost like it never happened," Georgia scoffs as her friends roll their eyes and say: *'aye right.'*

Chapter Twenty-Four:

2019

———

Turning into the small dirt car park indenting Ballykelly Forest, McNally had made the 13-odd mile journey in record time. Just under 20 minutes, thank God traffic was light, the wains not yet released from school. He'd driven past this forest numerous times, both to and from his parent's house, but never actually entered it. Despite it being a relatively good day, he's surprised to see he's the only car to pull up. Deciding to wait for the mole in the Ardóimid's underground organisation, strictly to be called Smyth and nothing more, he admires the beauty of nature.

This would be a good place for a walk, or to find a body. It's weird how being in this line of work makes you think about something as sinister as the latter. But after viewing Aaron Parker's corpse this morning, it's all he can think about. The forensic pathologist Peter, a man with a face as dead as the body's, and with a voice to match, explained the medical terms that lead him to believe the head injury was the cause of death, with no other tell-tale signs on the body to report. If he had to hazard a guess by examining the crack in the skull, he suggested the murder weapon to be a blunt object, like a tool of some kind.

This caused the SOCOs to return to the scene this morning to see if they can scour through the mess of the Parker's old land to find anything suggestable to a weapon. Of course, they're guessing he's been lying underground for three years, and with so much traffic coming in and out of the area in that time, it's ludicrous to suggest they'll find something. But they have to try. McNally had questioned the family this morning after calling off the FLO, asking them if anyone had heard anything strange that night. As guessed, they'd all shook their heads. Danielle was too drunk to even remember getting home, but had been escorted in out of the taxi by her ex-boyfriend, Chris Hewitt, who is on his list to speak to. Michelle had been in bed from 11, and Nuala joined her shortly after, stating she was sitting up watching a film.

She'd became quite defensive when he'd asked why she didn't join her husband at the party, stating that those things weren't for her and people looked down their noses at her at the few she had attended. Understandable, he had thought, but he still feels like they're hiding something. Ferguson shook his head when he'd met him at the station afterwards and suggested his hypothesis.

"They're innocent, boss. DI Quigley would've sniffed it out of them. They're just a grieving family. None are perfect, but they didn't deserve this, especially when Parker was trying his best to bring the people of this city together."

McNally acknowledged this, after indulging in the politician's manifesto. It seemed too good to be true. Money put into mental health and the NHS, taxes reduced and more employment in the city. Where the hell was he going to get all of this money? Perhaps by cuts on what the opposing parties held dear? Events which each party celebrated religiously, both resulting in government money spent on parades and street cleaning after celebrations, as well as reinforced police presence so bouts of violence could be dealt with swiftly. Maybe these were more motives? Not wanting Parker to take away what each community believed to be their form of *'culture.'*

His thoughts are interrupted as a figure emerges from the trees. Despite the sun beating down, whoever this is has a huge green raincoat, zipped right up with the hood covering their head. Frowning, McNally wonders what this strange character could be up to. They position their body facing the direction of his car, before cocking their head behind them and retreating again. They quickly disappear amongst the vegetation. Were they gesturing to him? Looking around, he sees he's still alone in the car park. A few moments later, wondering what to do, the figure reappears and repeats the transaction. Confused, McNally reaches for the door handle before halting. This could be an ambush. Walking into this wooded area and never coming out. Like something from a film.

After all, he has to remember he's back in Northern Ireland. The police are spat on here, called *'peelers'* and oinked at. And that's when people are being nice. Better than being shot, or pelted with petrol bombs. Deciding to call Ferguson and ask him for an update, he groans when he sees he has no signal. He looks up again and jumps. The figure had managed to sneak right up to the front of his vehicle. After several seconds, they bring both of their hands up to either side of their hood and slowly lower it to reveal a middle-aged man sporting a buzz cut. His eyes expand and he jerks his head in the direction he'd come from before mouthing *'come on, McNally.'*

Guessing this must be this mysterious Smyth, McNally steps out and locks the door, before following Smyth's footsteps, quickly being erased as the grass springs back up. As if no one ever trod on it.

Chapter Twenty-Five:

Chris wakes feeling groggy. Wanting to shift the blanket so it covers his head from the light protruding out from his curtains, but no energy to do so. Unsticking his lips from his teeth, he rolls over and takes one look at the clock on his bedside table and sighs. Gone 2pm. He hasn't slept until this time since he was a teenager. He just couldn't drop off last night. The five beers didn't help. But mostly, thinking about poor Danielle.

He'd gone back around to Steph's last night and she swore him to secrecy. This was not the time for Danielle to find out about the two of them. Not when they'd just found her dad's dead body. He knew she was right, but he was disgusted that he even had to be told.

"You aren't exactly the master of subtlety and compassion," Steph had said.

"What's that supposed to mean?"

"We're best friends, Chris. We talk. I know things you probably think she never shared. I probably know the most, if not everything. I'm like the third person in your relationship."

"Well ye definitely fuckin' are now, so get off your high horse."

He didn't mean to sound so harsh, but she'd triggered him. He lies now and regrets the fight they had. Her kicking him out. He needs a way in. A way to speak to Danielle. But she's blocked him on all social media and he deleted her number out of anger. He doesn't even know where she lives now. Or where her family home is, he should say. He knows that she shipped off to Newcastle after they broke up without a care or even a thought about how he would feel. He can't ask any of his mates, they'll be suspicious. He's in no form for a slagging this afternoon. And he definitely can't ask any other of her friends. That would be even worse. He'd sound like a stalker ex-boyfriend. But he needs to get in touch somehow.

Figuring Steph is his best bet, he scrolls to her name and inhales as he clicks *'call.'* It rings twice before cutting out. Exhaling frustratedly, he tries a few more times, just to be met with the same problem. Texting her he's sorry, he sees it's read within seconds. The three dots indicate she's replying, before they disappear. Waiting a few more minutes, he scrunches up his face and tries again. It just goes straight to voicemail. What the fuck?

Slamming his phone back down on the bedside table, he lifts the duvet and buries his head in the bed. How's he going to get around this one? He supposes the funeral will be in a few days, after the body is officially released, of course. But what evidence could you get from a body that has been left to rot for three years? He doubts it will be held for long. And if there's a funeral, there will be a wake. Everyone will be attending; he can join his friends and hopefully get a moment alone with her. Talk things out. He wonders if the family will let him back over the threshold. He wonders if Ritchie will. If Danielle will.

After a while of lying and planning, his ringtone blares and he scrambles around the bed to fight his way out of the duvet, but when he lifts the phone, he's disappointed to see that it isn't Steph.

"What, Dave?"

He doesn't mean to sound so curt, but he isn't in the form for Dave's boyish banter.

"Man, meet me at the uni now."

"The uni?"

"Aye, lad. It's important. I promise. You'll want to hear this."

Chapter Twenty-Six:

He follows Smyth's retreating figure through the trees at a safe distance for about five minutes. Finally, Smyth stops and allows McNally to join him.

"Smyth?" McNally's surprised to hear a gasp of exhaustion escape his lips.

He needs to get back to a gym, after not attending one since the big move over, and not having time to in the few months before with selling the house and getting everything ready. Smyth winces and shakes one hand at him, before pointing at him to stay and trotting off in the direction they came, leaving McNally with nothing but the cries of a bird high above him.

Moments later, after Smyth has circled the perimeter several times, he regroups with McNally, but not standing in front of him like you would with a normal conversation. He stands by his side. McNally fights the urge to ask why they're standing like two men at a urinal.

"You weren't followed?"

"No."

"No one suspicious looking hanging around the entrance?"

"What? No."

Smyth considers this for a moment, before nodding and turning towards McNally properly.

"Sorry, Detective. It's just if I'm ever caught passing on information to a peeler... I mean, you know the stories."

McNally nods. He's heard, and worked on, plenty of cases. Pissed off underground lords fuming that they were backstabbed, or the wool pulled over their eyes. These days, the number of layers in these organisations and what you have to do to climb the ladder of trust is shocking. Betrayal isn't accepted.

"I understand. Am I right in thinking that you have some information for me?"

Smyth nods, looking around one last time.

"So, word has spread about that politician Parker's body being found. Some of the lads were talking in the Bull's Horn last night, and were reminiscing. Nothing much was said, but apparently Boyle caught wind that Taylor was looking to recruit Parker. Make a sort of coalition government. To push Ardóimid out altogether, by the looks of it. He couldn't have that. As you know, Parker was getting the youths, unreligious and apolitical on his side. Boyle was worried about losing voters and being kicked out of office. He was assured that Parker wouldn't bite, he didn't have the same views as the Jacks, but he couldn't take any chances. So, he organised for someone to throw a brick through their living room window. They said something about a sectarian slur message tied around a brick. I understand the wife is a catholic? And the wains went to the catholic grammars?"

McNally nods.

"Aye, sounds about right then. They said it near killed them to write the words, but they wanted to put Parker off the track of joining the Jacks, and it was as good of an attempt as any. Any message with those words written on it... They'd automatically assume the Jacks were behind it."

"That would explain why, when questioned, they said they had nothing to do with it."

These underground organisations would have so much below their belts. A measly brick through a window is child's play.

"But wasn't that years ago?" McNally ponders, the station gossip revisiting him.

"Aye, so they said. But still thought it could be detrimental to the case."

"It still could be, Smyth. Thanks... So, do you think that maybe things went further? Did they want Parker to join *them?*"

"Fuck no," Smyth scoffs, "you know Boyle, he'd do the whole campaign by himself if he could."

"But do you think he might've killed him to get rid of the competition? I mean, he was basically a one man show. No violent supporters to start a riot or civil war."

Smyth shrugs and shakes his head.

"That's all that was said. They brought it up and laughed about it because apparently one of the lads I was with thought it was a stupid idea. He'd never say that to the boss though..."

"Right, thanks... You've been a huge help. Keep safe and be sure to report anything else back."

Chapter Twenty-Seven:

Stepping through into the kitchen to boil the kettle, Danielle leans back on the worktop and breathes out. As she listens to the water boil, she continues gazing out into the garden. As much as she appreciates Steph being here, something's up. She's twitchy, constantly looking at her phone and Danielle's heard it vibrate on and off as if someone were trying to contact her more than a few times now. Why won't she just answer? It would take two seconds to text back. She's hiding something. Does she have a boyfriend she hasn't shared? Not wanting to bring it up considering the way things are currently. She just wishes she would tell her the truth instead of walking on eggshells around her. She's not some big scary monster, she's her best friend. Nothing has changed... Has it?

As she fills two mugs, she forgets that Dermott is still in the dining room with Ma. Poking her head through, she asks if anyone would like some tea. Her mother is sitting with her head in her hands and Dermott smiles over to her.

"We're okay, but DI McNally is coming back to talk to us all in a while. We'll be out then."

That can't be good news. She nods before closing the door and retreats to the kitchen. Deliberating what it could be, she picks up the two mugs and turns around to see Richie standing in the doorway. He'd just been out for a run, and his grey t-shirt has a damp circle around the collar from perspiration.

"McNally's coming back in a while."

"Why?"

She shrugs.

"Dermott just told me."

Nodding, Ritchie bites his lip before crossing to the newly piled clean laundry in the discarded basket. Extracting a blue towel from the pile, he slinks it over one shoulder and turns to leave.

"Wait..."

He gazes at Danielle, who is speechless. Deciding that actions speak louder than words, Danielle puts down the mugs and pads over, wrapping two arms around his neck and leaning in for a cuddle. Seemingly surprised, it takes Ritchie a few seconds to react. Snapping out of it, he wraps his own arms around his sister. She smells the musty

164

stench of his sweat, but she doesn't care, she buries her head in his chest anyway. This should be weird. Awkward. But instead, it just feels like the past few years haven't happened. Like they were when they were younger. They used to be so close. Going to the same parties and having the same friends. Only a few years apart. They always got on so well. Until Chris had to ruin everything. Until she had to ruin everything. Seconds go by before they break apart, both not looking each other in the eye.

"Thanks..." Ritchie coughs before turning and opening the downstairs bathroom door.

Re-joining Steph in the living room, Danielle stares blankly at the TV. A re-run of some shit dating show Steph seems to love. The airhead American accents do her head in.

"Are you hiding something?"

Oh, fuck. Did she say that out loud?

"Wh... What?"

She turns to her best friend and tries to take the irritability out of her voice.

"You're quite distant today. I mean, thank you so much for being here for me. But I just feel like... You're somewhere else. Your phone keeps going off... Are you hiding something? Something you don't want me to know?"

Steph looks like she's been caught in headlights. She just stares at Danielle, shaking her head and stuttering.

"I... I..."

She gulps and blows out, before taking Danielle's hand. And just as she goes to open her mouth, the doorbell goes.

Chapter Twenty-Eight:

'The uni' as it was dubbed by young people is the bunch of trees behind Altnagelvin Hospital, just before the hill down to the underground tunnels beneath the Altnagelvin Roundabout which connect through to Lisnagelvin Shopping Centre. The trees, although being in close proximity to the Tesco and other off-licences, are hidden away enough that underage drinkers can't be caught by the police, but central enough in the Waterside for people to congregate easily. Rumour has it the name was derived from being close to the buildings that once housed the nursing students.

Why the hell would Dave want to meet here? They haven't been here in years. Not since they were maybe 16 years old. Falling down the hill drunk, clinging to each other and laughing and tripping into the shopping centre to get a huge bag of Tesco Value salt and vinegar crisps. Looking around, he feels silly climbing the hill as a full-grown adult, wary of the many onlookers on the Glenshane Road. When the grass levels out, he makes his way into the trees and perches on the bank at the side, his back to the underground tunnel at the bottom of the vertiginous drop.

Moments later, he sees Dave marching across towards him. He stands to greet him, but Dave silences him with a finger to his lips. Looking around, he waves him further into the trees. Confused, he follows him for a few moments until they come out into a clearing. From here, he sees he's leading him to the bushes surrounding the main road. The hum of traffic takes over the eerie silence. What is going on with Dave? He's jittering about like he's set to vibrate. Squatting at the bushes, Chris pulls up his trousers to join him.

"What the hell's goin' on?"

"You need to hear this from me, but don't tell anyone how you heard, you hear me?"

"Dave, what's your pro-"

Dave grabs him from the scruff of his t-shirt, making Chris lose his balance and fall forward until they're both on the ground.

"Get off me ye mad bastard. What's-"

"Ssssh!"

Sitting back up and brushing themselves off, Dave looks around before glaring into Chris's face. His eyes are massive, manic looking.

"Have ye been takin' somethin'?"

"Listen, lad... I need to tell you something. Something huge. What you do with this information is down to yourself... But whatever you do, this doesn't come back to me? Alright?"

Chapter Twenty-Nine:

Stepping off the bus outside the old Foyle College grounds on Duncreggan Road, Cathal takes in the sun as he marches home, reflecting on his story. The interview with DC Fleming didn't tell him anything he didn't already know, short of the confirmation that the body was that of Parker, and how he died. Therefore, the afternoon story online was just regurgitated facts about Parker's disappearance and quotes from the construction worker last night, as well as a few lines from Fleming reassuring the public they're doing everything they can. It infuriated Cathal seeing the by-line *'written by staff reporter.'* It was so impersonal. So unappreciative of his hard work... But he understands he needs to be careful.

The mystery of Aaron Parker's disappearance was splashed across all the local rags, as well as social media, at the time. With no clues as to where he went, the story quickly lost velocity, with nothing but anniversaries being published since. It seemed the police had pretty much closed the case. Something else took precedence and it slowly moved down the *'to-do'* list until it vanished off it completely. Manpower and expenses needed for more pressing matters. There were rumours that he'd jumped the bridge, or ran off down south with some mystery woman, but the family always stood defiant that he wasn't that sort of man. It was plain to see that he was passionate about politics and moving the city forward towards unity, why would he up and go and leave all his hard work behind?

The fact that he has been found now, dead, has opened a murder inquiry. Could whoever killed him be after Cathal, or specifically Orla, now too? These aren't the kind of people to mess with. No matter which religion did this to Parker, both underground organisations have reputations that precede them. He'd written about people losing family members, being hounded out of their homes or getting limbs blasted by all kinds of gangs. But he's just doing his job. Surely if he doesn't write the story, someone else will? They can't go after every journalist, and every comment on social media. It's in the public domain. No, he'll just soldier on, albeit anonymously, writing and updating the Letter's loyal readers. Starting with Orla. His first source into the Parker family.

He calls out as he locks the front door, dropping his bag down and stepping out of his groaning loafers. Opening the living room door, he mutters irritably before turning down the TV volume, blasting some techno tune, and files into the kitchen. There he finds Orla, tiptoes balancing on the kitchen stool, rooting around in the cupboard above the sink. Better known as the drink cupboard. He leans against the threshold and crosses his arms, but she still doesn't turn around. Elbow deep in the cupboard, she finally manages to prise out the bottle of vodka, making Cathal's eyes twitch with the sound of clinking glasses, half expecting one to come barrelling onto the tiles with a smash.

Closing the cupboard door and climbing down from her makeshift step ladder, she smiles over towards her brother as she puts the vodka in the open Tesco bag, where a litre bottle of Diet Pepsi and a huge bag of cheese and onion crisps also rest.

"Alright, Cath?"

"What are you at?"

"What you mean?"

"I mean where are you away with *my* vodka."

"Awk, fuck off. Stop going on all parental, and don't act like you weren't drinking at my age."

"I wasn't, naw. I was too busy working full time to put you through school, keep clothes on your back and a roof over your head."

"Awk, such a nice sob story, should try out for *The X Factor* with that one," she punches him playfully on the arm, making Cathal unable to resist a dry smirk. "Naw, a girl from work asked me around to hers tonight for a Chinese and to watch a film. She only lives up at the top of Brooke Park there, so I won't be home late. We're both off tomorrow anyway, but I don't feel up to a mad one, so just gonna have a few... What's wrong with you?"

She frowns and edges her neck back in disgust as she takes in Cathal's stance.

"You're not going."

"Am I not?"

"Naw, you're only 17."

"Oh, fuck up, Cath. You've bought us drink before, like."

"That's different."

"How?"

How indeed, what way could he tell her...

"Because it's been in this house, in my house. I can keep an eye on you."

"'*Keep an eye on me?*' Oh, piss off, Cathal. I'm not going to go runaway on you, I'm not fucking Dad."

The look on her face for blurting that out shows that she's as shocked as Cathal is. Their father is still a sore subject, and not often is his name breathed in this house, despite it being his originally before it was signed over to Cathal after his death the year before last.

"I... I'm sorry, I went too far."

"It's fine, Orl... Just... Please, trust me. I don't want you going there tonight."

"Why? Because you don't know her?"

"No, I-"

"She's 23, she's not some silly schoolgirl like you obviously think I am."

"I don't think that, Orla. Look, I can only ask that you trust me."

"And I ask that you stop treating me like a wain. I'm 17, Cathal. As you said, when you were my age you were out working full time to keep this house," she brandishes her flailing arms above her to the ceiling, "I'm not stupid, I know how hard you worked. And I'm grateful for it. But you're fucking suffocating me, Cathal. It's either no parents, or overparenting. And at the moment, I prefer neither."

She lifts the bag and pushes past him. Several seconds later, he winces as he hears the front door slam. Bringing the stool back over to the table, Cathal sighs as he sinks into it, folding his arms on the table and resting his head in them. What a day. At least it's the start of September, so the nights are still bright. The thought of her traipsing about in the dark would make him feel worse. He'll sit down with her later and try and think of a rational explanation for his actions.

He sits up and gazes out the window at the shed in the back garden. Bad people do bad things, he thinks, biting his lip. He knows that all too well. A vibration in his pocket makes him reach into his jacket.

'Sorry, I just need some space.'

He nods, leaving the message from his sister on read as he places the phone on the table. Deciding to make a dinner for one, with leftovers for lunch tomorrow, he goes over to the sink and washes his hands, his eyes still roaming to the shed. He's nothing like their dad, he tells himself. That's why he wants to keep her safe. But the night their dad died he found out some revelations, and did something he isn't proud of, that would beg to differ.

As he starts cutting a slab of chicken from the fridge into slices, another vibration lights up his phone. A new email. Swiping the screen with a curled knuckle, intent on not getting uncooked chicken juice on his phone, he startles when he sees it's from the same user from earlier. The jumbled letters and numbers of the email giving him Deja vu. Another picture file, but with no message this time. Clicking on download, his heart jolts. He sees a picture of what looks to be his street... Yes, he can make out Mr Graham's untrimmed hedges leaking over the pavement. But in the middle of the road is the back of a retreating girl. He recognises her blonde ponytail. The Tesco shopping bag. And the same pink sweatshirt Orla had on when she left just moments ago.

"Orla!"

Thundering out of the kitchen, crossing the living room and speeding out of the unlocked door, Cathal reaches the road and looks up and down... But there's no one to be seen.

Chapter Thirty:

"So, what are you going to do with this new information?"

McNally rests back in his chair and smiles sympathetically. On the sofa sit the four Parkers, the blonde girl, who he guesses must be a family friend, was sent upstairs upon his arrival. Dermott Curry, after introducing himself, sits in the chair beside him where its hard to believe that Ferguson sat only yesterday. He was expecting this. The family wanting him to blast through all guns blazing into Boyle's house and the relatively known nationalist pub, the Bull's Horn, in the west of the city.

"We need to treat this information sensitively. We-"

"Sensitively?" Nuala practically shrieks, startling her children, "I said from the word go that these scumbags were the culprits behind my husband's disap... Death. Yet because he's Boyle big bollox in the underground scene, he's basically untouchable. It's a fucking joke. I want to find out what they know because they sure as hell know something. And that's if I have to find it out my fucking self!"

"I understand that, Mrs Parker... We fully respect you're angry about the whole situation.... But we have, just today, found out this information by an undercover officer. If he's found out to be our mole by the organisation, who knows what they could do to him or his family. Boyle will be expecting us to go knocking on his door regardless of us finding this out, as the leader of Ardóimid... Which is what I'll be doing straight after this."

They don't look happy, he thinks, as he looks to Dermott for support. He avoids his eye and bites his lip. Maybe he's too close to the case? Was this a bad idea after all?

"We aren't just going to sweep this under the carpet, believe me."

"Like Quigley did," Danielle mutters.

"Sorry?"

Michelle digs Danielle in the ribs and she exclaims, rubbing them in pain.

"Sorry, Danielle, isn't it? Did you say something?" McNally tries again.

She looks in the corner, fumbling with the zip on her hoody. She only repeats herself after Nuala leans in and says, *'it's okay, sweetheart.'*

"Can I ask why you said that?"

"Because he was a useless bastard," she ignores the negative tone her mother takes with her after the cuss, "he just wanted to be the face of the investigation, but I don't think he could investigate his way out of a paper bag."

McNally nods and turns to Dermott.

"Can I speak to you outside, please?"

Raising his eyebrows at the family in a sign of affection, Dermott follows McNally out the front.

"Were you aware the family felt like this?" McNally turns to him when the door snaps shut.

"Well... They occasionally seemed to question his motives."

"Meaning?"

"They always said how he would just show up to give good news, which was rare. He got Ferguson to deliver them bad news, like another failed search or when they came away from a tip off unsuccessful. They just felt like his head wasn't really in the game..."

"And you?"

"Me, sir?"

"Everyone in the station seems to think the sun shines out of Quigley's arse."

Dermott stifles a smirk.

"How did you feel he handled the investigation?"

"No different to others to be honest... But I do see where the family are coming from. He'd be the first to throw himself in front of a TV camera for good news, despite putting little or no work into an investigation. But if something bad was up... He'd quickly pawn it off to someone below him."

"I spoke with him this morning and he seemed off when I brought up this case... I understand he moved to Belfast shortly after?"

"That's what I was told, sir."

"And during the case... When did he lose interest, or... Heart, should I say? Better turn of phrase."

"Er... Probably a few weeks in. He was very motivated at the start and convinced that he was going to find him alive. Calling all airports and banks to keep an eye on any activity if he tried to use cards or leave the country... Then, when nothing came up, and the insights into the political sides of things came up fruitless, he just kind of... Deflated, should I say?"

"And do you think there was a turning point of some sorts?"

Maybe this is the person he needs to speak to. To find out what really happened with this case.

180

"No."

He feels deflated himself now, almost cursing out loud.

"He just sort of showed up one day and said there were more important cases to be doing, stockpiled on his desk, he said they were. A few weeks later, a Wednesday I believe it was, he said his goodbyes. Word got round that he was offered DCI in Belfast, but he would hear nothing about a leaving party or that. We thought the case had knocked his confidence, but we were mistaken when we found out he'd been taken on for DCI... I mean, that's a whole different ball game, isn't it?"

McNally nods as Dermott turns to go back into the house.

"Wait."

Dermott halts at the doorstep and gives him an inquisitive look.

"If it was a few weeks in... How come no one talks about who took the job between me and him? I mean, that's a good few years."

Dermott smiles.

"That's because Ferguson was promised the job... He agreed to step into his shoes, as an acting role, but he had to take a step back a few months ago."

Why wasn't McNally made aware of this? He's been in Derry, and Strand Road Police Station, for nearly three weeks now.

"Why?"

Dermott's smile turns concerned.

"I'm not one to gossip, maybe it's best you ask him that yourself."

Nodding, McNally tells Dermott to inform the Parkers that he's going to speak to Boyle. When he hears the door close behind him, he crosses the lawn and reaches the gate. He sees a boy in a blue hoody resting against their fence, who averts his gaze when McNally rounds the gate. Frowning at the boy, who fidgets his hands inside his hoody pocket, at least that's what he hopes he's doing, he trods off to the car and calls Ferguson, who should be on his way back from the station now.

"Just the man I'm looking for."

"Ferguson, what do you have for me?"

"Well, nothing yet, but I'm on my way to Boyle's house to speak with him. Would you like to come with and lead?"

"I'll come with, but I've never met the little rat... So maybe best you lead on this one, Ferguson. I'm sure you have the expertise."

McNally winces. Was that too obvious? Ferguson goes quiet for a few seconds before laughing and confirming he'll swing by and pick him up now. Pocketing his phone, McNally thinks over this new information about Quigley as he gazes over at the boy outside the Parker's, who is still staring at the house and shuffling from foot to foot. Deciding to investigate, he rolls down his window.

"You alright, kid?"

The boy jumps and turns towards his car, smiling awkwardly.

"Uh... Aye, I am... Uh... Just, don't know if I've got the right house."

"Then maybe you should move on..."

The boy chuckles nervously, before realising that McNally's being serious.

"Er... Do ye know if that's the Parker's house?"

McNally narrows his eyes at the lad. Lanky, with piercing green eyes and brown hair just about noticeable under his hood. Despite being roughly the same age, his baggy jeans are way off what Ritchie is wearing in the house, which look like they are painted on.

"Who's asking?"

"Erm... I heard what happened, and I wanted to come pay my condolences... I... I used... Well, I used to a lot of things," he laughs again.

"Spit it out, boy."

"I used to be friends with Ritchie, and I'm Danielle's ex."

183

Nodding, McNally takes the boy in once more.

"Chris?"

The boy's eyes expand dramatically, and he takes a step back, nearly tripping over the pavement.

"Er... Aye, how'd ye know that?"

"You're on my list."

McNally steps out of the car and extends his hand.

"Detective Inspector Liam McNally, PSNI."

He feels the shakes of Chris's body as he takes his limp hand in his. What would anyone ever see in a weedy lad like him?

"Was actually looking to speak to you in a while about the night Aaron Parker went missing."

"Why? What happened Quigley?"

"He's moved on to greener pastures." The look of unrecognition on his face almost makes McNally roll his eyes. "Belfast."

"Ohhh," Chris nods.

"Anyway, what are you doing sulking around here?"

"Like I said... Just wantin' to pay my respects, but I didn't know if I had the right house. I haven't seen them since they left the house on the Glenshane Road."

Nodding, McNally hears the hum of a car approaching behind. Turning, he sees it's Ferguson pulling up.

"Grand... Are you planning on staying a while?"

"I... I d-"

"We'll be back in an hour or so, maybe we can get a good chat then?"

The boy looks alarmed as McNally nods at him before falling into the passenger seat.

"Is that your man... Danielle's ex-boyfriend?" Ferguson looks after him as he sulks towards the front door of the Parker's house.

"Chris Hewitt... Aye."

"Why does he look like he's just shit himself?"

The two burst into laughter.

"I'm not sure... Police presence, maybe? Or because he's not spoken to the family since they moved... Might still have a thing for the daughter. Who knows? We'll find out after speaking to Boyle anyway."

Ferguson does a three-point turn at the end of the road. By the time they drive past the Parker's again, Chris has vanished.

Chapter Thirty-One:

Standing at the front door, Chris blows out in apprehension. Have they really lived here all this time? Only down the road from him? He was shocked when Dave told him, but not as shocked as he was to hear what else he had to say. He has to tell them. That detective had spooked him, even more so than that old Quigley guy, but he's glad he's left. It's better to come from him now, with no police breathing down his neck. He can take his time, at his own pace. Decide what to tell and what to leave out. And he'd rather Danielle and her family hear it from him, not the police.

He raises a wrist to knock, before he halts. Had he imagined it? A hissing sound? Shaking his head, he curls his hand into a fist again, only to be met with the same noise.

"Pssssssssssst."

Cocking his head to the left, the source of the noise, he sees a mop of blonde hair curling itself around from the side of the house. Steph? Trudging over, he sees he's right, it is her.

"What are ye-"

But quicker than he'd ever seen her move, she jolts forward and grabs him by the scruff of the neck, dragging him around the side of the house. When they reach the bins by the back garden, she shoves him to the side, making him bang clumsily against the ivy-covered wall, wrenching his top back into place.

"What the fuck are you doing here?"

"Me? What're *ye* doin' here?"

"I'm her best friend, Chris. And I'm not gonna let you ruin that. Not now, Jesus Christ this is the last thing she needs."

"I'm not fuckin' stupid, Steph. I know what I'm doin'."

"No, you don't. She doesn't miss you, Chris. I asked her a few weeks ago when we were out one night. She says she's moved on. Has even started seeing someone she's working with over in England."

Chris stares at her dumbfounded, feeling a hollow pain in his chest.

"It's just a few dates, nothing serious, but still... It's progress. You broke her heart!"

"I fuckin' know what I did, Steph. I think about it every single day. It might be over for her... But it isn't for me. Not yet, anyway. And besides, I'm not here for that. I have to-"

"Oh, she's right. You really are an inconsiderate prick, you know, Chris? Spill your guts to her fuckin' best friend, why don't you? What the hell has the past week been, then? A way to slither back into her life?"

"What? No, I-"

"I have no idea why I even bothered. Well, I know why it started... Completely plastered and vulnerable and upset... Just how you managed to wangle your way into her life too."

Chris's mouth falls open. Is this really what they think of him? Sure, Danielle was drunk... But she wasn't vulnerable or upset. He was pissed too. And it was only a kiss. It isn't like he fucking raped her. But he has no leg to stand on with Steph. After all, she kissed him. She climbed on top of him. She... Initiated things. But how would that stand up in court? Or put forward to Danielle or any of their friends? He decides he isn't going to open that can of worms. Not tonight. He came for one reason and one reason only.

"Let's not get into that right now, Steph. Like I've been try-"

"Chris?"

Jerking their heads to the back door, they see Danielle standing peering through the crack. When she sees it's him, she pushes it open and steps onto the grass, wrapping her arms around herself. Protection, he guesses, as it's still relatively warm. Steph looks up at him with pleading eyes, but he ignores her and takes a step forward, ignoring Danielle's initial retreat, whether impulse or not. This is the first time he's seen her in years. His heart hurts, like someone has actually punched him in the chest. She looks the same, yet completely different. Ignoring her striking beauty, he physically shakes his head. This needs to be said. It needs to come out.

"Chris... What are you doing here?"

"D... Please, I need to speak to ye."

Chapter Thirty-Two:

"So, tell me a bit about this Boyle character."

McNally had heard bits and pieces about him whilst trying to stay up to date with news and politics back home whilst he was still living in England, but being from Portrush himself, he found it hard to keep up with everything that went on in the majority of Northern Ireland as a whole. They're just crossing the Foyle Bridge, or the new bridge as some of the locals call it, and are indicating left to pull onto the Culmore Road, off of which, Boyle lives. Ferguson shuffles in the driver's seat, making McNally observe him suspiciously.

"What would you like to know?"

"Well, as much as you can disclose before we get there."

Ferguson laughs.

"Well... He graduated from Queen's University in Belfast with a degree in politics before moving home and beginning his political journey by being elected to Derry City Council. He was unsuccessful in his run for Mayor of Derry in the 2000s, something he's very touchy about so don't bring it up. He then went on to climb the ranks in Ardóimid, before finally becoming leader, including health minister for a little while.

"As well as this, although he strongly refuses his participation, he is rumoured to be the big boss in the underground organisation, as you well know. We haven't been able to get anything in stone against him, although a few... Touts, for a lack of a better term, have given us insights over the years. Strangely enough though, days later they all seem to end up in tragic accidents. Whether that's being blasted in the knees or being found dead at the bottom of their stairs."

"Yes, very strange," McNally nods as they pull up outside a grand house overlooking the main road.

The prestigious three story boasts high ceilings and long clear windows looking into luxurious rooms filled with fluffy rugs and expensive paintings.

"We even gave a guy police protection after he stated that Boyle was behind the shooting of a local known drug dealer, but we still found him in the safe house with his throat slit. Aye, he still pleads his innocence. States he's only got the city's best interests at heart and doesn't agree with violence, says the city has seen enough already."

"At least we can agree on that," McNally sighs.

As the two detectives step out of the car and climb the drive, McNally takes a quick glance at Ferguson, who seems fidgety.

"Everything alright, Ferguson?"

"He's just a pompous prick, sir. Hate having to speak with him."

"Had a few run-ins with him before?"

"Aye, and he always tries to get the better of you. Despite knowing you're right, he still has the ability to make you walk away feeling this small," he says, sticking his thumb and pointing finger out and barely letting them touch, "he's just a nasty piece of work."

"Dangerous?"

Ferguson blows a raspberry.

"He wouldn't touch you himself."

"Well then, looks like we have nothing to worry about, do we?"

And with that, McNally knocks on the impressive red oak door and stands back.

****

Going an arse about face way of getting there, but determined not to be seen, I follow the Glenshane Road right up until I see Altnagelvin Hospital on my right. Indicating at the lights, I swerve the two mini roundabouts and continue up Belt Road. Heart in my throat. Steering wheel soaking with my clammy hands. I can't help it. I can't be stopped. I can't be seen. Turning into Trench Road, I pull up at the bus stop and flick my lights. I'm shaking, but it needs to be done. It needs to be moved.

Out of instinct, I reach for my phone, before thinking better of it. It's switched off anyway. If shit hits the fan, there'll be no trace of me here. I'll make sure of it. Stepping out and giving the road a good look up and down, I close the door carefully, making sure it doesn't echo, before trotting back down the way I came. Turning into the cul-de-sac, I hope I'm going to the right place. I'd heard they'd moved a good while back, but not 100% sure where. Gossip that I hope has a touch of truth in it. I don't know what I'm going to do when I actually get there, still to devise a plan. Until then, I'm just standing in the dark... Literally.

Drawing close with the house I think it is, I start to slow. There's a light on in a neighbouring house. I can see an older man sitting with his back to me watching an episode of Dad's Army *through his living room window. Fuck sake, it's the middle of the night. I'm sure the repeats are on most of the time. Why tonight? Crossing the road to the other side, I sneak past, but he's too engrossed in his programme. I slide through undetected. Looking up at the house they're rumoured to be in, I can see why they've moved. New place. New memories. And a bloody nice house. Luckily, every window facing out onto the street, and I count five, have all got their blinds shut.*

Crossing the garden, I stick to as close to the wall as I can. That is, before the shrubbery gets in the way. Hopefully its shadow will hide me from the moon looming above my head. Peering around the side of the house, I'm just at the bins by the side door when the automatic sensor outside light comes on. I freeze. Expecting an alarm to sound. A dog to bark. Blue beacons to appear. But I'm met with silence. An owl hooting to my left makes me jump and fall forward onto the ground.

Deciding this is a better idea, I start to crawl around the side of the house until I'm in the back garden. From here, I can see through the conservatory perfectly. Wicker furniture with uncomfortable-looking cushions thrust over them. A giant radio resting on a floating shelf that looks like its groaning under the weight. A painted picture of a pear idly resting below. Sliding doors through to the kitchen.

I wonder if they remembered to lock the door. Surely, they did. I mean, how many times do you shout at a burglar on the TV shows and films that they wouldn't be able to get access into the house so easily? Worth a try though, right? Creeping over, I rattle the handle as quietly as I can. It's locked, as I figured. Stepping back a few metres, I survey the back of the house. Directly in front of me on the first floor is a large window where you see the stairs break off onto a landing, before resuming again on the opposite side. A dying plant the only thing perched on the level. Another frosted glass window indicates it must be the bathroom. Short of the window on the ground floor, there's nothing else to go by. I spot two more of what I presume to be bedroom windows on either side of the house. But whose is who?

A light beams down on me, making me jolt my head towards the source. The bathroom window. Stepping back and away from it, shining down on the garden, I'm just about to escape its beam when I misplace my footing. I fall to the ground with a sharp clap. Looking down, I see I've reached the edge of the garden, and have just fallen into a plant pot, lying broken beneath my feet. A sharp pain tells me that I've scraped my leg against it on my descent. I sit there in the darkness and silence, hoping whoever has made a late-night trip to the toilet hasn't heard me. The sound of the pipes bursting to life tells me that they haven't and I exhale, not realising that I was holding my breath. Counting to 20 after the light goes off, I stand and start brushing myself down. Leaning down and unpeeling my sock from the cut, I wince as the fabric catches on the blood, already sticking things together. I'll need to be more careful.

"Oi!"

I jump, looking over at my left where the noise came from. Through the neighbouring fence, I see a woman standing at her back door with a cigarette lit and pointed towards me. Her nightie swaying in the breeze like a banshee.

"Fuck do you think you're doing?"

I scrabble around me, running back the way I came, around the other side of the house away from the woman, now shrieking after me and shouting for Alan, presumably her husband. I don't stop until I'm back in the car and have screeched it along Trench Road and down Fountain Hill. Flying across the

Craigavon Bridge and circling the roundabout to finally come to a stop in the carpark on Foyle Road, I relax and rest my head on the steering wheel. What am I going to do?

Chapter Thirty-Three:

2016

———

God, he looks awful, Danielle thinks, as her brother drops his bag on the floor and goes over to kiss their mum on the cheek. His hair is dishevelled and hasn't been washed in days, and needs cut. His clothes look wrinkled and musty, obviously thrown on to catch the flight that Ma bought for him, albeit a few days earlier than planned.

As he goes over to sit on the single armchair, he ruffles Michelle's hair, who snoozes on their mum's knee, her face still puffy and red from when she cried herself to sleep. Too drained from the day to stay awake for the 10 o'clock news, where a repeat will air for requests for anyone who knows anything about their father's disappearance to come forward. Not that it will suddenly tell them where he is, they know that's what Dermott's for, although he'd left barely a half hour ago. They aren't going to hear anything new from the TV, but they know that they must do something. Sitting in deafening silence is driving them crazy.

"No trouble renting a car, love?"

"Naw, Ma. Was grand. Sure, it's just at arrivals."

"Good man, I'm sorry I couldn't lift you... I was runnin' around that town 50 times over..."

"I understand, Ma."

"I'll get you the money you spent on it anyway."

He nods and resumes his attention to his phone. Not once has he looked over in Danielle's direction, where she sits on the loveseat with Chris. She felt Chris tense when Ritchie had opened the door, and he's still to settle. Taking his hand, she stares at him until he looks up at her and they both smile warmly at each other. She had been stupid last night; he would never cheat on her. With all the playboy stories that Ritchie had told her to deter her from going out with him, it had made her very insecure. She constantly second guesses her outfit and makes more of an effort when she knows she's going to see him. He never really complements her anyway, which makes her feel she isn't good enough for him. Like he's just waiting for something better to come along...

"Police are asking the public for information regarding the disappearance of Everyone Unite Party leader Aaron Parker. It seems the well-known politician attended the cancer charity night in the Waterfoot Hotel last night but never made it home. Jessica Deany reports."

There stands Jessica Deany in her tight blue blouse outside the Waterfoot Hotel, as she tells the camera that police have opened an ongoing investigation to track his last known movements, finishing with stating that the family are worried and heartbroken and just want him back safe. Back to the newsroom where the anchor moves on to the next segment, as if their father's disappearance isn't the most awful thing to happen to them. Just another story to be forgotten about.

"Maybe we should go looking again?" Danielle asks the room in general.

She'd been stuck inside all day; she's getting cabin fever.

"There's no point, darling," Nuala doesn't take her eyes off the TV, seemingly forgiving Danielle for their earlier spat, "the police are on top of it. They're still out searching now... Doing everything they can. We have to trust them. All we can do is wait... If anything has happened, we need to be here in case they ring, or they arrive... Or in case he tries to get in contact with us... Dermott will be in touch."

It sounds like she's given up, Danielle almost says out loud, but bites her tongue. Her mother had been out all day, she's probably exhausted. She thinks against asking if her and Chris can go looking, thinking that if something happens while she's away that she'll never forgive herself for not being here.

But the silence is unbearable. They sit like this for ages. Some ITV crime drama broken up by adverts, but no one actually paying attention to what's going on. Everyone in their own world of thoughts and worries.

"What's happening with your coursework, Ritchie, love?" Nuala says, when the awkwardness can no longer be ignored.

"I've basically finished... Been finished for a few days. Have just been leaving it to come back and edit with a fresh eye and see if I've missed anything... I'm able to submit everything online, anyway. I sent most of it away at the airport there when I was waiting for the flight. Just a few essays that I need to add the finishing touches to. Bibliographies and stuff," he shrugs.

"Oh, well that's good," Nuala nods, although everyone knows she has no idea what he means, before reverting her eyes back to the TV.

Another few moments of silence. Chris shuffles about uncomfortably and opens his mouth,

Danielle frowning at him. Is he going to try to talk to him? They haven't spoken in months.

"Ye know Dave's brother, Thomas? He's studying at Magee here, just finished his final year. He said there's a good website that he found that really helped him with his dissertation. Set up his bibliography for him, apparently. Ye should get in touch with him, might be of some help."

Danielle looks over to Ritchie, who, apart from tensing slightly when Chris began to speak, had not shown any acknowledgement that he was being addressed. Nuala looks from Chris to Ritchie and back to Chris again, giving him a sweet smile as if that's good enough. It fucking isn't, Danielle thinks.

"Ritchie?" Danielle clears her throat.

He bristles.

"Ritchie, Chris was talking to you..."

Ritchie coughs and nods so subtly it could've been perceived as a flicker of the light as he sits in the shadows of the TV and the big lamp. Nuala just looks between them both, her jaw jutted out in worry. This is the last thing she needs.

"Why do you have to be such a dick?"

"Now, Danni..." Nuala raises a hand to stop her.

"Enough is going on at the moment without this added tension and ongoing argument."

"Danielle, that's enough."

"What, Ma? How am I to blame? At least Chris actually just made an effort then. He just pied him off. Honestly, Ritchie... Grow up. I'm a big girl. We're a couple. Get the fuck over it."

For the first time, Ritchie glares over towards them. Right at Danielle. He opens his mouth to say something, but thinks better of it.

"What? You know you're in the wrong?" Danielle ignores her mother's continued protests to stop them. "Now apologise to my boyfriend, 'cause it looks like you'll be seeing an awful lot more of him."

"Ma?" Everyone's eyes fly to Michelle, who had been stirring on Nuala's lap, their raised voices wakening her. "What's going on?"

"Nothing, sweetie. Let's get you to bed, will we?"

Glaring at her two elder children, Nuala coos Michelle as she asks if there's been any updates on her father. They both leave the room and the atmosphere makes the space crank up a few degrees. Probably coming from the fuming brains of the siblings. Chris fidgets beside Danielle, before going to stand.

"Maybe I sh-"

"No!" Danielle grabs him and shoves him back down beside her, looking seethingly over at her brother.

They stay like that for several more moments before Ritchie snorts, stands and storms out of the room, muttering something about having no idea. Seconds later, Chris jolts at the slam of the front door.

Chapter Thirty-Four:

2019

———

A beautiful woman in her late forties with shoulder length black hair strains an awkward smile out at them on the porch.

"Can I help you?" she can't contain her bluntness, and it may have come out ruder than intended.

"Hi… Mrs Boyle, is it?" McNally reaches his hand out.

She nods, not even entertaining the idea of looking down at his hand.

"Detective Inspector Liam McNally and Detective Sergeant Cian Ferguson," they show their IDs, "is your husband in?"

She almost rolls her eyes, and without another word retreats back into the house, leaving the door ajar. Through it, they hear the scraping of plates and the collection of voices, including a booming laugh. The latter seems to get louder as its owner migrates down the hall towards them. The door swings open once more, revealing a balding man in his mid-fifties. His pinstriped shirt is unbuttoned way below what is fashionable, and his white teeth don't disappear once he sees the detectives. In fact, McNally can't help but feel like he recognises a glint in his eye.

"Gentlemen, gentlemen, come on in."

He swings around and starts walking up his marble hall again. The detectives look at each other quizzingly before stepping through and following him out into an opening where a long dining table rests. The windows behind give the room an picturesque view of the River Foyle and the bridge they just recently came off, as well as a natural source of light shining through them onto the table, where over a dozen guests sit, munching on cheese boards and sipping red wine.

"Where are my manners, detectives? This is Cathair Barr, MP for West Tyrone, and his wife Enda. Fearghal O'Carroll from social protection and his wife Dearbhla..."

This goes on for several more moments, the guests raising a toast to the detectives, who nod politely in return.

"And finally, Vice President of Ardóimid and my right-hand man, Cormac Byrne, with his lovely wife Rose."

The couple furthest from them, sitting beside Boyle's bored looking wife, are the last to raise their glasses. McNally notices that he described everyone that was invited to this social event by their job titles, and then their wives. Seems he's a bit of a misogynist. But why would he be inviting other people from surrounding constituencies to his house for a dinner party? He's obviously trying to build and expand his rapport and reputation, slowly working his way around to impress and win over the people of Stormont, where the Northern Ireland Assembly is held.

"Would you good men like a drink?"

"No, thanks, Darrell..." Ferguson smiles towards the table before stepping forward and close into his face so none of his dinner guests can hear, "actually, can we speak in private?"

Boyle gasps loudly, making his guests look over once more, before he brings his hand up to his face, mocking biting his nails in worry. Then, he bursts into laughter again, forcefully smacking Ferguson on the shoulder and swinging him in the direction of the back of the house, not taking his eyes off his guests.

"Looks like I'm needed in my office, away from prying ears. You know me, looking to help as much as I can. But don't worry guys, I'll be out soon. Roisin, darling, don't forget there's more wine in the basement if we run out," his cackle echoes around the hall before he leads them into the last room on the right.

His office is bigger than McNally's living room, he notices, as he looks around. Every wall is plastered in something or another. Whether it be the framed and signed Celtic football shirt, the tabloid front covers displaying the woes of the Bloody Sunday tragedy or the memorabilia of Irish flags with famous nationalist figures imprinted on them. Taking a seat facing them, Boyle begins swinging on his chair, looking at them amusedly.

"So, detectives... How can I be of assistance?"

"Well, I'm sure you've heard the news..." Ferguson cocks his head to the side.

"No, I haven't... What's happened?"

"The body of Aaron Parker has been found behind his garage last night."

"Who?" he sits forward and puts his chin in a clenched fist, protruding his lip and looking at them with as much innocence as a dog caught chewing the carpet.

"Aaron Parker, the leader of the Everyone Unite Party," McNally sneers at him.

"Oh... That silly little man," Boyle waves his hand at them dismissively, "I'd forgotten all about him. Yes, he went missing a while back. It's good you've finally found him. Suicide, was it?"

"No," Ferguson leans back, "we're actually opening a murder inquiry."

Boyle's bold demeaner drops for a nano-second, but McNally notices it, and he's sure Ferguson does too. The split second of shock that had lit up his eyes.

"I'm sorry to hear that. So, how can I help?" he gives his toothiest grin, taunting them.

McNally bites his bottom lip. He'd love nothing more than to smack that look off his face.

"We'd like to know where you were the night he went missing... June 18th 2016."

Boyle exclaims, half laughing.

"Am I a suspect?"

"Let's just say we're eliminating you from our enquiries," Ferguson raises his eyebrows.

McNally gazes into the politician's face. Surely, he'd be smarter than this? He'd demand that he'd already given his statement and kick them out. At least, that's what he was expecting. But it looks like Boyle loves having them hanging on his every word.

"Well, if it was June 18th, then I was in Galway."

"And you're sure about that?"

"100%. The 18th is my wedding anniversary. We got married in the Galway Bay Hotel in 1991. We go back there every year to celebrate. 2016 was our 25th year. Silver, it is. I got my wife an expensive silver bracelet which I'm sure she has on tonight. It has 25 engraved on the back of it, if you'd like to check?"

He levers out of the chair, looking at the detectives. Knowing that they'll stop him. Daring them to question him.

"That won't be necessary, Darrell."

Smirking, like he's won the war, Boyle falls back into his seat and tucks himself beneath his desk.

"So," McNally decides to take over, sitting forward to get Boyle's attention, who looks at him with as much enthusiasm as if he were paint drying on his hallway wall, "I understand that night was a big charity event in the Waterfoot Hotel. A political do, so to speak?"

"Yes, I believe it was."

"And you didn't go?"

"As I've previously stated, Detective, it was our anniversary, of which every year we return to the place we got married. Which part of that is so hard to understand?"

McNally almost snarls at him as he gives a toothy grin once more.

"I just find it hard to believe that such a political do would be occurring, and you wouldn't attend? Did anyone else from your party take your place?"

"They didn't."

"And why not?"

He rolls his eyes.

"It was an argument waiting to happen."

"What was?"

"The event. The whole night. They were glad I couldn't attend; it was almost like they picked that night on purpose."

Both detectives raise their brows at him once more. As if this man's ego could be so large.

"Can you indulge on why you feel like this?"

"Because the night was to raise money for the new cancer centre in Altnagelvin Hospital. Being health minister at the time, I was already under scrutiny for fighting for a United Ireland. The Jacks were saying that I was trying to ruin all the hard work that went into the centre by abolishing the NHS with the rest of the UK's policies. There were already arguments that month about *'boarder hoppers,'*" he air quotes, "who rented their homes in Derry to live full time in their holiday homes in Donegal, yet still benefit from free health care up north. It was a headache in the making, even if it wasn't my anniversary, I would've found a way out of it. And before you ask, yes I donated generously to the cause."

"And you haven't heard any rumours or anything through the grapevine on what might've happened Mr Parker?"

Boyle feigns concern.

"No, of course not. And the PSNI would be the first people I would tell if I did."

McNally looks at him disgustedly.

"No... Upset between you and him?"

"Why would there be?"

"Well, I understand he was trying to overthrow your party from power?"

Boyle chuckles.

"I doubt he had the chance. Our supporters have every faith in us, why would we be re-elected year in, year out if they didn't?"

"So, no ill feelings... No falling outs... Threats?"

"I'm not a violent man, DI McNally... You will learn that about me in time."

Sneering, McNally nods, before standing and thanking him, giving him the respect Boyle's wife had showed them by ignoring his outstretched hand as they go to retreat out of the office. But just as they reach the door, McNally turns back.

"Wait..."

He'd said that he was health minister back then, therefore wasn't the leader of Ardóimid.

"Am I right in thinking that you weren't the leader of your party at the time?"

Boyle regards him with amusement, even Ferguson turns to him blankly.

"No, DI McNally, I wasn't. I only got appointed last year."

That's why he wasn't questioned. He hadn't heard of another Boyle to be in power, especially working with Ardóimid. And he was sure he read on the paperwork they had spoken to a Darrell Boyle.

"Well then, excuse me, Darrell. But I've been in England for the better part of 20 years. Who *was* in power, then?"

Darrell looks at him confused.

"My father."

"Darrell Boyle Senior?"

"Yes, I was first born and so inherited his name and followed in his footsteps."

That explains it.

"Terribly sorry for the confusion, Darrell. It looks like we've got to speak to your father."

How had Ferguson made such a silly mistake? McNally goes to give him an annoyed glance, but Ferguson looks away as Darrell stares at him darkly.

"I'm afraid you can't, DI McNally. As he died last year."

Chapter Thirty-Five:

Taking the pouffe was a bad choice, Chris thinks, as he's in the centre of the room. Blocking the muted TV. All eyes on him. Dermott, whom he remembers from the original case, and Steph sit in the armchairs, whilst all of the Parkers squeeze onto the sofa. Danielle looking at him with such beauty and concern. Ritchie a cold glare, his jaw tight. Almost matching Steph's daggered stare. The other three look inquisitive, which he's sure they are. He hasn't shown his face in over two years. But he has good reason to now, he believes. He coughs and bites the side of his mouth in thought.

"Er... So..."

Ritchie rolls his eyes and looks out of the window, shaking his head. Chris can see his left foot jitter impatiently.

"I have some news."

Nuala nods, sitting forward.

"So, Dave... He asked to meet. And... Well... He was in the Crown for an afterwork drink..."

He gets the anticipated reaction of pursed lips. The Crown, in the east of the city, is well known for being a hot spot for trouble in the Waterside. And the rumours are that the underground organisation linked to the Jacks both own and run the pub. Anyone who enters the bar who are not in the organisation, or with some form of link to it, are stared at begrudgingly until they get uncomfortable and leave. It's almost like a clubhouse. Dave's uncle, Harry Wayne, was rumoured to be in the Jacks, and had taken part in some dodgy affairs that had led to his life tragically being cut short after getting into his car one day without checking under it first.

Because of this, he was an unsung hero in the Jacks' community, and their entire family were always welcomed in there. Dave's dad and Harry's brother, Stewart, pays his respects in the bar every weekend. It was often criticised within their friendship group, but Dave had the gift of shutting down any guileful comments with a look. Many were too afraid to say anything after that, in case he was deeper in the organisation than he let on.

"Anyway... Er... So..."

"It's alright, son," Dermott nods encouragingly, "go on ahead."

"Sorry... So, Dave heard some guys in a booth behind him talkin' about them diggin' up your da..." he blushes towards Danielle, "... they said that the police will be at Taylor's door soon enough sniffin' around. Said that it's funny because there's somethin' they don't know."

Nuala nods, sitting forward as much as she can without toppling off the sofa.

"Apparently, on the night that he went missin'... The night of the charity event... Taylor had cornered your da... Er... Aaron..."

It feels weird saying his name, Chris thinks. He never addressed him, never had to... He wasn't overly friendly. But he's sure not many girl's dads are very welcoming to the lad who's riding their daughter.

"... They said Taylor asked him to join their party. They wanted to team up against Ardóimid and push them out of power."

Everyone in front of him look away deflated, Michelle even curses under her breath, but apologises after a disapproving look from her mother. Dermott sits forward and raps his knee.

"We know all that already, son. There were rumours for months-"

"Wait, I'm not finished!"

That had come out a lot more forceful than intended, but the nerves and their instant dismissal had triggered him.

"Go on..."

"So, aye... He asked him over a drink. And they said that Aaron accepted the drink, but politely declined his offer and walked away. A few of his buddies watchin' and knowin' what was happenin' saw the look on Taylor's face... Doesn't take well to people sayin' no to him apparently."

Dermott nods, his mouth pulled to the side in a half smile. Chris is sure he could tell them stories about Taylor to make their toes curl.

"That's when Taylor got quite... Hostile. Shoved him around a bit. Discreetly, of course, as they were still in the hotel... I don't know whether it was on the way to the toilet or in a side room or somethin', sorry... They said that's when he threatened him, but they didn't say with what... Aaron declines again, respectively, they said... And walked back into the function room. Well, by this stage... Taylor is seethin', like... And that's when Aaron leaves. They said Taylor must've rattled him so much that he left. But apparently during the conversation and the... You know, *'roughin' him up a bit,'*" he air quotes and shrugs, "Taylor had managed to steal his phone. So he couldn't call a taxi. He looked around the hall a bit, where he was sittin' and all that, tryin' to find it, but came up short... They guessed he would walk out onto the main road to try and flag one down, 'cause if he had to return to reception to request one then he'd have to walk past them again. So apparently that's what he did, and when he came away from the hotel and the cameras, Taylor's cronies jumped him and shoved him into the boot of their car."

Everyone looks at him shocked. Michelle's hands are over her mouth and Danielle and Steph have silent tears running down their faces. Nuala looks confused more than anything, even more so now when Chris stops talking.

"Well?" she finally cracks, waving her hand in his direction, "then what happened?"

"Dave said they wouldn't say any more. One shushed the guy who was chattin' after that... He thinks it might've been 'cause they realised he was earwigging, but he was too scared to look around. So, he finished his pint and left. Called me and told me everythin'. But he made me promise that this wouldn't come back to bite him... So, ye have to promise that it doesn't."

Nuala stands and puts her hands behind her head, circling laps of the coffee table. Everyone else continues to look at Chris like he has just burst into flames. Dermott coughs and sits forward, a hand to his mouth.

"Okay, okay... We won't, won't we not guys? But, Chris... Son... You're going to have to tell DI McNally all of this. Officially."

Chapter Thirty-Six:

"What an absolute arsehole."

They're coming back over the bridge towards the Waterside, McNally cocking his head around Ferguson to take a better look at Boyle's house from this angle. He half expects to see his figure gleefully looking out from the giant window, tracing their movements like a villain in a film. The sergeant just chuckles along, putting down his sun visor to see the road better.

"I hate to say I told you so..."

"I'm an absolute idiot," McNally scrunches his face up as he digs his fingers into his hands, falling against the headrest once more, "how the hell could I have been so stupid?"

"Well... Easy mistake, sir."

It isn't, but McNally admires him for his attempts to make him feel better.

"Anyway," Ferguson clears his throat, quick to change the subject, "I'm sure you've seen in the records that Boyle Senior was questioned, but there was apparently no beef between neither himself nor Parker. Not dissimilar to his son, he wasn't entirely worried about Parker taking his voters. The majority of them have been voting for the party since its founding decades ago, nothing anyone can say or do would or will change that."

McNally considers this.

"True... So, you think that Boyle Senior had nothing to do with this?"

"Well, that's what Quigley and everyone in the station came to an agreement on. I mean, don't get me wrong, he was heavily involved in the underground scene in his younger political days, but stopped shortly before the Good Friday Agreement. Since then, he was often criticised by republicans for not listening to their requests or taking their advice, which he seemingly did before.

"You could say he was paving the way for Boyle Junior, who seems very different to his father. He became immersed in history and politics at a very young age, and is said to have been in the underground scene from when he was a teen. Once he got a taste of power, it engulfed him. To be honest, I think he enjoys the money and fame, as I'm sure you can guess after being in his house. I mean, compared to his son's luxurious house, Boyle Senior lived and died in a pokey little hole at the top of Rosemount. Bought the house for what we would consider to be near pocket money now and never left. Seems he was not one to forget where he came from. Believed to have been *'the voice of the people'* of his generation. Well, before he turned a political curve, so it seems."

"What do you think happened?"

Ferguson shrugs.

"Old age? The decline in the Troubles? I don't know... I suppose we'll never know now."

McNally nods, looking at his phone where he had Googled Boyle Senior's name. It's incredible how alike they are. They could pass as twins when they were the same age. He clicks onto a photo of him in his late fifties. He notices Boyle Senior has a more rounded nose and slightly darker hair, but apart from that it's truly hard to tell them apart. That, and the name, makes him believe that he isn't the only one to make such a silly schoolboy error, blaming his time in England for his carelessness.

"How come I never heard he died?" McNally asks as he continues scrolling through a short article on the Londonderry Letter, detailing what kind of cancer he had.

"Boyle Senior kept his illness a secret for as long as he could. I don't even think his family knew...

Not of the extent of his illness anyway. He had a simple funeral, only close family and no media presence. That seems to be the only thing that Boyle Junior keeps close to his chest... He doesn't flash and boast about his dad... I'm guessing he was very close with him."

"So, Boyle Senior wasn't a suspect?" McNally sighs. "What about the brick through the window? Boyle Junior's work?"

"If I was a betting man..." Ferguson shrugs. "Although he's very cool in suggesting that they weren't concerned... I don't know... Maybe they were more worried than they let on? Not wanting to show weakness... Or give a motive. Then again, it might've had nothing to do with either of them. Or nothing to do with the political party and just the organisation's work. Or it could've been a few youths who thought they were doing good by their community... We don't know."

"So, where do we go from here?"

Just as McNally speaks his thoughts aloud, the handsfree on Ferguson's phone lights up, showing Dermott's number.

Chapter Thirty-Seven:

The ticking Guinness clock on the wall is all that can be heard apart from the soft chewing. Cathal and Orla sit at the kitchen table. Their battered sausages devoured. The discarded chips dampening with the layer of vinegar, sinking into the moist paper. They have no idea what to say to each other. Cathal is disgusted with himself for putting her at risk, so God knows how Orla is feeling. He had rung and managed to catch her before she had reached Creggan Burn Park. Explained to her the situation and showed her the photos. They returned home and the police arrived. They took statements and copies of the photos and messages, but apart from that they couldn't offer much more. After the police had left, Cathal suggested a chippy, too agitated to cook. They'd gone together to the handy one up the street and returned, not a word said between them the whole time. Both consumed in their own thoughts.

"Cath..." Orla finally musters.

He looks up with a nod.

"Could this maybe have something to do with Dad?"

Cathal is instantly cagey. Standing, he scrunches up the takeaway leftovers and lobs them in the bin. Migrating over to the counter, he slides the dinner he had begun before the email back into the packaging and drops it in the fridge. He hates discussing their father, even more so when it revolves around his criminality. They knew he was into dangerous shit even before he up and left five years ago. Despite the common knowledge, as well as news surrounding him, Cathal never indulged Orla in the secrets he found out about him two years ago. But he can't hide forever, Orla has commented on the difference in him since that night... Since he found out what his dad done. Since...

"You never talk about him. You barely told me what happened that ni-"

"Orla, stop it. I've told you before. He's gone, that's all that matters. Just leave it at that."

"What are you hiding from me?" she's suddenly on her feet, screaming. "You just seen what could happen to me if you continue to do this... If you continue to block me out. Let me in, Cath... We used to be so close... What the fuck has happened?"

She sounds like she's close to tears, but Cathal doesn't dare turn around to look. He just stares out into the back garden. At the shed. He can't. He just can't. He's protecting her... And he's protecting himself.

Thankfully, the doorbell goes. Cathal almost exclaims aloud in rejoice. He turns to see fear in Orla's eyes, her face dropping, and he almost laughs. Like someone coming to attack you would be so polite as to ask to be invited in first. They aren't vampires.

"Don't worry, it's only Ava. The police advised us to stay somewhere else tonight, and she offered for us to stay with her."

Chapter Thirty-Eight:

Pulling up to the house on the Limavady Road, McNally whistles at the expensive sports cars underneath the bricked carport. Three all in shiny cherry colour, with a white Mercedes just in front of them, out in the light of dusk. Facing the elements. Presumably the most used, although it doesn't take a detective to figure that out. The white bricked house has the odd flint grey thrown in here and there. Odd, but it works well. There aren't many windows, they seem to be thin and up high like at the station. He presumes this is to deter potential terrorists. Members of Ardóimid, or other enemies. Who knows how many this guy has?

"So, what's our best strategy, boss?"

McNally leans back, thinking.

"We can't just barge in and say we heard what happened that night. We have to be subtle... For our sake, the family's sake, and the boy's sake. Who knows what could happen if it came back to him? ... Taylor has done some nasty stuff to people for doing less. And he might not talk to us at all without a lawyer if we come across as hostile. Let's just go in and see if we can rattle his cage, and if not... We say we heard rumours... See his reaction. See if we can bleed a reason for a warrant or arrest out of him."

"You don't know this guy, boss. He's a hard nut, a right slippery bastard. He's almost likeable... Tries to be your friend. He'll always be one step ahead."

"Maybe... But we have to try."

Slamming their car doors, they crunch along the gravel until they reach the front door, but can't seem to find a doorbell. They knock before seeing the blinking camera above their heads.

"Who is it?" a tinny gruff voice asks.

They introduce themselves and hold their IDs up towards the camera, but receive nothing in return. Seconds later, the black door opens and there stands a six-foot man with a buzz cut in a dressing gown far too small for him, showing off four or five strands of dark curly hairs on his chest. It's almost laughable. He looks like Biff from *Back To The Future*, McNally almost smirks.

"Hello, detectives. How can I help you?" Billy Taylor looks sheepish, like they've caught him doing something he isn't supposed to be doing.

"We'd just like to ask you a few questions, may we come in?"

Nodding, he stands back to let them through, before apologising and excusing himself, climbing what looks like floating shelves as stairs to change into something a bit more appropriate. They gaze around at the room he had pointed them into. A large glass table with coffee coloured leather chairs either side of it. The walls adorning classical paintings and pictures that make you want to cock your head to the side to see if that makes you understand them any better. A big, empty house. Devoid of laughter. A complete contrast to Boyle's. The more people who fear you, the lonelier you are, McNally thinks.

Moments later, Taylor returns downstairs, sporting a more presentable pair of jeans and a navy jumper. He shakes their hands and gestures for them to sit.

"How can I help you tonight?"

It looks like his house isn't the only thing that's the opposite to Boyle, McNally registers. Boyle is a pompous, arrogant show off, or a slimy weasel, as McNally would like to call him. Whereas Taylor is calm and collected, actually quite polite... He doesn't come across as your typical baddie, but then again there have been psychopaths before that have presented themselves as the most charming people in the world.

"I think you know why we're here," McNally begins, giving him a nudge to see what he thinks they know.

"I'm judging it's to do with finding Aaron Parker's body?"

At least he isn't trying to feign ignorance.

"It is," Ferguson nods.

"Should I be worried?" he chuckles, an arm inside the neck of his jumper, caressing his armpit distractedly.

"Just doing some follow up questioning since we're opening a murder enquiry," McNally narrows his eyes at him, a subtle smile on his face, "can I ask you, please, Mr Taylor, if you attended the charity night at the Waterfoot Hotel on June 18th 2016, the night Aaron Parker went missing?"

"I did."

Without hesitation, he wasn't expecting this.

"And is it true that you were trying to seduce him into abandoning his party and joining the Ulster Jacks?"

He closes his eyes for a few seconds, before reopening them, focusing his attention between the detective's heads, on the back wall. Like he's trying to remember a recital.

"I'm not sure *'seducing'* is the word I would use, personally. But, yes. We were trying to get him on board. He was getting young people involved. Are you aware of the contrast between young and old people that turn out to their polling stations? It's frightening. I wanted him to join us, only a fool wouldn't. Together, we would've been an unbreakable force... He was our missing link."

He cocks his head to the side when his attention returns to their faces.

"Sorry, but I can't help but to feel like I've said all of this already. To a Detective Inspector Quigley, if I remember correctly. Should I be contacting my solicitor?"

"Not at all," Ferguson fake laughs, "this is an informal chat, after all."

Taylor nods and tells them to proceed, seemingly relaxing.

"You see, we've had some new evidence come to light as of late... Including a few eyewitness accounts from that night," McNally stares into his face, "saying you were being quite abrasive with Mr Parker."

"Oh?"

Is he sweating, or is it the shine from the chandelier above their heads?

"Aye, seems that you didn't like taking no for an answer. Is that true?"

Taylor shuffles about in the seat uncomfortably.

"Well, I was worried about my party's reputation and future, obviously. I didn't want to be overpowered by a busy body like him."

"*'A busy body?'* Why, just seconds ago you were calling him your missing link."

"He had no political background; he was an independent party... He just had the gift of the gab..."

He's definitely sweating, droplets running down the side of his ears.

"Something wrong, Mr Taylor? You do look awfully hot."

"It's just this jumper," he flusters, pulling it from his neck, "and with the small windows this house can retain heat awfully easily... Hence why I was in my dressing gown when you arrived. Save a fortune on my heating bill, though. Excuse me whilst I get myself a drink, would you two like anything?"

The detectives look at each other triumphantly after they decline. Several moments later, he returns with a glass of water, a slither left at the bottom.

"So, what other new evidence do you think we have?"

"I don't know, you tell me."

"Nothing you'd like to own up to? Maybe tell us why Mr Parker's phone was found in the bushes surrounding the hotel a few weeks after he went missing?"

Taylor looks stumped, just sitting in silence. If he's lying, he's a fucking brilliant actor, McNally thinks. Both McNally and Ferguson know from reports that the mobile phone was free of any prints, was that intentional? Wiped clean and left there to deter the investigation away from somewhere else?

"We've heard from a source that when Mr Parker declined your advances that night, twice, that you had him picked up. Kidnapped, I think the word they used was... From outside the hotel, away from any CCTV to keep your nose clean, of course. Now, why would someone come to us with such accusations? What would give them that idea?"

It's like a switch has gone on inside Taylor. His face darkens and he sits forward, chuckling demonically. This must be the sinister side that he uses with his underground boys, McNally is almost sure of it.

"Where have you heard that?"

"We couldn't possibly say."

Taylor observes them for a few more seconds, a half-smile curling on his lip.

"Terribly sorry to be wasting your time, officers. But this is just hearsay. Where are the facts? The evidence? This is all just a stab in the dark... A cold case with nothing new except a body found. So, you come creeping around with this absolute crap that you all have somehow conjured up in your station. You have absolutely nothing on me, so... I'd like to ask you to either leave, or arrest me. Your call."

Chapter Thirty-Nine:

Dermott and Nuala's hushed tones can be heard
from the kitchen, although no one can properly hear
what they're saying. Only the odd word thrown in
here and there. Ritchie and Michelle have migrated
upstairs to digest the new information whilst Chris,
Danielle and Steph all sit where they were. No one
has moved. They haven't even attempted small talk.
Danielle stares at the flame inside the tealight,
flickering lazily on top of the coffee table. Steph and
Chris catch each other looking at one another a few
times, before dodging their eyes to other sides of the
room. The tension is palpable, even more so than
when he arrived. He thought unloading onto the
family, and then eventually McNally and Ferguson,
would've helped, but it hasn't.

"I..."

The girls look up at Chris, as he picks at his
nails.

"I'm sorry it had to come from me... Dave just wanted to protect himself... I'm sure he would've told ye himself if situations were different..."

Danielle nods and smiles innocently. Steph continues to glare at him as he gives her side eyes.

"Anyway, er... D... Could we talk in private?"

Chris bites his lip and turns towards Steph, who doesn't budge. Surprisingly though, it's Danielle who protests.

"Steph is my best friend, Chris. You know that. She's been there for me during everything and anything... So, whatever you want to say to me, you can say in front of her."

And with that, she marches over and plants herself beside Steph, linking arms with her and resting her head on Steph's shoulder. Chris growls as Steph sneers over at him, a look of smug triumph on her face.

"Okay... I suppose I just want to properly apologise. I know I never really got the chance, and I had every reason to. I was very dismissive and self-centred. I've had a lot of time to think, and I know I was in the wrong. Even before all this stuff with your da... I was very quick to fly off the handle, but if ye did the same then I called ye a psycho... I wasn't very sympathetic, or empathetic... I just wasn't a nice person, and I know that now. I'm sorry."

Danielle nods along, tears brimming in her eyes whilst Steph has her head cocked to the side, a slight frown prominent above her eyebrows.

"I just wish there was more I could've done, or more I could do now. I want-"

The living room door opens. In steps Ritchie, who scowls over towards Chris, his chin tilted. They stay like that, in silence, for a few more seconds, before Chris sighs.

"Anyway, I best be goin'... I really hope the new information helps bring you all closure... Or justice, or whatever it is you're lookin' for. I'm sure I'll see ye at the wake, and the funeral. That is... If you'll let me."

Danielle looks down at the rug, her tongue out to the side and her foot kicking off the coffee table. A sure sign she's trying not to cry. Finally, when he's just about to give up and leave, she nods slightly before clearing her throat.

"Aye... I... I'd like that."

Smiling down at her, Chris thanks her before excusing himself and saying his goodbyes, bypassing Ritchie at a safe distance, who continues to just stare at the place where he once stood. Danielle clutches Steph's arm, unsure whether she actually wants him to leave.

Chapter Forty:

"First room up on the right there, Orla."

Orla shouts her thanks over her shoulder as she hammers up the stairs, before discarding her pink overnight bag down on the landing and closing the bathroom door. Ava and Cathal step through into the living room, where Cathal drops his own bag, before kicking it under the sofa.

"Thanks again for having us, Ave."

She waves away his gratitude.

"Not at all, don't worry about it. I'm just sorry I only have two bedrooms."

I'm not, Cathal almost says out loud. He wondered if she was going to offer the space in her bed beside her to him, but it looks like the sofa is going to have to do. It's now his turn to act modest, reaching for her elbow and giving it a squeeze.

"The sofa is just fine."

She scrunches up her shoulders and smiles over to him, before gliding over to the single armchair by the window and parking herself in it, much to Cathal's annoyance. Taking the sofa on the other side of the room, he nestles into get comfortable as he hears Orla thunder down the stairs.

"Orla! You aren't in your own house now."

"Aye, I know we aren't. Sure, we don't have stairs."

She smacks him in the arm and Ava laughs along.

"What do you say to Ava?"

"Jesus Christ, Cathal. I'm not a wain. I thanked her back at the house."

Ava smiles as she leans back, stretching.

"Honestly, don't mention it. Is the room warm enough?"

"It is, aye. I have my warm fluffy pyjamas with me anyway if not."

"Awk, Jesus. How do you sleep in those? I can barely cope with a vest and shorts. Many a night in the summer I sleep naked."

Ava and Orla start cackling, whilst Cathal wonders whether he can strategically press the cushion beside him against his groin without either of them becoming suspicious. Ava turns on the TV and presses the Netflix icon, asking Orla what she's currently watching. Cathal likes how they both get along, like sisters that neither of them had. It would be great if they could, indeed, someday be sisters-in-law. Orla indulges that she's hooked on something that sounds painstakingly like every other show she watches, and Ava can't find it on Netflix. Cathal discloses that their TV at home is chipped and she was streaming it illegally. Ava tuts before wagging her remote at them, smiling and putting on some other shit show about dresses and makeup which makes Cathal roll his eyes ungratefully.

"So, I can't get over all of this," Ava pushes her shoes off and crosses her feet beneath her to get comfortable, "like, why would you be getting targeted?"

"Because I wrote the story," Cathal shrugs, feeling a lot safer here.

It's innocent enough, but he knows why Ava feels so strongly about this, being the victim of something similar a few years ago.

"But I mean... Anyone could've got that story – no offence," she laughs. "You aren't connected to the story or the case in any way, like. Are you?"

That reminds Cathal.

"I seen that you're friends with the youngest daughter, Michelle, on Facebook, Orla?"

Orla's lip twitches in acknowledgement, her eyes stuck to her phone.

"Do you think you could get in touch with her for me?"

"'*For you?*'" Ava squints over at him. "You're not seriously going to continue this story, are you? After all that?"

"Of course I am. It's one of the biggest local news stories to break in years. I'm not letting that slip past me. Anyway, like you basically said, if I don't do it, then someone else will. It'll all be anonymous anyway, so even if they did continue without me, whoever is behind this will still think it's me."

Ava reverts her eyes back to the TV, a disapproving look on her face, but she bites her tongue.

"Anyway, Orla. How about it?"

"I don't really know her that well, Cath... We were in the same class for science at GCSE, but we never spoke. She was very popular, well liked... Probably because of her dad, and then when he went missing, she got the sympathy card. That, and she's minted. I mean, there were some girls whose Dads obviously supported Ardóimid, or might've been big boys in the underground running of things. They didn't take kindly to her... But no one ever really said anything bad against her. Not to her face, anyway."

Just as Cathal almost curses and tries to think of a better way to sneak into the family's circle without door stepping, Ava nostalgically looks out of the window.

"I remember Dermott saying that she was lovely and quiet."

Cathal glares over in her direction.

"Dermott? That policeman you know?"

"Aye, he was their family liaison officer when their dad disappeared."

That's it! The way in.

"I wonder if... Ave, could you talk to him? I mean, see if he'll talk to me, about anything? Try and get me some inside information, or be the first point of call? That would be great for my career. My editor is already buzzing with me, I don't want to lose this story to someone else or get it taken off me... Even if it does run dry."

Ava doesn't look too happy, but agrees regardless, bringing out her phone. She feels indebted to him, has done so for years. She'd do anything he asks, even if she doesn't agree with it. That's why he'll never ask her out. One, in case he loses their friendship and his source. And two, in case she feels obliged to agree. No, if they're ever going to be a couple, it needs to be on her terms... Her that initiates it, and Christ knows he's gave plenty of hints that he's interested.

Chapter Forty-One:

Sighing after that long day, McNally has never been so happy to see his own car, parked inside the station grounds. On the way back from Taylor's house, Ferguson and himself had talked things through. Antagonizing Taylor wasn't the way forward, even Ferguson had said that he'd never seen the side to him as they did when he kicked them both out. But that means something is up, McNally had suggested. If it was all rumours, then he wouldn't have reacted like that and let his mask slip. They're onto something, he just knows they are.

Leaving Ardóimid for now, seeing as the Galway Bay Hotel was able to confirm Boyle's alibi, they've agreed that first thing tomorrow they'll start by speaking with any members of the Jacks' underground group who have been arrested in the past few years. Ferguson had said a few of the Jacks are awaiting trial for joyriding several cars over the space of a few weeks. Although their true intentions are still to be found out, they guess they were possibly something similar to this. Transporting drugs or bodies... They will offer them lighter sentences, immunity and even police protection if they have anything decent to tell them about Taylor and what happened that night. There's also a few more charged with violent offences, so they're as good a place to start as any.

"Right, boss," Ferguson stretches, "can't wait to get back to the missus's curry."

"Oh, Chinese?"

"Naw, I wish. It'll be some sugar free, gluten free, chicken free, taste free shite."

McNally laughs before stepping out of the car. As he turns to close the door, he stares in at his DS.

"You alright, sir?"

"You know what, Ferguson? Set me up."

"You want some of that stankin' curry, sir?" McNally smiles.

"No, with your sister-in-law. Niamh, wasn't it?" Ferguson arches a brow.

"You sure, sir? She's a rocket."

"I can guess that, but... I don't want to end up like Taylor."

"Meaning?"

"That big empty house, all alone. No friends or family around. I'm far enough from my family as it is."

He makes a mental note to try and get an hour up with his parents this weekend, if this case allows it.

"Hmm... Fine, sir. Although I don't think you have anything to worry about in that respect, unless you're orchestrating murders on your days off."

The pair laugh as McNally wiggles his eyebrows.

"Believe me, though, sir. You don't know what you have yourself in for. When?"

"How about tomorrow night?"

"Keen bean, well... Why don't you come over to mine, and we'll ask her around? I'll get Jane to make something for dinner and we can have a few drinks."

"Will it be gluten free, fat free, taste free..."

"Almost definitely," he laughs, "no, she only suggests doing that to keep us healthy. I have enough buns in work, I can't blame her." He pats his stomach. "She'll make something nice tomorrow, or we can just get a takeaway."

"Whatever's less bother for Jane," McNally taps Ferguson's car roof, "thanks, Ferguson. I'll see you at 8am for the briefing."

Saluting him as he closes the door, Ferguson yanks the car into reverse as McNally slinks over to his own car. A date, at his age? Maybe this new city *has* changed him after all.

Chapter Forty-Two:

6am comes too soon. Uncurling his arm and reaching it out of the covers, Paul turns the alarm off at a much slower pace this morning. That'll teach his wife for waking him several times in the very late hours of last night. Laughing with her whole body at some silly video or picture from Facebook on that stupid tablet of hers. Worst thing she ever bought. He preferred it when she had the lamp on until all hours, her nose engrossed in a book. At least she was quiet then. But it seems the wonders of the Kindle surpass just reading nowadays.

Placing his bare feet on the fluffy rug below their bed, he yawns and winces as his bones crack on his ascent to standing. Pulling on a pair of shorts and an old t-shirt, he blindly searches in the dark for his discarded trainers, which he finally finds kicked through into the ensuite. Giving the wife shaped lump in the duvet a dagger glare, knowing she is the culprit for this, he shakes his head before trotting down the stairs and out the front door.

Picking up pace, he decides he'll cross the Craigavon Bridge this morning, before looping back over the Peace Bridge to the Cityside again. He continues up Foyle Road, passing the old Railway Museum, and crosses the deserted T-junction at the bottom deck of the old bridge. Jogging across, he takes in the spectacular views of the old buildings embanking the Waterside. He loves the bright mornings, it sure as hell beats the miserable and dull wet ones, which are fast approaching, with September leaking away in front of them with each passing day. He may enjoy them whilst they last. Putting that foul thought to the back of his head, he begins to plan his day. It may be a Saturday, but that doesn't mean he can lounge around and watch TV all day. He would be so lucky.

What needs done today? Glenn had messaged before lunch yesterday, requesting for an informal meeting in the Marks and Spencers café in Foyleside this afternoon. Business talk. That'll be an expensive lunch, he can barely afford a McDonald's Happy Meal until pay day, still two weeks from now. And it's Jacquie from the office's birthday on Tuesday. She always asks around for a few bob each for a cake and a card whenever it's someone else's, so he supposes they'll have to do something for her too. He may grab a card on his way home from the meeting, none of the other soft bastards would bother their arse.

His thoughts escape him as he nears the Waterside, specifically where the bridge melts away into the quay, separating the River Foyle from the local businesses right up until the railway station. Is that a scarecrow on the fence dividing the walkway and the carpark? It couldn't be. Why would someone have a scarecrow stuck up? But the clothes make it look almost human shaped. Perhaps he's seeing things. He'll come level with it and it'll just be some stupid sign. *'Lordy lordy, Wendy's forty,'* or the sorts. Needs to get his eyes checked. He's nearing 50 now, he's done well to escape the shackles of glasses this long.

But no, as he comes off the bridge, the shape starts wriggling. Oh, fuck. It's a person. A man in his early twenties. Alive. Rushing to his aid, Paul's mouth falls open as he sees his arms and legs pinned to the fence with cable ties. His eyes wide and pleading desperately. His mouth pissing with blood.

Chapter Forty-Three:

2016

——

After a sleepless night all round, the Parkers and Chris, all still in yesterday's clothing, congregate at the island, facing a standing Dermott, DI Quigley and DS Ferguson. They'd just been told that there was no progress so far. All CCTV around the hotel had been checked, and guests were contacted but none saw him leave. They also said he was in brilliant form, helping support a good cause, and didn't notice anything out of the ordinary. The Foyle Search and Rescue are still looking, they are reassured, despite all their protests that he wouldn't have killed himself.

"We have to explore every avenue," DI Quigley looks irritable, perhaps they weren't the only ones running on no sleep, "if he didn't enter the river voluntarily, he also could've been pushed. We have to take that into consideration also."

"And the CCTV on the bridges?" Nuala taps her nails off the island's top.

With three bridges in total connecting the Waterside and the Cityside, and one being a walking bridge, there are several hours of footage that need to be inspected. Surely they couldn't have finished all that already?

"Still under review. Believe me, we have all our men on this investigation and doing everything we can."

"It's one of those underground organisations, I'm telling y-"

"Nuala, I understand you're frustrated and scared and you want to get your husband back, but pointing the finger of blame towards a paramilitary-style action without significant evidence won't get us anywhere."

"The fucking Jacks done our windows in with a rock and a sheet around it calling us all kinds of names."

"And where is that evidence now?"

"It was years ago, Aaron got rid of it at the time."

"Then we don't have a lot to go on with that, Nuala. Both parties will be questioned today, and we will bring it up, but without evidence then we can't go much further. But-" he interrupts her as she goes to protest again, "there may be something we can go on."

Everyone leans forward, including Dermott.

"You have to understand that your father..." he smiles at the children, including Chris, who blinks at him confusedly, "... he's a very popular man. A man in demand, some may say. Now, he could be detrimental on how this country is run if he goes all the way. He's already making waves in the Foyle constituency. He's a valuable pawn... And therefore, there's a few who could want..."

He almost says *'to take him out.'*

"Er... Him to lay low... For the sake of their own party or organisation or what have you. It's been over 24 hours, as I'm sure you're aware... That isn't good. I think we need to be realistic and keep an eye and ear on the ground as things might get a bit... Drastic," he flinches. "Now everyone knows of this man's wealth... We need to stay open to the very real possibility that you could be receiving a letter or a phone call asking for money."

"You think he's been kidnapped?" Danielle's mouth drops open, "being held for ransom?"

"I'm not saying that... But, I'm saying there's a chance that he could be, yes... If he has been, I'm sure you will hear something very soon, that is why it's critical that you all trust Dermott."

Dermott nods and smiles warmly at the family, who eye him suspiciously.

"He is here to help. He's one of the best in the business. We need you to trust him... For your father's sake."

Chapter Forty-Four:

2019

———

The incident room is full of chatter as Ferguson and McNally march in, and it takes a glare over their heads from the latter to finally silence them.

"Thank you," he nods as he stands by the board, "now, judging by the gossiping I've just walked in on, I'm guessing word has spread, so I may confirm it. David Wayne was found this morning tied to a fence just off the Craigavon Bridge on the Waterside with his tongue cut out."

Everyone winces, one even musters a gag.

"Yes, disgusting, although not a very uncommon punishment for *'touts,'*" he air quotes, "for those who don't know, David Wayne used to run around in the same friendship group as none other than Danielle Parker."

Murmurs begin again.

"In fact, Wayne is the best friend of Danielle's ex-boyfriend, Chris Hewitt. According to Hewitt, Wayne was in the Crown pub in the late afternoon yesterday and heard some guys discussing how members of their organisation had shipped Parker into the boot of their car and sped off with him. He informed Hewitt to tell us, and the Parkers, in an attempt for it not to be brought back to him. As I'm sure you all can guess, this was unsuccessful. Wayne is now in A&E in Altnagelvin Hospital and is, thankfully, going to be okay. The same, though, can't be said about his tongue, which was nowhere to be seen. Whether the Jacks moved him there after cutting his tongue out, or did it on site is unclear, but I'm sure we will hear back from the blood splatter analysist in due course. This is all great as Wayne, for a lack of a better term, isn't speaking."

A few titters from the back of the room.

"He refuses to write anything down on paper or make a statement, so it looks like this case will be pretty much closed soon enough. But we all know why he was targeted. We spoke to early morning jogger Paul McMullen, who is, understandably, in shock, but our guess is Wayne was up there for a good while before being spotted by McMullen."

After lifting the tepid coffee to his lips, O'Connor raises a diffident hand.

"Yes, O'Connor?"

"Maybe this was a hoax to get rid of Wayne? I understand his uncle is the famous Harry Wayne?"

The room as a whole nod.

"So, here's my theory. The entire Wayne family were basically welcomed into the Crown due to Harry's death, right? But what if, after a while, they didn't like that? I mean, Harry's nephew was running around with girls from the catholic grammars, including Danielle, who also has Parker as a dad... Surely they wouldn't be able to trust him? What if the story was false and they wanted to use it to see if he'd go running to his friend... Which he did?"

"Or, it could be a set up," Fleming stands, pointing at O'Connor, "what if the people Wayne heard in the Crown were members of Ardóimid?"

A few chortles come from around him, even McNally manages a smile.

"There's no way any members of Ardóimid would be allowed within spittin' distance of the Crown," O'Connor narrows his eyes at Fleming, "are you mad?"

"Right, as I was saying," McNally calms the situation before there's another domestic between the two, who seemingly work well together, opposites must attract. "Some good points there, but there's no evidence. It's all hearsay at the moment, but until... or *if* would be a better word to use, David Wayne decides to speak... Then we're in the doghouse. At this moment in time, I'm guessing that it was punishment for ratting them out, so we need to investigate further."

Gesturing to Ferguson to continue, McNally falls into his seat, draining the last of his coffee and willing the oncoming headache to disband.

"So, as I'm sure we all know, we are currently looking into members of the Jacks who are still incarcerated. They would have little, or no, communication with Taylor since they've been arrested. And we have leverage. We can dangle deals in front of them, see if anyone will bite. See if anything interesting will come out of the woodwork. Let's begin with this, the more severe cases first, would be a good start. Alright, guys?"

McNally claps his hands together as the excited whispers begin again, shouting over their retreating heads that this remains out of the press and public domain for now. He then climbs out of his seat and stares at the picture of David Wayne, plucked from his social media account, as it rests on the top left side of the board.

"You alright, sir?"

McNally turns to see Ferguson lagging back from the crowded exit.

"Fine, Ferguson. Just brainstorming," he resumes his attention to the board.

"Very good, boss. By the way, everything's set for tonight."

McNally looks around with wide eyes.

"It is?"

"Yes, sir. Jane says she'll make steak, hope that's okay?"

"Happy days, well I can't come empty handed, that would be awfully rude of me... Red or white?"

"You're the one who's going to have to deal with Niamh, I'd suggest both!"

They both cackle.

"Naw, only joking. She's really excited, according to Jane. You must've left a lasting impression on her the other night."

McNally barely manages to hide his blush.

"Then again, she's probably just looking to have us both around her little fingers in case she ever needs a get out of jail free card."

Chapter Forty-Five:

Danielle sits with her head in her hands, staring at the carpet. She can't believe what she's just heard. Dave? Really? This is insane. This is just too much. This doesn't happen in Derry. Well, it does. But it happens to someone you don't know. Your Facebook friend's cousin's boyfriend, or something. Not to poor old Dave. Sure, he was a mouth, but he wouldn't hurt a fly. They always said that his tongue would get him in trouble one day, but they never thought it would be something like this. And it looks like it never will again.

"I know you're really shocked," Dermott nods, looking at the family, "but I also have another bit of news."

Their attention resumes to him.

"They're releasing your father's body today. Turns out there's no other evidence to go on. So, you can start preparing things for the wake and the funeral. I could help with that as well, as a friend, if you wish?"

"Dermott, that would be lovely," Nuala nods, tears still streaming, "thank you."

"Don't even think about worrying about the coffin, I've already spoken to a friend who is sorting it as we speak. It'll arrive with the body inside, so you won't have to do anything in that regard... Just you focus on getting through the next few days."

"Thank you, Dermott," Nuala nods, a hankie to her face, "what would we do without you?"

"Er... Tea?" Dermott eyes her, before she nods and stands, following him into the kitchen.

When the kettle is boiling and the door through to the hall is closed, Dermott addresses her again.

"There's something else I'd like to ask you."

"Anything, Dermott."

"Cathal O'Flaherty, a journalist from the Londonderry Letter, has been in contact through a mutual friend. No, wait... Hear me out."

Nuala had already rolled her eyes and stomped to the cupboard, retrieving cups and biscuits, seemingly washing her hands of the thought of allowing press access to them.

"I understand you're suspicious and reluctant, but remember how they hounded you? Parked outside your house? If you give this boy an exclusive, it will keep them off your back. Give him everything you can, and there will be no more questions to ask... Not yet, anyway."

Nuala sighs as she pours the boiling water into two cups, adding the teabags in as an afterthought. It was true. The press had basically lived at the bottom of her garden for weeks. Little did they all know that the answer to everyone's questions was only metres away the whole time. Aaron's body resting just behind their garage. Begging to be found. And what if they'd found him sooner? Would it have been any easier? Would someone be in prison right now? Fresh evidence? Or, if one of them had found him... Would it have torn their family apart even more? Her seeing her husband, or the wains seeing their da, in a vulnerable position like that. When he used to be their superhero... Their papa bear. It's hard to tell.

"To be honest, I'm surprised how they haven't found me yet," Nuala mumbles, mind reverting back to Dermott's request, who looks longingly at her across the table. "I mean, I used my middle and maiden names to rent this house, and I won't let any of my details go online or in the address and phone books... But I thought they would've sniffed me out by now. I knew I'd have to face the music one day."

"I would strongly advise that it's in your best interest. And I'll be here the whole time. I can make him stop when you want him to or nudge the journalist into the right territory if he tries to sway off topic. It's better to have the media on this side of the door, rather than the other."

Nuala hesitantly nods, rattling the spoon stirring the sugar off the side of the cup and dropping it onto the coaster.

"Okay, I'll do it."

Chapter Forty-Six:

Slamming his door, McNally tries hard not to scream out in frustration, but can't manage to stop his closed fist coming down on his desk. Flinching, he raises his hand and stretches it out, hoping he hasn't broken anything.

All morning had been spent speaking with several members of the Jacks. Locked up for sentences from GBH to dealing. And not one of them would utter a word against Taylor. He'd been met with so many *'no comments'* it felt like it was burned into his skull. And all they did was laugh at him when he asked if Taylor had anything to do with Parker's disappearance. Seeing he has an unread email; he growls as he takes a seat and tucks himself behind his desk. More bad news. It's from the council, and he almost, unjustly, throws the screen at the wall when he sees that they haven't kept their CCTV from almost 40 months ago.

He knows that the ones they had sent over at the time are still resting in the online folders, he doesn't know what he was expecting... Some fresh new tape with all the answers? And anyway, who knows who, or what, he is looking for? He couldn't exactly go through ANPR (Automatic Number Plate Recognition) and contact every single person seen out driving that night. It was a Saturday night; the town was booming. Taxis full of sloppy students celebrating end of exams and drunken adults enjoying the good weather. It would be near impossible.

They need something to pin Taylor down. Something for an arrest or a warrant. They don't have sufficient evidence, just rumours. He can't even think of a good enough reason to revisit him. Is he poking holes in stories? Seeing red flags when there aren't any there? Dawson taught him to look at all the facts and to go by instinct, but even he had his let-downs throughout his career.

Just as he's continuing to think about looking elsewhere, Ferguson knocks on his door. By this stage he's calmed himself down. If Ferguson had have knocked five minutes ago, the pig-shaped mug that Dawson himself had bought him for a leaving present, with an assortment of pens sticking out of it, would've been smashed against the door. Sighing

and inviting him in, his mood instantly lifts when he
sees the look of determination on Ferguson's face.

"What's up?"

"We've got him," Ferguson jeers, smashing
down a file on his desk, "young boy, Kyle Bagley, he's
called. Arrested with a few of his brothers and
cousins for joyriding. Anyway, he's just turned 18 and,
unlike the others, hasn't been in prison... Yet. Seems
we've broken him a good bit, he just looks like he
was acting hard in front of his family and friends.
Started squealing like a little piggy when we offered
him immunity."

McNally punches the air.

"What does he know?"

"He admitted he doesn't know much, but he's
heard from hanging out at the bar that a certain
Victor Sargent was one of the guys who picked
Parker up that night."

"Well, let's get him in."

Chapter Forty-Seven:

Stepping through the threshold, Cathal almost exclaims with joy. He'd done it. He'd been able to do what every other journalist had yearned to do for years. Actually get in through the Parker's door, albeit in a different house, but it still counts. He gives himself a momentous metaphorical pat on the back, before following Dermott through into the living room, where all the Parkers are collected on the sofa. Himself and Dermott take the two armchairs, and he stands again to retrieve his notepad from his back pocket. Resting it on his knee, he looks up into the miserable faces of the family and gives them a reassuring smile.

"Hi, thank you so much for agreeing to talk with me."

The three children barely take their eyes off him, whilst Nuala just nods sullenly. They all look like they haven't slept in several days. Worn slippers or blackened socks on their feet. Tracksuit bottoms or leggings and old jumpers pulled on to make themselves look half presentable. Although his dad is also dead, it feels strange to think that these people could mourn the death of theirs. It's an alien feeling to him.

"Can I just say I'm so sorry for everything that's happened. I can't begin to imagine what you are all going through. And although this is an opportunity to inform the public of what's happened, it's also a great time to let our readers know what kind of a man he was. Give personal memories of him which will build empathy amongst the community, and working together with the PSNI-"

He nods towards Dermott, who smiles briefly.

"-we can hopefully help bring this person to justice. Whether that's through rejigging people's memories, or keeping everything in the public interest."

He frowns slightly at Danielle, who has begun to look at him with as much disgust as you would if you trod in some shit on your walk back from the shops.

"Well, thank you for your interest," Nuala clears her throat, intentionally, he presumes, trying to think of something nice to say. "Aaron was a loving father and husband. Papa Bear, we would fondly call him... Sometimes... Well, more so when the wains were wee."

"Any fun memories together?" Cathal directs the conversation towards Michelle, who shrugs.

"He would take us to Benone some Sundays in the summer," Danielle reminisces, still not meeting Cathal's eye.

Benone Strand is a seven-mile long beach about three quarters of an hour away from Derry, stretching from Magilligan Point to Castlerock.

"That was years ago though," Michelle pouts, "we didn't have many excursions after his political career took off."

"And rightly so," Nuala angles a narrowed brow towards her daughter, "you were all growing up. None of you wanted to spend time together as a family. So, instead, he intended in bringing the people of this city together. Despite religion or politics or the history. He wanted to move this city, and country, forward into something prosperous, instead of being stuck in the past. But, it seems, the city, and its residents, weren't ready for that..."

The sofa groans as Ritchie sobs and stands, shielding his face with his shaking hand. He ignores his mother's moaning of his name and slams the living room door closed, before everyone hears him start to climb the stairs.

Chapter Forty-Eight:

McNally sneers at the pompous attitude of Victor Sargent. Leaning back in the chair, chewing what he guesses to be the inside of his mouth, though an aftermath of too many drugs is unknown. His eyes, although alert and darting between McNally and Ferguson, don't seem to be unusually wide. Maybe his consistent chewing is a coping mechanism, some anxiety thing? He's unsure.

But he is sure about the look on Sargent's face when he turned around to see them standing in the Crown and asking him to come into the station for a chat. He'd been taken completely by surprise. Probably never thought the police would have the balls to step through into the pub, which was a shit hole if McNally ever saw one. Why it was rumoured to be the headquarters for the Jacks' underground trade was unknown. Surely they'd be rolling in it if all their criminal activity was anything to go by?

But where that money was tied up wasn't their problem this evening. Sargent had bluntly asked for a solicitor before even being escorted into the car, never mind the station. Stephen Beattie, another arrogant man, rocked up an hour later like he owned the place and demanded for some time alone with his client before they began questioning. Overly smug for someone who didn't know Sargent personally and has been given to him free from the government. Now, here he sits. His purple tie, with a stain that they hope is tomato soup, pulled out from his collar slightly. Signs of a difficult conversation. He folds his arms as the interview begins.

"Now, Mr Sargent," McNally sits back after the formalities are out of the way, "we would like to know where you were on the night of June 18th 2016?"

"No comment," Sargent smirks.

"You aren't going to tell us?"

"No comment."

"Because we have reason to believe that you might've been mixed up in something that may interest us. What have you got to say to that?"

"No comment."

"Do you spend a lot of your time in the Crown?" McNally attempts to try a different tactic.

"No comment."

"Funny how many of the people who drink at the Crown seem to always end up in criminal activity, isn't it?"

"No... No comment," Sargent narrows his eyes at him.

Looks like they're starting to get somewhere. Of course, they'd checked his file. And, surprisingly, he was squeaky clean. It definitely didn't suit his attitude. Which only means one thing. He's good.

"But not you, huh?"

"No comment," Sargent yawns.

"So, anyway, back to the 18th June 2016."

He continues to look at them with a bored expression on his face.

"No *'no comment?'*"

"You didn't ask me anything."

"He speaks! Let's try to keep this up, shall we?"

"No comment."

McNally grips the pen in his hand tighter, before looking over towards Ferguson, who coughs and sits forward, eager to takeover.

"We have reason to believe that on the night of June 18th 2016, the night Everyone Unite Party leader Aaron Parker went missing, that you had something to do with it."

Sargent rolls his eyes and leans back further in his chair, sucking his teeth now.

"We've heard from a source that you were one of the guys in the car who snatched him from the Waterfoot Hotel. Is this true?"

"No comment."

"Where did you take him?"

"No comment."

"And why?"

"No comment."

"How did his body end up behind his garage?"

"No comment."

"Why Parker? What did he do?"

"No comment."

McNally, cracking up, slams a closed fist down on the table, even making Ferguson jump.

"Just answer the damn questions, Victor!"

"Now, Detective Inspector McNally, that is extremely unprofessional..."

As Beattie goes into a rant about how he's being physically violent and aggressive towards his client, Sargent just chuckles away. He rests his hands behind his head and continues to smile whilst swinging on his chair.

"Why am I even being questioned? Yous have nothing on me. Why am I here? I'm not under arrest. You should be talking to big Taylor... Not me," he beams, showing yellow stained teeth.

McNally takes a deep breath to get ready to bring this little shit down a peg or two... But then he realises... Joining his smile, he also starts swinging on his chair, almost miming Sargent's every move.

"Billy Taylor? The leader of the Ulster Jacks Party? ... Well, who said anything about him?"

Sargent's face drops. He sits forward, all four legs of the chair now safely on the floor.

"Billy Taylor? I... I never said anything about Billy Taylor. What are you lads talking about?" he forces a laugh, which is cut short as he stares at McNally.

"May I remind you, Mr Sargent, that this interview *is* being recorded..." Ferguson cocks his head to the side.

Sargent is sheet white. He splutters a few times, before diving his head towards his solicitor. Ferguson and McNally almost jolt up, thinking it was an attack and a chance to escape. But it was only to confer. After a few seconds of hushed tones, Beattie nodding and staring at them the whole time whilst Sargent's mouth is pressed against his ear, he clears his throat.

"My client and I would like some more time alone to discuss things."

****

I should just go in. Come clean. Clear my conscience. But I can't. My feet won't let me. It's like they're cemented to the ground. My heart beats frantically within my chest and my brain screams at me to just go in and do it. It'll only take a few seconds. Sure, more is to follow, but if I'm compliant then they'll go easy on me. Lesser sentence. Lighter punishment. Who knows? But my body just won't respond, like it's having a battle against my brain and my heart, and my muscles are winning. Standing tall and clinging on.

I'm standing outside the Strand Bingo Hall. Gazing across the road at the police station. The high walls with the higher fences built on top. The metal gates shut to everyone except police cars, none of which have entered or left the premises since I've been standing here. Where do I even enter? I suppose that's a stupid question. The station is built to keep people out. People who see police as scum. Not let people in. The station has had its fair share of terrorist attacks. This street blown to pieces; shop windows smashed from the impact. The walls impenetrable, not unlike the city walls that make this town so famous.

But how do you get in if you mean no harm? Not anymore, anyway. I thought about ringing 999, or 111, but I can't do it over the phone. Not after holding this secret in for so long. I need to look into someone's eyes and admit it. If I rang, I could easily just chicken out and hang up. They'd probably take it as a prank call anyway, God knows there are enough of those. No, I need to be sat down in a room with a police officer. A red blinking light on me. Recording everything I say. No return... But how?

Mustering the courage after an elderly couple excuse themselves by breaking their link and passing around me, I slink across the road without checking traffic. Maybe it's better if I'm run down now. An easy way out. Karma. But I glide over unharmed, although narrowly missing a black BMW within the last few steps, which honks at me, the driver gesturing out of the window. I hop onto the pavement and turn to wave my apologies, but the driver has already sped off towards the traffic lights.

Resuming my attention to the walls, I see a big black door to my right with a camera above.

Presuming that's a good place to try, I cross over and bite my lip. 'Pedestrian gate enter here.' But how? There's no call button, and if there was, what would I say? What reason could I give for requesting access? Information? Confession? I'm hardly going to blurt everything out right here in the middle of the street.

I'm just about to try my hand at knocking on the door when a squeal comes from beside me. I jump and turn around to see the metal gates sliding open, revealing a police land rover crawling onto the street. The uniformed officer in the passenger seat looks out at me inquisitively before I turn and march away.

Chapter Forty-Nine:

"So, is there any more news on what has happened?"

Nuala goes to speak, before Dermott cuts in.

"May I remind you, Cathal, that there is still an ongoing investigation underway. Anything that can be made public has been, anything else could corrupt a trial, and so is being kept private at this time."

Cathal nods, biting his pen lid.

"Anyway," Dermott stands, "if that's all?"

Cathal, disappointed that it's over so soon, even though he's got about ten pages filled with shorthand, memories of Aaron Parker and direct quotes from the family, stands and fishes out two business cards from his jacket. He hands one to Nuala and the other to Dermott.

"Please, I would love to be first contact, now you know you can trust me," he smiles at them both.

Nuala continues to stare at the card as Dermott tucks his into his shirt pocket.

"Aye, sure thing, kid. Now, if you don't mind..."

Cathal thanks them again for speaking with him as Dermott leads him to the door. He shakes Dermott's hand again gratefully and crosses the driveway. When he comes out onto Church Brae, he can't hide the huge grin on his face. He'd done it, he'd really done it. Deciding to catch the bus into the office, the worrying clouds above his head threatening to burst, he climbs the steep hill before levelling out near the hospital and waits at the bus stop, looking back over his notes.

Danielle barely spoke, but when she did they were perfect quotes. Must've been daddy's girl. Michelle was helpful too, but she seems to still be at that awkward teenage stage where she hates the world, he knows all about that with Orla at home. He's sure with all that has happened, that hasn't helped her outlook on life much either. He's surprised with Ritchie's behaviour, what with being the eldest and the only boy. The new man of the house, some may say in olden style terms. Nuala had apologised and said that his father's death had hit him hard as they were really close. She believes it to be one of the main reasons why he rarely comes home. Cathal would've liked to have gotten the chance to have talked to him a bit more, but he was cagey. He guesses it takes men a lot longer to open up. If they were five pints deep in a pub it might've been a different story.

As he pays the bus driver, he takes a window seat and continues examining his notes. Nuala was typical reporter gold. The grief-stricken widow who wanted the world to know how much she was hurting, whilst bumming her husband up as much as she could. Even when Michelle tried to badmouth him for not spending as much time at home in his later years, she had instantly come to his aid. He wonders if he'll ever be able to meet someone like that. Would Ava ever be like that with him? Dermott was exactly as Ava had described him, although he can guarantee that he's being kept at arm's length.

Still, he's so thankful for getting the exclusive, he brings out his phone to text Ava that the interview went well, when he sees he's got an unread email. Panic rising within him, he registers that it's the same user, and clicks on through to see it's another picture file. It's a photo of him taken through a window, his eyes on his notes, sitting on a bus. It's like looking down at a live feed. Jerking up, he looks out at the street, but there are dozens of people going about their everyday lives. Shoppers with trolleys blustering in and out of TK Maxx. Teenagers talking with friends or their attentions on their phones. A woman jogging with her white earphones in, her ponytail pushed through her navy cap. It could've been anyone.

There's a message below the photo. Written in the text box.

'I fucking warned you.'

Chapter Fifty:

Knocking on the door into the spare room, Danielle steps through to see Ritchie's motionless body angled towards the wall facing her. Settling herself at the edge of his bed, she places a hand on his back, but retreats it once she feels him tense. Sighing, she looks around at the bare walls. The room feels empty, despite them both being here. Just like their relationship with each other.

"How are you?"

He shrugs, not even turning around. She knows he's taken his death bad; they all have. But whereas the women in the house collect together to cry, he's happy to seclude himself. As if them seeing him cry will make him less of a man.

"It's going to be okay, you know? We're all going to be grand..."

She stops. She hardly believes it herself, never mind trying to convince him. But she has to do something. He barely talks about his feelings; she's worried they'll swallow him up. The majority of suicides in this city especially are carried out by males. She'd even lost someone she used to run around with at youth club when they were younger. She hadn't spoken to him in years, but still thinks would he have done it if she had reached out to him? She won't let it happen with her brother, despite how bad their current situation and feelings towards each other might be. Standing, she opens the slide robes and starts unpacking all the shopping bags filled with things from Ritchie's room in the old house. They hadn't gotten around to unpacking them, and this is the first time he'd been home since they moved in. She throws a few bags on the bed, unsettling him. Curiosity kicking in, he turns towards her.

"What are you doing?"

"Decorating," she smirks, chucking him his old school Gaelic shirt she hopes is washed, "c'mon. Let's go through what you want and what you don't want. We can take some stuff to the tip, or give it to the charity shop. It'll be fun."

"I think you and I have different opinions on what *'fun'* is," Ritchie mutters, but still sits up and pulls a bag towards him despite the comment.

Half an hour later, the room is a bombsite. Posters of Bob Marley and *Scarface* are uncurling on the bed under school textbooks he definitely hadn't returned. His clothes lie in piles. A pile to throw out and a pile for the charity shops. He's gained almost two stone since he's shipped off to Wales, there's no way he could fit into any of them. Pictures litter the floor, surrounding the two who sit cross-legged facing one another, laughing and brandishing their new finds in one another's face.

"Fuck," Ritchie yelps, tossing a picture over to his sister, who has to scurry under the bed to retrieve it, "remember this night?"

When Danielle finally finds it, she bursts into laughter once more, her cheeks blushing. The photo shows her guzzling an electric blue WKD, an arm slung around her brother, who is looking at her with mild amusement.

"That was the worst night of my life."

"First night I've seen you drunk."

They laugh some more.

"You made me promise not to tell Da," Ritchie giggles, "because you boked in the bath when you got home."

"The toilet was too far away," Danielle huffs, "he found out anyway."

"Aye, 'cause I told him," Ritchie sniggers, "that was the first night you snogged Chris. I wanted to teach you a lesson."

"Fuck he was ragin'," Danielle elongates the *'a,'* "I mean, it was only a few WKDs, imagine if he saw the sight of me after a few gins now."

The laughter dies out and they look away from each other. Embarrassed at how they both acted. When Ritchie looks back up, he sees his sister wiping away tears. Skirting over, ignoring the collection of memories, he pulls his sister into an embrace. After a few moments, she says she's grand, and he slides back to where he was. They continue to stare at each other. So many unspoken words, just lingering in the air between them.

"Are you going to see him again?"

"Chris?"

Ritchie nods.

"I don't know..."

She honestly doesn't, Danielle thinks. The feelings are obviously still there, on both sides, by what she could figure last night. She almost went to unblock him on her Facebook, in case he needed to make contact, but it was just too hard. She wouldn't have been able to stop herself from looking back over his life without her.

"I don't think right now is a good time to be making any rash decisions," Ritchie squeezes her hand.

She smiles and nods, before they break apart and start collecting the pictures back into the old shoebox.

"Ritchie! Danielle! Michelle!"

It's Dermott, calling from downstairs.

"Yeah?" Michelle has opened her bedroom door, closest to Ritchie's at the back of the house.

"Come downstairs, I think you're going to want to hear this."

Chapter Fifty-One:

Victor Sargent remains silent as McNally and Ferguson file back into the room and take their seats. When the recording commences, he continues to look at the floor, his hands entwined on his lap. McNally and Ferguson wait for him to break down. If word got out that he brought Billy Taylor's name into a police investigation, the man will be a dead man walking. The best thing he can do now is comply.

"My client would like to make a statement," Beattie looks up at them from his glasses as he lifts the piece of paper in front of them. "On the night of the 18th June 2016, my client was instructed by Billy Taylor that he was needed to help with a pickup and drop off."

McNally snorts. He's making it sound like Taylor's running a fast food delivery service. The real passengers could be drugs, weapons or, in this case, bodies.

"My client left his own house after getting the phone call from Taylor at around 11:40pm. He was picked up in a stolen car by three other men just before midni-"

"Names?" Ferguson requests.

"Johnny Spratt, Stuart Riddles and Lee McKay."

Ferguson, seemingly surprised that it was so easy, nods for him to continue.

"He was picked up in a stolen car by three other men just before midnight, and taken to the Waterfoot Hotel. There, they waited out of sight for Aaron Parker to emerge. Once he levelled with them, they jumped out and threw him into the boot of the car. Once they did this, they took him to the Bay Road."

The Bay Road is a secluded area embanking the River Foyle typically reserved for industrial traffic making their way to and from their jobs. But at that time of night it would've been deserted.

"There, they were told to threaten him, but not to touch him. They told him that Billy Taylor gave them instructions to kill him unless he agreed to join forces with the Ulster Jacks. Despite this, Aaron Parker still said no. Thinking that he'd seen through their bluff, they contacted Taylor again. He commanded them to take him to an old farm on the Ardmore Road away from the city. Rumours are that the farmhouse is his, although it's currently empty. So, they took him there and tied him to a chair in the barn, as Taylor requested. When Taylor arrived, he instructed them to leave. And no one has heard anything since."

He leans back and takes off his glasses, giving the detectives a second to digest this. Sargent physically shakes beside him, seemingly terrified for his own safety. Finally, McNally and Ferguson exchange looks before clearing their throats and regrouping themselves.

"Okay..." McNally begins, "...so no one has any kind of idea what could've happened to Parker?"

Sargent shrugs.

"My client stated that there were rumours, but nothing set in stone. Taylor keeps his cards close to his chest. And, of course, no one has the courage to ask him. After all, we all know that Taylor is a dangerous man... Parker wouldn't have been the first person to get on the wrong side of him, and I'm sure we can all agree that he will not have been the last."

McNally and Ferguson share grave expressions as they look back at one another sullenly.

"Before this goes any further," Beattie holds up a hand just as McNally goes to speak once more, "I would strongly urge, for my client's safety, that he receives police protection, as well as immunity in this circus act. He was simply taking orders from Taylor, who has a reputation as big as his ego. I'm sure you can understand why he wouldn't want to argue with him."

McNally doubts there was much arguing on his part, but agrees that this had certainly turned more interesting.

"Okay," McNally nods after much deliberation, "I will personally deliver your client's request myself. Thank you, Mr Sargent. You are free to stay here until we find out if and where we can place you."

Chapter Fifty-Two:

"DI McNally and DS Ferguson have just come out of an interview with a potential suspect."

The tension lies heavy in the air of the living room. All eyes fixated on Dermott.

"The member of the Jacks has reportedly stated that himself and three other men were instructed to capture your father on the night he went missing. They took him to the Bay Road to threaten him to join their party. However, he refused again. I'm assured that it was only verbal threats, and Taylor instructed them not to touch him anymore than was necessary. After your father declined once more, it seems they grew frustrated."

A single tear falls down Michelle's cheek as the family sit forward, hands entwined.

"Taylor ordered them to take him to his farmhouse on the Ardmore Road. There, he was tied to a chair and left with only Taylor for company."

Ritchie physically shivers.

"And?" Nuala shrieks, making her children jump with fright, "then what?"

"They're on their way to speak to Taylor now, Nuala."

Nuala lets out an almighty squeal and falls forward. Ritchie jolts across to grab his mum, but by that time it's too late. She lies on the floor sobbing into the carpet, both of the elder kids either side of her, consoling her. Whilst Michelle just stares at the scene, silent tears still streaming down her cheeks.

"I knew it," Nuala bellows, muffled by the fluff on the carpet, "I fucking knew it. All these years, I fucking told them. But they wouldn't listen. Why wouldn't they listen? That bastard. That bastard!"

Dermott leans forward and strokes her tear-drenched hair out of her face, before lifting her up and placing her on the sofa again.

"We'll get to the bottom of this, Nuala. I know it's hard. The PSNI have been trying to get something on Taylor for years. He's a slippery one, we all know that. There's been no cold hard facts. Hopefully this Sargent character is willing to stand up in court and fight this. For your sake. For all of your sakes," he glances up at the other three, a fond smile on his face.

After it seems like she's cried herself out, Nuala blows her nose and stands abruptly. Sniffing, she steps forward towards the huge mirror resting on the mantlepiece, fixing her hair back into place.

"Ma?" Michelle raises a brow.

"Can't look an absolute mess going to Tescos now, can I?"

"Tescos?" Danielle narrows her eyes at her.

"Aye, sure we'll be having people around tonight for the wake. I've half a loaf and hardly any butter, never mind any fillings."

"Nuala," Dermott rises, "don't worry about any of that, we'll so-"

"Ritchie," Nuala points her finger at her son, "you collect Granny from her house to bring her round. Pack an overnight bag for her 'cause she'll probably want to stay here until after the funeral. We'll make a space for her in the dining room. Danielle, will you run and get an inflatable bed from Argos, there's no way she can climb those stairs. Michelle, I want you to start cleaning the house. The bathroom, the kitchen, in here... Anywhere where anyone is going to be."

"Nuala..."

"I'll be right back, just going to grab cheese and ham... Maybe a bit of tuna. Do people still have tuna and sweetcorn sandwiches?" she starts to giggle hysterically, "and I hardly have any teabags. Would 200 be too much? Oh, there's so much to do. Right, chop chop, guys. Let's get this sorted now before your father is home."

And with that, she marches out of the room, grabbing her keys from the shelf in the hall and slamming the door. They watch her trudge down the drive, waving at them to hurry, tapping her finger off her watch, before climbing in her car and reversing out onto the road and speeding off. They stare at the space where she was seconds ago, before all reverting their eyes to one another, confused expressions on all their faces. What just happened?

Chapter Fifty-Three:

2016

_____

The sounds of car doors slamming are the first inclination that something is wrong. Danielle hops up from the sofa and pods over to the living room window, overlooking the front garden. From there, she can see the approach of DI Quigley and DS Ferguson, climbing the drive. Shouting for her mum, she stirs a snoozing Ritchie on the armchair next to her. Dermott and Michelle are already in the kitchen, the latter trying and failing to eat a slab of dry toast.

When the detectives make it to the back door and knock twice, Nuala has skirted to the island just as Dermott opens the door. Stepping through, they smile at the family. But it isn't a confident smile. More of a sympathetic smile. They've come up short. Again. Collecting at the island, DI Quigley sighs as he takes a seat.

"It's not good news, I'm afraid."

There had been a call that someone reported seeing their father working in a bookies in Letterkenny, a large town in County Donegal, about a half hour west of Derry. They hadn't had their hopes up, if he was looking to up and leave, you'd think he would go somewhere a bit further away? Somewhere with no trace of him or chance of being spotted. He was a relatively well-known man, even in Letterkenny they would have recognised him.

"It wasn't your father, although there was a bit of a resemblance, I can see where he had gotten the idea."

It has been over two weeks since Aaron's disappearance. Both underground organisations and opposing parties had been spoken with, but neither had heard anything that had happened that night. All CCTV was checked, but there was no sign of him. It's almost as if he had vanished off the face of the earth. The only sign that he existed, and was at the party at the Waterfoot Hotel at all, was the finding of his phone several days ago. However, it brought no new leads.

"Them bastards have something to do with it, I just know it."

Nuala glares at the detectives, nursing Michelle's head in her arms.

"Nuala... We've been through this," Quigley takes a deep breath in.

"I still think there's more to it. Some things they aren't saying... He wouldn't leave us. He wouldn't leave all his hard work. He wouldn't..."

She can't bring herself to say *'kill himself.'* The search of the River Foyle had been called off. It's summer, so the water is relatively warm. Warm enough for a dead body to float anyway. She just has a twisting feeling in her gut that he never entered the river. That something has happened. Something awful.

"Look... Nuala, I'm sorry to tell you this..." DI Quigley stares at the hob on the island instead of at Nuala, or any other family member, directly. "But people go missing all the time... Some, only for hours. Others... Days. Many of them children, the vast majority of them showing up. Missing adults? Now, that's a different story... If he has disappeared, I'm sure there is a good enough reason as to why. He doesn't want to be found... And maybe, for the sake of yourself and your children... Well, maybe that's a good thing?"

Chapter Fifty-Four:

2019

———

"Maybe we should call in back-up?"

McNally accelerates down the Limavady Road towards the Crown. Taylor's cleaner had rudely informed them that he spends every Saturday evening down there, and that's the only time she can come in and clean up after him. Not that the place looked like it needed a tidy yesterday evening when they last visited him.

"I mean... Boss... Going in all guns blazing hasn't worked well in the past. And especially not after already lifting Sargent hours ago... Word will have gotten round. Backs will be up; tensions will be high... They might be suspecting something."

"Call it in if you wish, Ferguson. I just want to get to him before he hears that we're looking for him.

I don't want to give him the chance to skip town or go into hiding."

"Sir, there's no way Sargent will tell him we're looking for him. There's not a chance he could do that without shooting himself in the foot. Unless he has a death wish."

"Be that as it may, I'm not taking any chances."

Ferguson decides to send Fleming and O'Connor a courteous message informing them of their strategy just as they round the corner to the Crown pub to the east of the city. There, they see him standing, slouched against the outside wall right in front of them, phone to his ear. Alone. Pulling up right beside him, McNally jerks off his seatbelt and looks over towards Ferguson, eyebrows raised and eyes wide.

"After me."

Stepping out resistantly, Ferguson crosses the road to see Taylor looking at them with amusement.

"Right, I've company here... I'll have to speak to you later. Right, right, bye."

Ending the call, Taylor pockets the phone and takes one final drag of his cigarette before grinding it into the ashtray on the table in front of him.

"Well, gentlemen... Long time, no see," the lines of his forehead prominent as he observes them, "on another wild goose chase, are we?"

Does he know?

"William Taylor, I am arresting you on suspicion of the murder of Aaron Parker on or around the 19th of June 2016."

Billy lets out a cackle, his arms wide open at his side.

"You do not have to say anything, but it may harm your defence if you do not mention when questioned something which you later rely on in court. Anything you do say may be given in evidence. Do you understand?"

"Balls, absolute balls," Taylor continues to guffaw, before McNally brings out his handcuffs.

Shaking his head, his body still vibrating with laughter, he agrees to be led to the car uncuffed. Ferguson spies a few heads peeking out at them from the dimly lit windows of the pub. Thankfully, they're all safely in the car when a few boisterous lads appear at the front door. Shouting *get tae fuck'* and *'peeler scum.'* Taylor just continues to chuckle as a group start snorting after them, one even launching a full pint glass at the car, which narrowly misses Ferguson's passenger-side mirror.

"Nice friends you have there," McNally grumbles.

Ferguson looks into the rear-view mirror to see Taylor glaring back at them playfully.

"You have no idea."

298

Chapter Fifty-Five:

"Can I speak with you a moment?"

Jodie looks up from her computer and nods, minimizing whatever she was working on to display the Londonderry Letter's emblem which is the standard screensaver for all the office's computers. Taking the proffered seat, Cathal looks at his feet.

"How were the Parkers?"

"Oh, you know... As you'd expect... Bereaved."

"Any good quotes?"

"Aye, I've actually finished the article and it's been submitted for approval."

As if bursting to life, Jodie bustles with her mouse, bringing up the requested articles for the paper's online forum. Finding it close to the top, she opens it, silencing Cathal with a raised finger and a sharp *'shush.'* He sits awkwardly whilst she assesses his work. When she's finished reading, she looks back up at him with gleaming eyes.

"Very good, I love it. Although, I'd take out the part about the older brother leaving with tears in his eyes. That's a bit too... Creative writing for my tastes. And we want to keep them onside, we don't want to embarrass the boy."

"No, Jodie... You don't understand. I came in to be asked to be taken off the story."

Jodie cocks her head to the side, a frown prominent on her face.

"Is... Has there been more... Incidents?"

Cathal nods before bringing out his phone and passing it over the desk. Jodie pulls her glasses down from the top of her head and inspects the latest message, before gasping and looking up at him.

"Right... I understand completely. I'll give it to Ethan, he worked on the case three years ago."

"Thank you, Jodie."

"Can you pass him your source's number?"

"Of course, I'll send it over to him now."

"In the meantime, I want you to take annual leave."

Cathal goes to protest, but Jodie waves away his interruption.

"I'll hear nothing more of it. You have so much left, you refuse to take any. It's good for your mental health, you know? Even if you have nowhere to go."

Cathal desires to tell Jodie that keeping himself busy is the best thing for his mental health. That sitting alone at home is the worst possible thing he can do.

"Go home and spend time with your sister. Contact the police. Do whatever you can to keep yourselves safe. This isn't some silly jealous reporter; this could be serious... You have to look after yourself."

Nodding, disappointed, Cathal thanks her for her time, before exiting the office. Deciding not to make a song and dance about it, intent on messaging Ethan privately later, he walks straight out of the office, everyone too engrossed in their own stories to notice. If anyone did see him leave, they'd guess he was popping to the shops to buy something to eat at his desk. It's not uncommon to get something to bring to your desk when a story keeps you here well after office hours have finished.

Stepping out onto Spencer Road, Cathal sighs as he decides a walk will do him good. Crossing the road, he starts to walk across the upper deck of the Craigavon Bridge over to the Derryside, but stops, leaning against the railing, gazing down at where they found David Wayne earlier this morning. Of course, the news had shocked the city. There was no denying that an underground organisation was behind it. No one else would be that brutal. But what it was about, Joanna in the office still has to find out. The police are almost being as tight lipped as David will be going forward.

The office was gossiping earlier about what they think it could be. Of course, the *'tout'* route was the most obvious. Punished for blabbing something he shouldn't have. Maybe Cathal won't even find out now, having been forced to take leave. He'll miss the camaraderie of the excited office as someone gets a lead. It's addictive. He'd basically been forced to take holidays during the summer, and it was the longest two weeks of his life. He'd been in the office two or three times during those weeks, inquiring as to what his colleagues were working on before being chased out by Jodie. How is he going to last now, with God knows how long this investigation could carry on for?

His thoughts are broken as his phone vibrates in his pocket. Instinctively, he looks either side of him, wondering if a neighbouring car has their camera on their phone pointed towards him. Could they be following him now? Suddenly feeling very vulnerable by himself, especially so close to the river, he retreats back a few steps before pulling out his phone. Thankfully, it's just Dermott.

'Interesting update – will keep you in the loop when we know more. D.'

He yearns to know what's going on. He can't believe he has to stay in the dark. He can almost feel the pins and needles in his fingers, itching to get at a story that is no longer his to tell.

Chapter Fifty-Six:

Jumping as the overhead speakers blast a local voice asking for Andy to come to checkouts, Nuala continues to migrate down the same aisle again, lost in her own thoughts. She gazes into her trolley. Five big packets of crisps, two bags of KP nuts, four loaves of bread, two slabs of butter. What else does she need? Teabags, right. And fillings for the sandwiches.

She shouldn't have to do this alone, she thinks, as she bypasses pissed off shoppers who give her dirty looks for attempting to squeeze past them. But who else will help? Kealen hasn't returned from Australia in two years, and he's too busy with his own family anyway. She hasn't even bothered to message him to let him know that Aaron's been found. And if he has seen anything on social media, he hasn't attempted to make contact. They have never really been close, so why start now? He had rung her when Aaron initially went missing and gave his apologies.

He had tried to ring once a week thereafter, after only speaking maybe two or three times a year, but it started to dwindle down to once a month, before he stopped altogether. Last time they spoke was for her birthday three months ago. It was nothing more than a courteous *'happy birthday Auntie Nuala'* text with a picture of his two gorgeous girls.

Their mother is far too old to be blustering about a shop, she can barely make her way from the armchair to her bed in the tiny flat she rents just outside Newbuildings. She had been a huge help in the first few months after Aaron had gone missing. Helping out in the house and keeping them all sane. Agreeing to babysit Michelle when Nuala couldn't sleep and had wanted to search in the dead of night. She had even hidden her cancer scare from them all, deciding that they'd had enough on their plate. Her ill health continued, and after the diabetes diagnosis last Christmas, she's nothing more than the shell of the woman she once was. Kealen would sink to the ground if he seen the shape of her now. Thankfully, their mother doesn't agree to any FaceTime or Skype calls, deeming her wrinkly skin as the reason, wanting to remember herself as a younger woman.

And all her friends have as good as ditched her. They were all there for her at the start, but she more or less pushed them away after Aaron's disappearance. She refused to go on nights out or even brunch dates. She just wanted to wallow in her own self-pity. She understood that life goes on. For them, but not for her. Juggling the kids, fighting with the government and trying to keep up a search with dwindling interest. It was exhausting. She had to learn to do it on her own.

"Watch where you're going!"

She looks up to a woman with a trolley full of meal deals huffing away from her, giving her dagger glares. Nuala had almost trodden straight into her. Nuala apologises before reverting up the freezer aisle, how had she managed to make it here? The supermarket is so packed, it's doing nothing for her nerves. Finding the cooked meats section, she gasps when she sees there are only three packets of ham left. With six pieces in each pack. Surely that isn't enough? That would only make 30 sandwiches. She jumps again as a toddler springs past her, laughing ludicrously with a 20 packet of fish fingers in his sticky hands as his dad jogs after him.

The lights are so bright. The hum of the fridge is so loud. It's almost deafening. She claps a hand to one of her ears and squeezes her eyes closed. Just wanting to shut everything out. Shut everything up. What's going on? She finds herself struggling to breathe. Oh, God. Is she having a stroke? A heart attack? As she gasps for air, a teenage girl to her left gazes at her inquisitively. Is she asking if she's okay?

Her mouth is moving but no words are forming. She just hears a piercing sound in her left ear.

Leaning all her weight on the trolley, it skids away from her and she collapses onto the hard floor, landing on her hand and feeling a crunch of pain. She cries out but she can't hear even herself. Rolling over, she stares up at the white lights of the supermarket ceiling beaming down on her. Wondering if this is it. If this is when she's going to finally be reunited with Aaron.

Chapter Fifty-Seven:

They aren't expecting to see Taylor looking so smug in the interview room. As they go about the preliminaries, he just continues to glare at them with a broad grin. Even his solicitor looks uncomfortable.

"Well done, gentlemen," he erupts before they have a chance to ask the first question. "You've done it. You've always wanted me here... And now you've managed it. So, what silly little story have you conjured up now? It best be a good one, as you can't keep me in here much longer without any evidence."

He raises his eyebrows at them. He's toying with them. McNally leans back in his seat, observing him. He was expecting the cruel underground lord to come out like it did for half a second last night. But instead, he's still braving this front that he's in control. That won't last long.

"Why do you think you're here, Mr Taylor?"

Taylor snorts.

"Haven't a clue... Maybe... Jealousy?"

McNally and Ferguson can't help but share a concerned look between themselves.

"Jealousy, Mr Taylor?" Ferguson narrows his eyes at him.

"Aye. After all, you seen my house. You seen my cars. And I came from nothing. Didn't I? Brought up to two dole-head parents. I decided I wasn't going to be like that. That I was going to make something of my life... And I did. And you can't accept that. Because of me wanting to make this country a better place, I'm accused of paramilitary-style attacks, drugs, you name it... I've apparently done it."

"And what has any of this got to do with what happened with Mr Parker?"

Taylor sighs and looks down at his fingers. Rubbing his thumb off one of them, he lazily looks up at them.

"Mr Taylor, the best thing you can do now is to comply. We have a warrant to search your house, which officers are currently already combing through. What will we find there? We've also found out who the stolen car belonged to. We have even managed to track down the number plate and have ploughed through CCTV to see it crossing the Foyle Bridge shortly after midnight, with four men in the seats. It was then seen entering the Bay Road area, where it stayed for some time. An hour later, it is seen driving over to the Waterside towards the Ardmore Road, where it is ultimately lost. You have a property on the Ardmore Road, I believe? A derelict farmhouse... The perfect place to take someone for a slither of privacy."

Taylor stares at them, his eyes bouncing between them. Before finally, lifting a hand and scratching his unshaven chin, he pouts.

"What do you want to know?"

"Well... As you can tell, we know everything, Taylor... We want to hear you tell us what happened, in your own words."

Sighing once more, Taylor glances at his solicitor, his only moment of weakness, who nods.

"You don't know everything. You have the wrong end of the stick... Like I told you last night, only a fool wouldn't have been worried about Parker's party. Ardóimid and Boyle might tell you different... But I know they were. I could see they were getting nervous. And that's what spurred me on. I know Parker was a protestant, and although his wife is a catholic, and their kids went to the catholic grammars, that didn't concern me. We could've been a great team, I think. Move this country forward. You're right, I didn't like taking no for an answer that night, but show me someone who does. So, I think he needed a little... Persuasion."

McNally almost snorts audibly.

"You're right, I did get some lads to pick him up and take him to the Bay Road. There, they were asked to convince him that it was in his best interest whilst I mingled with the party. One eye on my phone."

"And Parker's phone?"

McNally almost stomps on Ferguson's foot for interrupting him.

"What about it?"

"Is it true that you stole it?"

Taylor raises a brow.

"Yes, but giving the light of the conversation and the fact that I've been arrested for murder, I didn't think that was an issue."

"Just wanting to know how it came to appear in the surrounding bushes of the Waterfoot Hotel."

"I planted it there after stealing it."

Ferguson nods as McNally glares at him.

"As you were saying, Mr Taylor."

Taylor rolls his eyes and coughs, leaning back and fidgeting with his shirt.

"Yes, well... Where was I?"

"You were still at the party."

"Aye, so... They rang and said that he still wouldn't budge. He wouldn't agree to join us. So, as I'm sure you're both aware, I asked them to move him to my farmhouse."

He goes quiet, pursing his lips.

"And then?"

"I must say, gentlemen. What I'm about to disclose next will almost indefinitely incriminate me, but I must urge you to keep an open mind. I arrived, drunk and annoyed. I requested that they leave me alone with him. At first, we started out just talking. Discussing politics... As you do. He was trying to establish that we would never agree on anything if we were to join. We had different views on religion. On abortion. On the LGBT community," he air quotes the latter. "It seems I wasn't getting through to him. His job was not to agree with my terms. It was to just do as I say. Get the people interested and voting for him. Therefore, voting for me!"

The frustration in his voice is obvious, as he clears his throat in an attempt to calm himself down.

"When he refused time and time again, I do admit... I did do something I'm still not very proud of..."

They sit forward. Eager to await his confession.

"I cracked up... And I... Threw a bottle at the wall. It smashed, showering us in glass. I marched over and I grabbed him by the scruff of the neck. Bellowing in his face that if he didn't join me... That I was a very powerful man. I knew people. And I knew where he lived. I knew he had a son and two daughters. And a wife... I'm not proud of it, detectives... But I threatened the life of his family. That's when he finally caved... He agreed.

"Shortly after that, I threw him into the back of my car. Off a back road, I tossed him out, freeing him and drove off. But I swear, detectives, when I looked in my rear-view mirror as I sped off, I saw him standing up and brushing himself off. Glaring after my car and turning in the direction of the Glenshane Road and, ultimately, his home."

The detectives stare at him. Unconvinced.

"And then what?" McNally scrunches up his face.

"I went home and I went to bed. The next day, I saw on the news that he went missing. It's the *truth!*"

Both McNally and Ferguson shuffle defiantly in their seats.

"So, what do you suggest happened to him, then?" McNally shakes his head.

"I honestly don't know. I'm sure you've heard all the rumours about me. Not all of them are true. And I didn't kill that man. Why would I want to kill him after he agreed to join forces with me? With both of us, we could've knocked Ardóimid out of the race. We could've gone on to become massive political figures in Northern Irish history. Think about it!"

Chapter Fifty-Eight:

Is that... It is. It's her. Chris trots across the car park, reaching for the passenger-side door handle just as she outstretches her hand towards it. Taking her completely by surprise. Danielle startles, collecting herself and laughing. Dropping the blow-up mattress into the car, she turns towards him once more.

"How have ye been?"

"Good," she smiles, "well... As good as I can be, obviously."

Chris nods, staring at her. This is the first time they've been alone together in years. He has so much to tell her, but can't seem to find the words to actually express himself. Instead, he nods through into the passenger-side window.

"No bed?"

She laughs again, he had no idea how much he missed it until he finally heard it again.

"It's for my granny, it'd be a whole handling bringing her back and forth when she'll want to be there for the wake and the funeral... So, we may as well just have her sleep over at ours."

He nods.

"So, the body's been released then?"

"Aye, we're sorting everything now... With all being well, we should be having the funeral on Monday."

"Long time comin'."

She smiles again, tears collecting in her eyes. He rests a reassuring hand on her shoulder as she looks down at it. Alien to her after all this time. They used to know each other inside out, but now...

"What about you?" she shakes away her tears and points at his gym bag, "didn't see you as a gym-goer."

"Me neither," he laughs, sliding the bag behind his back embarrassedly, "I've only been once or twice. When I could be arsed."

"Which is never, I bet," she chuckles.

Maybe she still does know him after all, he smirks.

"Hi, how about a milkshake?" he turns and jolts his head towards the golden arches of McDonald's.

"And ruin your hard work at the gym?" she leans her head to the side.

"I'll just end up goin' home and gettin' a chippy anyway," he laughs, not disclosing that he actually hasn't made it in yet, "and sure, it's only a milkshake, what harm would it do?"

She bites her bottom lip before nodding. Half an hour later, they're parked up beside the Homebase in Chris's car, their milkshakes melting in their hands as they catch up on the past two years. What they've been up to. What they've missed. What's in store for them in the next few weeks, months and years. A lot of it they already know. What they learned during the part of their relationship where they got to know one another. Got to understand their hopes and dreams. But now... They continue telling each other funny anecdotes they'd know the other would love. Laughing along and reminiscing.

When their laughs finally subside and Danielle lifts the straw to her lips, sipping her banana milkshake, Chris reaches over and takes her other hand. Both of them look down at it expectedly. Excitedly. Like the start of their relationship. When everything was new. Could they start again? Could they forget everything that happened? They both look up from their hands and into each other's eyes. Danielle blinks repeatedly, opening her mouth to speak. But before she can say anything, her ringtone penetrates the silence of the car. Almost as if bursting a bubble.

Suddenly, they're back in the car park. The hustle and bustle of the busy retail park can be heard, and they're suddenly aware of the shoppers flocking around the car. Fighting her hand out of his grasp, she struggles to pull her phone from her pocket.

"Hello?"

Her eyes widen as Chris takes a slurp of his own milkshake.

"What? When? Right, I'm on my way."

Pocketing her phone once more, she apologises, getting ready to escape the car.

"D? What's wrong? Chat to me."

"It's Ma... She's had a fall in Tescos... They think it was a panic attack. She's in A&E now, I have to get to her. I'm sorry. I..." she indicates the milkshake, "... Thank you. I'll be in touch."

How? Chris wants to scream as she flops out of the car and slams the door, running to her own. Chris leans back on the headrest and breathes out deeply. Like he can fully breathe again. It isn't over... It can't be over. He has to do something.

Chapter Fifty-Nine:

Turning the corner, Smyth narrows his eyes as he sees a collection of people outside the Bull's Horn, notorious for housing members of Ardóimid and other locals to the west of the city. But with its shutters down, it's obvious that something's happening. He observes skinheads in three quarter length shorts and bare, flabby chests hammering on the door, their abandoned t-shirts resting on the picnic bench on the pavement.

Levelling with the pub, Smyth cranes his neck over the revellers, looking for someone he would know. There are about 20 or 30 people all shouting and roaring, battering their fists off the shutters, vocally expressing their distaste for not being able to get into their local on a Saturday night. He would know some to see, a courteous nod when walking into the pub, but wouldn't talk to them. Doesn't know any of their names. He doubts they'd acknowledge him now, especially in their angry states.

Finally, on the other side of the crowd from him, he spots Macka rolling a fag. Stepping out onto the road to bypass the agitated congregation, he spits on the ground for added effect, before cocking his head towards the front doors.

"Fuck's happenin' here, Macka?"

Macka is the barman in the Bull's Horn. If he's not even allowed in, something massive must be wrong.

"Cannae say, hi," Macka lights his smoke before taking a long drag, "Boyle's holdin' some form of a meetin'."

"About what?" Smyth sneers, police training kicking in.

Could this have something to do with the Parker murder? Rumours circulated Facebook earlier that they'd arrested Billy Taylor from outside the Crown. He was expecting to land here tonight to a celebration. Keeping up appearances, he knew he had to join.

"No clue, boy," Macka attempts to hock a greener over the wall beside him, which misses, hitting the top of it and stringing down onto the pavement next to them, making Smyth's stomach turn, "but whatever it is, they mean business. Showed up here at six o'clock and told me out to fuck," he clenches his fingers and protrudes his thumb, bashing his arm backwards aggressively. "Big Stoner and Gurnsy were in there too. As ye can tell, they didn't wanny go quietly."

He nods towards the two shirtless guys bashing their bare shoulders against the doors in a means to penetrate their own clubhouse. Ultimately destroying their sanctuary, Smyth struggles not to shake his head at their stupidity, instead opting to stay in character and chortle along with Macka.

"Bustin' for a pint myself, might end up joinin' them. But fuck am I waitin' out in this. Told the wife I was only comin' for the one. Give me a shout when you're open."

Macka nods, sucking the last remnants of his cigarette as Smyth bids him farewell with a gravelly *good man.* Once out of eye and ear shot, Smyth plucks out his phone, desperate to inform the big bosses on what he's seen. Something's going on behind those closed doors. Something big. And whatever it is, there's no way it's good news.

Chapter Sixty:

The third glass of red wine is going down too smoothly. Opting to take on Ferguson's joke, McNally had landed to their house with both a red and white, one in each hand as Ferguson opened the door. The two had laughed, before McNally got invited into the living room, where an uncharacteristically shy Niamh rested. Her legs crossed, red lips to match the wine in her glass. She had looked up at McNally with a protruded lip, the smirk forming on the corner of her mouth. He had taken her hand delicately, deciding not to kiss it. Too formal.

He'd been introduced to Jane shortly after, popping out of the kitchen with a bizarre apron covering her sparkly top. They had cheered as they clunked their glasses together, before settling down to Jane's lovely spread. Sweet baby potatoes with an array of vegetables, and a piping hot steak. Medium/rare, just how McNally likes it.

Now, here they sit. Discussing their everyday lives and getting to know one another. Jane occasionally throwing Niamh a lifeline, telling her not to be so modest, as McNally smirks over the table towards her. Entranced by her beauty. Excited at the opportunity of getting to know her. She's a beautician at Suzie's Salon, although she studied a degree in psychology. Their mother and father had blatantly informed her that no child of theirs was going to be a beautician. *'Not when she has brains to burn,'* Niamh and Jane had giggled, mocking their late mother's apparent regular lecture.

After graduating, however, she decided she wanted to pursue her preferred career, and whilst claiming that she was actively looking for jobs to her parents, she took up a beautician course in the tech. Within ten months, she was hired and soaring in the beauty world. Getting requests for weddings and formals, and the money was nothing to be snubbed at, so eventually she won her parents over.

"I mean, surely studying psychology, you would've known how to get them wrapped around your wee finger anyway," McNally winks at Niamh as she giggles into her hand, clasped around her mouth, her shoulders raised defensively.

"Awk, little miss perfect," Jane scoffs, a few drinks in now, her words slurring, "couldn't do wrong from doing right with her," she hiccups, slurping more wine.

"What?" Ferguson turns to her, frowning and smiling in confusion.

Within seconds, all of them are laughing along, before McNally feels his phone vibrate in his pocket. Pulling it out, he puts down his glass and excuses himself.

"Incredibly rude," he eyes Ferguson, so he knows it's a work call, before stepping out into the hall to answer O'Connor.

"Sir, Smyth has just called in a mob of people from outside the Bull's Horn. Turns out there's a near riot going on because people can't get in for their drinks. Members of Ardóimid are holding court, including Boyle. We've sent some officers over there now to see if they can see what's going on."

Sobering up, McNally rubs his stubble thoughtfully.

"Has there been a disturbance?"

"Well, that's how they're going to downplay it..."

"You think it could be linked with Parker?"

"I don't know, sir. Smyth went there himself as he believed there'd be a big party with Taylor getting arrested... Something seems fishy to me."

"Right... You're right... Keep me in the loop."

"I will, sir."

Hanging up, McNally apologises again as he returns to the dining room, where Jane is bustling over the plates, Niamh in the toilet. The two ladies re-join them at the table just as McNally's coming to the end of the story.

"But I don't understand, why tonight?" Ferguson asks, "you'd think Boyle would know we'd be keeping a close eye on him."

"Ignorance, or arrogance," McNally shakes his head, lifting his glass to his lips before realising it's empty, "my vote is for the latter."

"Do you believe Taylor's story though, Liam?" Jane leans back in her chair, bringing her foot up to get more comfortable.

McNally gives a side glance to Ferguson, who shrugs and holds his two hands up, palms facing forward.

"What can I say, sir. No secrets with us. And if there were any, she'd beat them out of me... She's basically my sergeant in training."

"I don't know, Jane," McNally blows a raspberry, "I don't see why he would lie... I mean, he'd gotten what he'd wanted. Why try so hard to get it, just to take him out of the picture completely?"

"Maybe he's just saying that, though," Niamh sits forward, helping herself to a generous helping of wine, before offering to top up McNally's glass too, "he knows you're all onto him, so he made up the story that he complied. I mean, maybe he did kill him because he wouldn't join them, and that was just his cover story."

"I don't know," Ferguson shakes his head, "they've never hid bodies before, have the Jacks. They just leave them out in the open, or strategically placed so people know it's their handiwork. Look at David Wayne this morning."

"Good point," McNally nods. "And the threats on the O'Flaherty boy... The journalist," he adds, for the women's benefit, "that isn't like the Jacks either... Usually they're more action, less talk."

McNally and Ferguson had called in on Cathal on their way back to the station earlier this evening after getting a call from the incident room. They took his statement about the threats he was getting, but further investigation had come up short. The email has only been active for a number of days, and they were able to link it with a pay-as-you-go phone. It has only ever made contact with Cathal. Phone triangulations have zoned it in on Lisnagelvin Shopping Centre twice, as well as around the area of Cathal's house for the picture message of his retreating sister. Where the perpetrator was exactly is hard to pin down.

"But, what could Boyle have to do with this?" McNally brings this evening's antics back to the table.

"Maybe he's holding his own celebrations?" Niamh chuckles into her glass.

"Maybe," Ferguson nods, "or maybe they're planning something. Or panicking. Either way, it looks like we're one step closer to finding out the truth."

"Fancy a trip over? Just to check it out," McNally directs the question towards Ferguson.

He's over the limit, he knows that. But the eagerness to find out is too overwhelming. He'd book a taxi, or ask to see if a patrol car could pick them up. After all, they're not far from the Bull's Horn, what with Ferguson living so close to the Strand Road embanking the Foyle.

"Aye, just for a quick gander," Ferguson sloshes the last of his wine to the back of his throat and stands, flinching at the scraping of the chair legs off the wooden floor.

"Jane, I'm so sorry, we'll be right back," McNally also stands, before turning to Niamh and winking, "will you be here when I get back?"

"Hmm, I dunno," she raises her perfectly shaped brows at him, "it might be past my bedtime."

Chapter Sixty-One:

Stepping out of Dermott's car, Nuala thanks him as he holds out an arm to help her. Her wrist is badly sprained, and as she straightens up, she tries to tug at her sleeve to hide the brace again. She's so embarrassed. The doctor said she's lucky that that's all she hurt, but she doesn't feel lucky. All the horror stories of people hitting their heads when falling were told, almost as if rehearsed, whilst the brace was being adjusted. To be honest, she feels like a good blow to the head is what she needs. But she can't be selfish, she needs to think of her family. The three children who look up to her. She's all they have left.

She just wants to crawl into bed and hide her face in shame, but knows that people will be landing soon for the wake. They'll have to make do with glasses of water, and maybe some will land with casseroles and the likes. Would it be incredibly rude to use their food for the people coming? She thinks so, but they'll just have to grin and bear it. It's not like they'll say anything. Dermott had told her the body was on its way when he collected her from the hospital. Closed coffin, obviously. How is she going to get through the next few days if a trip to the Tescos is enough to land her in hospital? Panic attack, they had brushed it off as. Handed a few leaflets about counsellors and away she was sent. As if it were that simple. Panic attack? She felt like she was being swallowed alive. Turned inside out.

But the answer to all her questions park up in the next two cars. Out steps Danielle and Michelle from one, and Ritchie from the other, all three of them migrating to the latter's passenger-side door. Struggling out, feebler than she's ever seen her, is her mum. She totters over, walking stick in one hand, and gives Nuala a hug that must take every ounce of strength. Deceiving strength. Squeezing the negativity out of her. When she pulls away, Nuala has tears collected in her eyes as she looks at her little family, Dermott included. Taking them all in. She has to stick around. For them, rather than for herself.

"Right, let's get in and get the kettle on," her mother jabs the bottom of her stick towards the front door, giving a gummy grin.

Linking arms, they all march across the garden, before Michelle breaks the chain to open the door. They step through and sigh, before moving into the living room. That's where Nuala gasps, her good hand flying to her chest. All the sofas have been pushed back against one wall, and the coffee table is littered with finger food wrapped in cling film, from an array of sandwiches to cocktail sausages and sausage rolls. Dining room chairs scattered around the floor. Where their TV once stood is now a barren corner, wide enough for a six-foot coffin. The family are silent as they gaze around, the only sound coming from Granny's padding feet trotting over to the nearest settee, which she groans into, oblivious. Nuala turns around to her children, but they all look as confused as her.

Where's Dermott? The foursome turn and retreat into the kitchen, barely acknowledging their granny's shout for *'milk and two sugars.'* Once they open the door, they see Dermott slouched against one wall. He shrugs and nods towards the corner. Following his gaze, Danielle inhales excitedly, clapping her hands to her mouth. Beside the tower of polystyrene cups and packets of sugar stand Jase, Katie, Travis, Steph, Georgia (holding a squirming and smirking baby William), Jimmy and Chris. They all smile nervously at the family, before Danielle squeals and runs over, letting herself be enveloped by them all.

"Guys," Nuala shakes her head, hobbling into the kitchen properly, "did you do all this?"

The only one to hear her over the noise of babbling conversation is Jase, who nods politely.

"Honestly, guys," Nuala speaks up to be heard, a few of them breaking away and giving her their attention, "this is too much. We can't thank you enough, honestly."

"Don't worry about it, Nuala," Katie smiles over to her.

The collection of voices overrun the kitchen as Chris dodges past Ritchie and Michelle as they unpeel themselves from the doorway. Ritchie makes a beeline for Jimmy, whilst Michelle haunches down to speak to William, who has plonked himself down on the tiled floor. Turning to Dermott once more, a look of confusion on her face, Nuala sees him look away again shyly.

"Was this your handiwork?"

"Not at all," Dermott shakes his head, "I just found out from Michelle where the spare key was kept."

"Then, who?"

Dermott smirks and nods towards Chris, who has slumped back against the washing machine, looking over at Danielle hugging Jase with a satisfied look on his face.

Chapter Sixty-Two:

Crossing the wooden floor and twisting the rusted twin deadbolt locks on the top and bottom of the door, Boyle puts on his deepest frown as he goes to swing it open. Before he can, however, he jumps as the shutters protecting the window on his left make an almighty bang, being followed with jeers from the halfwits outside.

Anger escalating, he pulls open the door, fighting the urge to smirk as he's greeted with the sound of the shouting and cursing being cut short. 50 or more faces drop when they see him standing over the threshold. Silence. He looks over the collection of men staring at him with a brow raised. Some he knows well. Some, not so much. Obviously heard the commotion and wanted to come and give their two pence worth. A chance for a blowout. Well, they'll get it soon enough.

He steps forward and, instinctively, the people collected in front of him start to part, making a path for him. They continue to stare after him before he makes it to the edge, seeing Macka lazing against the back wall, smoke in his mouth. Boyle lags his head backwards towards the entrance, making Macka nod in understanding, before tossing the cigarette on the ground and stepping forward to return to work. As he retreats to his car, Boyle hears the excited whispers of the crowd as they start to flock into the pub. O'Carroll and Byrne are still in there having a pint, but he can trust them not to expose any information... Not yet, anyway.

Just as he presses the car keys to open the driver door, he looks up and smirks. Standing just beside his car on the pavement are DI McNally and DS Ferguson, a police car metres behind them on the other side of the road.

"Well, well, well... How may I help you gentlemen?"

"We were just in the neighbourhood," McNally scowls at him, "were wondering what all the roaring and shouting was about."

"You can't come between a man and his pint... Especially not on a Saturday night. Make life easier for yourselves, eh?" Boyle winks, before clicking open his driver's door.

"Something interesting going on in the Bull's Horn, was there, Boyle?" Ferguson rounds the back of his car to meet him.

"Nothing specifically, no," Boyle brings his bottom lip up to below his nose, a look of confusion on his face, "just a bit of political business. Ran on longer than I would've liked... Some of them politicians can talk."

As he falls into his seat, he looks up to see Ferguson glaring in at him.

"What are you up to, Boyle?"

Boyle widens his eyes and smiles, before slamming the door and speeding off towards the direction of Brooke Park, a customary glance in his rear-view mirror to watch the two shrinking figures helplessly looking after him.

Chapter Sixty-Three:

Seeing the two of them in the corner, laughing and touching, it makes her blood boil. She has no reason to be jealous. If anything, it's *her* that's in the wrong. But Steph can't help it. Lifting the granny's mug with a smile, she asks if she'd like a top up. The granny taps her on the forearm as confirmation, still engrossed in a story with the lady in the neighbouring settee. Stepping through into the hall, she pushes into the kitchen to see Ritchie looking out into the garden. Smiling at him as he turns towards her, she totters over to the kettle, filling it to the brim before pushing the button.

Waiting for it to boil, she stares at Ritchie's back. Tense. Uncomfortable. A lot heavier than he used to be. He used to be so fit, infamous on the Gaelic pitch. Oozed confidence. Now, he's like a completely different person. She's not sure if he's even stepped foot in the living room yet. His father's remains resting inside the coffin in the corner. He's been looking into this garden all evening, from when the guests started arriving. Barely bothering to greet them. A limp hand offered as a form of acceptance for their condolences.

When a couple whose names she'd forgotten almost instantly after being introduced to them decide to go back into the living room, they find themselves alone. She stares at the kettle, well aware of the age old saying, before turning back to Ritchie.

"How have you been?"

He shrugs. She joins him by the pane of glass, rubbing her shoulder off him playfully.

"Long time, no see. You should come home more often."

She looks at his side profile. His jaw tightened. Patchy stubble. Eyes blinking rapidly. Lines on his forehead that weren't there the last time she had been this close to him. His father's death had taken a massive toll on him, and on his family. She wouldn't wish it on her worst enemy.

"It's going to be alright, you know?"

She links arms with him, resting her head on his shoulder. She feels him tense more, but as she pulls him into a hug, she finally feels him relax. Placing a hand on the back of his head, she's surprised to feel her shoulder growing wet. He pulls away, apologising and retreating to the downstairs bathroom, but she follows him. As he goes to shut the door, she barges through, throwing it closed behind her.

"It's okay to cry, you know?"

He sits on the toilet and pulls a long wad of paper from the roll attached to the wall.

"You don't have to be *'Mr Cool'* all the time. Your dad is dead, Ritchie. No one expects you to be okay about it. It's okay to cry. It's okay to feel sad. It's okay to be absolutely fucking devastated."

She finds her throat straining and tears in her own eyes. Reaching for the bottom of the pile of paper he has collected on the floor, he grabs her hand, rubbing it gently. Their faces are level with one another, and they continue to gaze into each other's eyes. What's going on? Are they having a moment? Does he want her to... Yes, she thinks he does. She can't do this. Not now. Not in the downstairs toilet, of all places. And not with her best friend's brother. No matter how upset he is. He isn't in the right mind frame. He isn't...

But as he leans forward and their lips meet, all her worries float away. How had they known each other for so long and not kissed? It feels like this was always supposed to happen, despite the idea not cropping into either of their heads until this moment. It just feels... Right. And before she knows it, his tongue isn't the main problem. Sliding her down on top of him, she can feel him pressed against her, and is surprised to feel herself responding. This can't be happening. But it is. Within seconds, he's pushed himself inside her and she's moaning as she begs for the porcelain to be quiet. Shudders going up and down her body. Absolute bliss as she feels his lips pressed against her neck.

Chapter Sixty-Four:

2016

———

Throwing the monster multipack of crisps onto the coffee table in frustration, Danielle flops herself back onto the sofa. Seething with anger, the girls pick up on it.

"What's wrong, D?" Abbie goes to rub her back.

"Is it Chris?" Katie asks.

"No!" she spits, glaring at the latter, "why is it whenever something goes wrong it's always straight to fucking Chris?"

"Jeez, okay, sorry," Katie blushes as she reaches for a cheese and onion flavoured packet.

Danielle bites her bottom lip to steady herself. It isn't her friends' fault. And, in their defence, it isn't like herself and Chris have been getting along any better. She doubts they're going to be together much longer. He wants to break up with her, she knows he does. But breaking up with a girl when her dad has just gone missing is the lowest of the low. He'd never hear the end of it. So, until her da eventually turns up, or they get some answers, it looks like they're still stuck with one another.

"Sorry, Kate," Danielle blows out, taking a sip of her tea, "it's just that Quigley guy."

"When's the last time he's actually showed up?" Steph shakes her head.

"Last month," Danielle purses her lips, "after the fall through of the Letterkenny sighting. When he basically more or less said that there's a reason why he's gone missing and it's better we don't know why."

"What a prick," Abbie shakes her head, throwing a Haribo into her mouth, "maybe it's best he doesn't come around now."

"Doesn't help *us,* though, does it?" Danielle sighs, trying not to be short with her friend, "I mean, Dermott's lovely and that Ferguson guy seems nice enough, but we need some answers. They've hit a brick wall and they're just too afraid to tell us the truth, I think."

They all shake their heads or nod along, before reverting their attention back to the TV. Some mindless reality show that Danielle would tear her hair out watching. Bringing out her phone instead, she Googles more online forums for missing people, wondering if anyone has put up anything in the hour since she last checked. When the show takes a well-deserved ad break, everyone watching it tensed to see what will become of the couple's relationship when it returns, Georgia coughs to get everyone's attention.

"There's something I'd like to talk to you all about."

Sensing her nerves, they all sit forward, even muting the TV.

"What's up, Georgie?" Abbie flicks a stray bit of hair out of her face.

Georgia breathes out apprehensively, her fingers shaking before she bites her lip.

"I'm pregnant."

The room stays silent. Everyone just stares at her. Thinking she's going to start laughing. Ready to throw a pillow at her in disgust. The *that's not something to joke about* lecture about to burst out of their mouths. But the way she's fidgeting with the sofa cushion, tears rolling down her eyes, they know she isn't lying. Steph, Abbie and Katie fall onto the floor, crawling forward to be level with her. Holding her hand, squeezing her knees, pulling her in for a hug. Danielle just stares at her from the corner of the room. In complete shock.

"George... Are you sure?" Steph blinks.

"I took a test. I haven't gone to the doctors yet... But I missed my period, and you know me... I'm always regular. I just thought it would eventually come, but it hasn't. So, thinking that maybe it was stress related, I went to buy a test to prove to myself that I wasn't... To prove to myself, and my body. To calm me down. But, no... Positive," she coughs through tears.

"Whose is it?" Katie shakes her head, in complete disbelief herself.

"Is it Patrick's?" Abbie gasps, causing them all to inhale sharply.

"No, no, it isn't. We've been broken up for months," Georgia rubs her snotty nose off the back of her hand, "it's... It's..."

"Jimmy's," Danielle whispers.

Everyone whips their heads towards her, confused expressions on their faces before realisation steps in.

"Oh... My... God," Abbie's hand slaps to her mouth.

"The night of my party?" Katie mutters.

As Georgia nods, they all sit up to comfort her. Like all friends should. But not Danielle. Danielle just continues to stare at her. Georgia? Pregnant? And *'on the night of Katie's party?'* Surely, she means on the night Danielle's da went missing? How can all this be happening? Life moving forward when her da still hasn't arrived home. She can't believe the selfishness of them all. Shaking her head, she stands and thunders to the door, making sure it slams behind her.

Chapter Sixty-Five:

2019

———

Jane's frosty attitude hasn't warmed since the two detectives landed back hours ago. She just continues to give Ferguson dagger glares and adds snippets of conversation when she's invited to. McNally felt uncomfortable to start with, thinking about leaving, but the more wine that flowed and the more Niamh came out of her shell, the more he wanted to stay. They've just finished their fourth bottle between them all when Ferguson struggles to stand.

"Want another glass, love?" he directs the question towards his wife, who tuts and rolls her eyes in return.

"What? Give you an excuse to piss off again to the off licence, will it? You know there's none left."

Ferguson physically places himself in front of McNally, his back to him. As if that will shield him from their harsh tones towards one another.

"Actually, Liam brought two with him tonight. They're sitting on the coffee table in the living room. Let me go and get them."

"Of course, roll on into the living room," she slurs, pointing in the wrong direction, going to rest her head in her hand, but missing, "you'd rather be anywhere else than with me, anyway."

Her head juts out from behind her husband and her attention falls on McNally as Ferguson continues to eye her with disgust.

"Are you the same, Liam? Married to your job? Is that why you're still single? I mean, no offence, but you're bound to be in your forties by now, am I wrong? And still unmarried?"

She hiccups, nodding her head towards Niamh whilst Ferguson follows up with a *right let's get you to bed.*

"Is that why you're looking to court my sister? I hope you're not going to treat her the same as he treats me. All these druggies and murderers. They get more attention than I'll ever - get the fuck off me!"

She screams the last sentence as Ferguson puts a hand under each armpit in an attempt to lift her. She stands, slapping him across the face.

"Sir, I am so sorry," Ferguson blushes, and not from the slap, as he holds two hands up to McNally, "c'mon, Jane. That's enough."

Leading her through into the hallway, although he closes the door, their argument can still be heard through the crack at the bottom of the threshold. McNally and Niamh smile towards each other as they can hear *'that's my fucking boss'* and *'you're embarrassing us both'* as they ascend the stairs. Just when a scream of *'oh, I always fucking embarrass you, that's why you're never home'* reaches them, Niamh coughs and sits forward.

"They love each other really. It's just... Well, it's been a hard few months for them."

McNally nods, thinking about asking her if she knows the reason why Ferguson stepped down from the DI job, but thinks better of it. If Ferguson wanted him to know, he's sure he'd have found out why by now. And he doesn't want to upset their family dynamic anymore. Just as the couple reach the top of the stairs and they hear the floorboards above them creak, raised voices continuing to shout at one another, Niamh stands.

"Why don't I fetch those other bottles of wine from the living room?"

McNally joins her standing.

"Er... No, I think I've overstayed my welcome, to be honest. And anyway, we have a busy day tomorrow. Evidence to find, murderer to convict. You know," he laughs.

"That's a shame," Niamh follows him into the hall, watching him grab his coat from the rack on the wall, "there's a lovely wee pub just down the street. I know it well. After all, it's barely gone midnight on a Saturday night."

She's openly flirting with him again, liquid confidence. McNally smiles and holds out his arm for her to link onto.

"Sounds good."

Deciding against informing Ferguson and Jane where they're going, Niamh promises to text her sister in a while as they close the door, and the heated argument, behind them.

****

I see his face. Twisted in anger. The hammer falls to the ground. The blood splattering on the grass. Him falling, still looking at me. Glaring at me. Before I hear the crash at my feet. I fetch the shovel. The shallow grave. As close to the garage as I could get. I smell the earth. The moist air, telling me a storm is coming. Wanting to get it done whilst it's dry. More muck and more blood would make it harder. More difficult to hide evidence. Let the rain come and wash away everything, but not until I'm finished.

When I am, I pat the ground before retrieving the hammer. The shovel under one arm. It feels like I walk for miles. When I can't see any sign of civilisation on either side, I dig into the grass. Lifting the dirt up again. Bringing back memories of him lying beside me. When I'm satisfied with my hole, I wipe the hammer with my t-shirt. Evidence. DNA. Fingerprints. Dropping the hammer into the ground, I splutter as I start to cover it in earth once more. My vision clouded. I need to hide everything I can.

My second burial complete, I walk some more. Further away from both sites. Finally cracking, miles later, I turn and thrust the shovel into the air with a grunt. Hearing it clatter away from me in the darkness, I turn and retreat the way I came. I'm exhausted, adrenaline depleting. It takes me twice as long to get back. But when I approach the scene, I see blues and twos. Sneaking around the land rovers, I gasp. Two bulky officers with their arms crossed at the back door. Waiting for me.

I wake with a start. Heart hammering in my chest. My sheets cling to my sweaty body. Gasping for air, I whip them off me and fall over to the window, opening it the full way and look out onto the street. The busy city noises greet me. Soothe me. The honk of a car horn. The squeal of a cat, followed by a few barks. I start to relax as I rest on the windowsill, my head against the cold surface. The nightmares are getting worse. More realistic. Always getting caught. It's like I'm being hunted.

I know the case has run dry, there's no way they could link his disappearance to me... But a niggling feeling in my head just keeps me up at night, and when I do drift off, I wake screaming. I need to do something. Get help. Speak to someone. Obviously, I can't indulge everything, but I can start with little things. Describe the nightmares. Ask someone what they mean. I know what they mean, of course. A confession of guilt. But why all of a sudden, again? I wouldn't say they disappeared, but they became less frequent... Especially in the months after. But it's been years.

So why now? Is it an omen, telling me I'm going to be found out? Warning me. I need to go back. I need to move him. Before it's too late.

Chapter Sixty-Six:

Car doors slamming jolts him from his half sleep. Sitting up in bed, Victor strains his ears for any sound of movement from outside, but all he can hear is his heart thumping in his chest. Sighing, he tries to settle himself back into his damp sheets. Despite the two police officers parked up at the front door, he just can't seem to relax. Staring at the ceiling above him, he thinks back on the last few hours.

Getting lead out of the station into an unmarked police car and told to lie down in the back seat, a blanket covering him. Taken to this safe house, he doesn't even know where he is. Is he still in Derry? He doubts he's very far out of it, he hadn't been in the car that long. Not that it matters. He doubts he'll be able to show his face around Derry for a long time. Maybe even ever. He'd heard of people that had betrayed Taylor before. And it never ended well for them.

He only has himself to blame. Bringing Taylor's name into an open murder investigation. How could he have been so stupid? He's just glad he hasn't got any family that the organisation can threaten, or to put through this as well. The sad thing is, the closest thing he had to a family were the guys at the Crown, who are now probably plotting their revenge against him. That ship has well and truly sunk.

Deciding the car doors were probably officers changing shifts, he rolls over, facing the window. Willing sleep to overpower him. Moments later, he hears the creak of a floorboard. His ears perk up, and he struggles to keep his eyes closed. Was that another one? He's being too hypersensitive. It's his imagination. But is it? They sound too... Rhythmic. And they're getting louder. Almost as if they're sneaking down the hall towards him. A gurgle of a pipe behind the wall makes him jump and almost topple out of bed. He nearly laughs aloud, but stops himself. As he moved, the creaks stopped.

Refocusing his attention on them again, they resume. He can't be imagining this. Is it an officer making their way down? Making sure he hasn't tried to escape? No, they wouldn't be so stealthy. Surely, they'd just announce themselves? Whoever this is doesn't want to be heard. It has to be someone here to kill him. Or shut him up. He's sure of it. He's a

wanted man in his former community... They'll be
after him. How they've found his hiding space or
bypassed the police, he's not so sure. Either way, he
needs to get out of here.

Stepping out of bed as quietly as he can, he
pulls on his shoes and tiptoes over to the window.
Looking out through his curtains, all he sees are
fields. Straining his neck around to see further along
the garden, he sees a bunch of trees collected
together. He'll go there, he'll be able to survey the
scene undetected. Making sure the coast is clear, he
struggles to open the window to his left without
making a sound. It's an old house, so the screech of
the window pierces the night. Waiting a few more
seconds, expecting an officer to round the corner and
order him back into his bed, he's surprised when
nothing happens. Lifting his foot, he drapes one leg
out of the window, content when he feels his shoe
pad onto the concrete beneath him.

Just as he's pulled his body through, and is
about to lift the second leg through the window, his
door bursts open and he's met with the wails of
gunfire. Falling through onto the ground, he's
momentarily stunned as he looks up at the stars.
Flashes of light illuminate the dark garden as bullets
continue to fly about the room he was in seconds
before. Finally coming to his senses, he stands,
doubles over and makes a run for the back of the

house towards the surrounding trees, away from the window.

Jolting through the vegetation, Victor doesn't stop. Whoever is behind him is looking him dead. This wasn't a kidnap, or a lesson to be learned. This was pure murder. He can still hear the gunfire ringing in his ears, and isn't sure whether it's his flashbacks or the echoes from the room he left behind. He isn't sticking around to find out. The ground starts to slope, and before he knows it, he's tripped over himself. Struggling to grab hold of something or to regain his balance, he continues to fall, beating every bit of his body off something or another, before he hits the water with a splash.

Lying there, face up, gazing at the night's sky. Just like he did moments before, only this time... It's peaceful. Every bone in his body is sore, but he's safe. He feels the water pushing against him, but it's shallow. He lies and catches his breath, although it hurts his lungs, as he continues to look upwards. Thinking about everything he's done and whether, after all that's said and done, he deserves this.

Bradd Chambers

Chapter Sixty-Seven:

Ferguson looks as furry as McNally feels. He nods over towards his superior as he joins everyone at the huge table. Murmurs are buzzing around the incident room before O'Connor shuffles in with a steaming cup of coffee, taking his seat as McNally stands to address the room.

"Now, I'm sure you're all aware of why we're here this early on a Sunday morning. In the early hours of this morning, shortly before 3am, to be precise, two figures somehow pulled up outside the safe house where Victor Sargent was resting. We can presume these to be members of the Jacks, given their track record. They approached the police vehicle, before retreating when confronted. However, this is suspected to have been a distraction, as another member or members managed to sneak in the back door whilst the officers were busy. The officers had no idea until, moments later, they heard gunfire. They rushed into the house, but whoever had been inside had fled out of the back door once more. They were greeted with an empty room; the bed tore apart with bullets.

"Luckily, Sargent had heard the intruder approaching in the hall and was able to escape out of the window before they had reached his bedroom. Sargent fled through the woods on foot before falling into the River Faughan. From there, he travelled upstream, injured, until he pulled himself out at the bottom of a lady's garden on the Ardground Road. Almost a mile and a half from the safe house. He hammered on the door and got Mrs Hamilton out of her bed before she called the police.

"After receiving some treatment in hospital, he has been moved to another safe house at the bottom of the Glenshane Mountain. Hopefully that is further enough away to not be discovered, although we still have no idea how he was found in the first place. And we also have no clue who the people were in the original safe house. The two the officers saw coming were wearing balaclavas, and disappeared as quickly as they arrived. Officers will be inquiring at the Crown later today, but I think we can all agree that everyone will be keeping tight lipped. Especially considering the attempt on the life of the last person to betray the organisation, as well as David Wayne yesterday.

"Investigations are also underway into what was happening at the Bull's Horn last night, although the same can be said for that... Seemingly fruitless. As for the Parker case, Lee McKay, Stuart Riddles and Johnny Spratt, the other three guys who took part in the abduction of the politician, have been questioned. They've been giving *'no comments,'* which I'm sure we aren't surprised about. This is proving hard to pin Taylor down, with very little evidence. We've got him in custody for another 10 hours. We need to apply for an extension, but for that we need facts. And that's what I need from you all today. Any questions?"

The eyes in the room continue to look at him before his phone starts going off. Nodding that they're finished here, they start to collect their things as McNally pulls out his phone. A look of confusion on his face as he sees who it is calling him.

Chapter Sixty-Eight:

After the coffin being in there for over 12 hours, Ritchie finally brings himself to step into the living room. He eyes it hesitantly, before taking a seat beside his family on the sofa. They all continue to stare at it. Each engrossed in their own thoughts. Their own memories. They turn down the offer of tea as Granny slides in in her nightie. The thought of another cup sickening them. The front door opens as Granny shuffles into the kitchen, Dermott calling out that it's *'only me.'* He pops his head around the living room door and offers them a sombre smile, before holding up two trays of tinfoil goodies.

"Treats from the missus, who sends her best wishes. There's lasagne and a tart. I'll throw the lasagne in the freezer if you want?"

Nuala smiles and nods, still not taking her eyes off the coffin. It's a weird form of grief they're going through. It was a bit of a shock, but was also expected. They'd have been stupid to think he would just turn up out of the blue one day, still in his suit, having not aged a day. Smiling and asking them what they want from the chippy that evening. At least now the *'what ifs'* and *'buts'* are gone. They'll get closure. They can finally move on, as much as they don't actually want to. Now, they know, or hope, he didn't want to leave them. There wasn't another woman, another family. They can remember him as he was.

"Thank your friends again for me, Danielle," Nuala finally stands, brushing her hair out of her face, "it was incredibly kind of them. There's still some things left over, but I'll run to the shops for tea cakes and biscuits."

Danielle nods, creating a group chat on Facebook Messenger with everyone that was there, before she realises that she still has Chris blocked. Hovering her finger over the *'unblock'* button, she bites her lip as she clicks it. Adding him into the chat, she writes a short paragraph, thanking them all for everything and stating she owes them all a drink next time they're out. She smiles as some 'heart' her comment, others send the thumbs up emoji or type *'no bother.'*

Just as she goes to put her phone away, she sees a new private message from Chris.

'Hello stranger.'

She can't contain her smile.

'Hiya.'

'Nice of you to unblock me,' with the tongue out emoji.

She snorts, making Ritchie glare over towards her confusedly.

'Don't flatter yourself. You're out on bail. Can easily just block you again with a click of a button,' crying with laughter face emoji.

'Please don't :(. It's nice seeing your face on my timeline again.'

She blinks. What to say back to that? She decides a simple *'you too x'* will suffice, but sees he's typing again. The three dots disappear, then reappear again. This repeats a few times, before the three dots blink at her for what feels like ages. Is he writing an essay? She starts to get nervous. Just as she's about to type *'what's wrong?'* he finally sends it.

'Want to go a drive?'

She stares at the message, her lips pulled to the side. This could mean anything...

'When and where?'

The reply is instant.

'Can collect you in an hour.'

She glances at her watch.

'And you know where...'

She narrows her eyes, before nodding as if he can see her.

'Sounds good. See you then x.'

Chapter Sixty-Nine:

Pulling into a space and switching the car off, McNally leans back in his seat and observes the area around him. Despite it just turning midday, the KFC behind him is already blustering with people in and out for their lunch. The 212 bus from Derry to Belfast had just collected a group of people, sunglasses on, ready for a day of shopping in the capital. Still no sign of Quigley though.

He thinks back on their conversation. He had stepped through into his office for privacy and cleared his throat before he answered the phone.

"DCI Quigley?"

Silence had greeted him down the line.

"Hello?" McNally repeated.

"DI McNally?" the timid voice asked.

"Speaking..."

Quigley sighed, before McNally could hear scuttling on the line, as if the phone was getting moved from one ear to the other.

"I've just seen the news... About Taylor."

"Yes, sir..."

"What has happened?"

And so, McNally had indulged the former DI on what had happened over the past few days since they last spoke. He had listened attentively, not asking questions or interrupting. When he'd finished, Quigley had continued to sit in silence for several more seconds, ingesting everything that was said. When McNally was just about to speak once more, Quigley had spat back at him.

"What are your plans for today?"

McNally had narrowed his eyes. Did he think because it was a Sunday that he was going to be sitting in church? Praying that this investigation would solve itself? Or hop off to the beach and have an ice cream? And why was he speaking to him like that? He had nothing to do with this case. Hadn't had in over three years.

"Investigations are still underway; we need to find some evidence to keep him behind bars. At the moment, nothing has turned up out of the ordinary at his house."

"Meet me at the Castledawson Park and Ride at noon."

McNally had opened his mouth to speak, but was cut off. He continued to stare at the phone. What was going on? The impulse to find out had been too great, and had made him come today. Ferguson had instructed that he'd join him, but McNally had ordered for him to stay in the station and take care of things. Ferguson had given him a sombre look, perhaps embarrassed by his wife's actions the previous night, feeling like he was getting punished for them, but that wasn't the case. McNally didn't want his presence to deter Quigley from saying what he wanted to say. The two had never met one another, and perhaps speaking, or pleading guilty, to a stranger would be easier for Quigley. Bringing in his old DS could throw a spanner in the works. No, better off that he arrives alone.

And now, here is where he sits. The Castledawson Park and Ride, just off the Castledawson Roundabout, on the outskirts of Magherafelt. As close as possible to halfway between Belfast and Derry, give or take a few miles. He watches a black Mercedes park up behind him, but strains to see the face of the driver, having the uneasy feeling that he's being watched. The car stays like that for several moments before it turns and start slowly reversing into a car parking space to McNally's right. When the driver doors are level with one another, he watches as the driver's window slides down.

Chapter Seventy:

They're just leaving Drumahoe as Chris steals a glance at Danielle. Her hair blowing in the wind from the open passenger-side window. Her eyes, staring right in front, barely visible through her sunglasses. Light make-up on her face. Her singing along to the Becky Hill single he deliberately added to the playlist, knowing she was always a fan of hers.

She had insisted on walking up to his new house since it was only up the road. She was greeted by his mum like the past few years had never happened. Instantly enveloped in a hug and a mug of tea offered. Asking her to catch them up on everything they'd missed, before being dragged on a tour, despite Chris urging for them to leave.

He needs to tell her. If they're going to get back together, or whatever it is they're doing, he doesn't want it to be under false pretences. And he needs to do it now, while he has her alone and while he has the courage. That's why he had messaged her and asked to meet.

She stops singing and turns her head towards him. He gives her a grin, but realises she looks unhappy. He goes to speak, to ask what's wrong, before he realises. They're driving past her old demolished house. Now only rubble and upturned soil. No sign of her dad or the police investigation currently underway. How could he have been so stupid? He should've gone the long way round.

"I... I'm so sorry."

He feels like slapping himself in the face. He had wanted to bring her to Ness Woods. A country park on the outskirts of the Waterside of the city.

"It's okay, honestly. It's obviously still just a little bit of a shock. But I have to get used to it, it's on the main road in and out of Derry, for God's sake."

He smiles over towards her once again sympathetically. They travel the rest of the five-minute journey in comfortable silence, his playlist blasting out another nostalgic track before they clamber out and start down the hill and through the trees towards the river. They'd come here a few times during their initial dating phase. Against Ritchie's wishes, of course, so they'd had to do it in secret. Luckily, it had been the end of summer, and although they were going back to school in September, the weather was still bright and relatively dry.

They got to know one another beneath the canopy of the trees. As they stumble down the steep incline now, it's as if they've stepped back in time. Listening to the flow of the river ahead of them. Dodging under low hanging branches as they thunder down, narrowly missing scraping their faces. Laughing adolescently. They'd never got a chance to come back since they'd gotten into a relationship. What with exams and other school stresses, not to mention the bad weather, so it seems like the perfect place to start again. If they're going to start again, that is. Chris just hopes what he's about to indulge won't ruin the memory of them, or this place, forever.

They reach the wooden bridge overlooking the waterfall and come to a rest. Danielle stares at its beauty, whilst Chris looks at hers as she spiels off into a story about her flatmates. It's when he doesn't pass judgement that she looks at him and smiles.

"What?"

"Nothin'..."

"Tell me!"

"I... I'm just happy ye agreed to come. I-"

"To be honest, I'm glad you texted me. I'm just so happy to get out of the house. I was starting to get claustrophobic; you know... How I got at the start? At least now, it's a new house. And since I've moved to Newcastle, it's like a new start. A new city. New friends. It's just all... It all works. I feel like a completely different person... Especially after what happened with... After finding out everything that happened.

"It makes me think that... Well, back then... I was so overdramatic. Such little things I'd blow completely out of proportion. Make mountains out of molehills. And for what? A fight? Insecurities? Wanting you... Or, you know... Others, to tell me everything was going to be okay? It was stupid. It was juvenile. I wish those were my biggest problems again, fuck sake."

Her voice croaks at the last statement, and he wraps an arm around her waist, expecting her to pull away, but she doesn't. Instead, she leans into him, brushing her hair out of her face.

"I want to continue my life like this... Start again. No worries, no cares... Because, at the end of the day, something you're stressing about seems so mediocre in comparison, and will I even remember what I was worrying about in another three years? You know what I mean?"

Chris nods as she leans her head back into his chest. He smells her shampoo and closes his eyes. Hearing the waterfall. Wishing that they could leave here and still feel like they're back in time. Take her back to her old house with her pissed off father and brother. Eventually win them both over. Make an alternative reality. But now...

As she turns and wraps both arms around his neck, he feels his t-shirt dampen with her silent tears. And that's when he can't bring himself to tell her. He can't take away this new lease of life. This new courageous Danielle. He shakes his head at his own foolishness, which Danielle perceives to be towards her. She apologises, looking at her feet in embarrassment and goes to step away, but Chris says *'no.'* When she looks back up, he has already moved in for a kiss.

Chapter Seventy-One:

DCI Quigley is nothing like McNally expected. Well, if he's honest, he didn't know what to expect. But not this. His silver hair is almost white, and cut into a short style, old before his years. His freshly shaved face shows deep lines of wrinkles. His hooked nose gives him a Disney villain look. He smiles timidly at him from the safety of his car.

"DI McNally?"

"Yes, sir."

"Stop with the *'sir,'* we don't even work together."

"Er... Okay, sorry... Quigley?"

He nods sombrely, before cutting his engine and turning down his music.

"How was the drive down?" McNally tries to get him comfortable.

"It wasn't too bad. A lot of Sunday drivers. Usually when you get to the motorway, it isn't too bad. It's after that that's the problem."

McNally nods, knowing that talking about the main road between the two biggest cities will inevitably lead back to the finding of Parker's body.

"Well, hopefully the commute will be a bit smoother soon."

The two officers lock gazes, McNally raising his brows. They both know what they're here for, so they might as well get on with it. But Quigley doesn't look like he's going to spill the beans easily.

"I understand you have some information for me?"

"What makes you think that?"

"Well, what other reason would you have for dragging me 30 miles away from Derry when we're this deep into an investigation?"

Quigley smiles.

"You don't have to be a detective to figure that out, eh?"

McNally joins him in a light chuckle.

"You're right, McNally. I'm just struggling to find the way to put it into words. Even with the long drive, and the hours before where I argued with myself back and forth, I still don't know how to put it."

He sighs again, reaching across for a bottle of water.

"Well... How about we start at wherever you think is necessary?"

Quigley swallows and nods, before recapping the bottle and throwing it across to his passenger seat. He wipes his mouth with the back of his hand and resumes his attention to his front windscreen. Seconds later, he begins.

"You have to believe that I was just as eager to find out what happened Aaron Parker as you currently are. I'd done everything that was needed. There were no reviews against how I handled the case. And I know as well as you do that people can just... Disappear. Very rare in babies and young children, rarer still in teenagers... But full-grown adults? I mean... They have their own life. If they decide someday that they don't want to answer their phone, well what's stopping them? Guilt? Pride? Love? A mixture of the three?"

McNally shrugs and nods his head. It's true. Plenty of misper cases end with a happy ending. Well, if that's what you could call it. An aggravated wife assaulted that her husband up and left in the middle of the night, simply not bothered for the argument on why he wouldn't stay. A young girl fed up with her friends and life, making a new image for herself. Not wanting to drag her old friends along to remind her of previous times. It's not uncommon.

"I was close to a conviction with Taylor, you know? I was following a strong lead from a hint in the Jacks. A rumour had gone around the Crown that he'd taken him. However, because of who my source was, I couldn't tell anyone else. You know what happens touts. I heard that he'd taken him to the farmhouse, probably as far as you have come in your inquiry so far, but then...

"I was questioning him, and he told me I was getting into dangerous territory. I told him not to threaten a police officer. He claimed his innocence, but said that if I continued to suspect him that I'd find myself in serious hot water. I laughed it off. Started a new line of questioning before he simply said my wife's name. I asked him to repeat himself, he told me my wife's name again, and her place of work. I asked him what he was playing at, before he read to me my kid's names, their ages and their school. And he knew that the missus was pregnant again. It wasn't common knowledge; only close family knew. So, naturally, I started to get a bit worried.

"I told him I wasn't finished with him and left. Enraged that he could threaten my family. I rang my wife, but her and the kids were in the house grand. I told her to lock the doors. Made up some bullshit excuse about a lot of robberies in our area that week. I arrived home and saw a mysterious car parked in front of my house, on the other side of the road. Blackened windows and a number plate that didn't exist, believe me, I got everything checked. When I stepped out of my car, it sped off in the opposite direction. So... And I'm not proud of this... I didn't inform anyone. I was so scared for my family's sake. I was hoping someone would come forward or... Something. An easy way to get out of the situation. Someone else arrest him and charge him. I don't know..."

He places his hand on his neck and swivels it around. McNally can hear the cracks from way over here.

"I just felt like I was stuck between a rock and a hard place. And then, shortly after that, I left. I had to," he pleads his case as McNally shakes his head in disgust. "The cars still came. Parked outside until all hours of the morning. Every time I approached them, they sped off, just to return half an hour or so later. Followed me and my kids to school. I was petrified. I wouldn't let the girls go to their friends or even play outside on the street. They all knew something was up, so eventually I had to tell my wife, after many sleepless nights. The next day, I handed in my notice at work. A rumour circulated that I was promoted to DCI in Belfast, but I never confirmed or denied it. The next night, we went out and chased the car away, and then, when it was safely out of the way, we did a moonlight flit of some sort."

McNally has no idea how to take this information. A detective inspector acting like this?

"I know what you must think of me, and I can only apologise. I did what was best to protect my family. That was my main priority. I've been living off my police pension and my wife has been working full time in an office. I've basically become a house husband... Of course, this isn't what I wanted. But if it keeps my family alive, I'll do it. I know I was cocky, going after Taylor myself, but I wouldn't change it. Because if I went and told someone else and got it on file... Well, it would've been a lot harder to cover up."

Quigley looks like a massive load has been lifted off his shoulders. He almost deflates onto the chair, rubbing his brow with a shaking hand.

"Thank you for your honesty, Quigley... But, I must ask, what do you think will happen now?"

Quigley shrugs.

"I don't care, to be honest. These past few days I've had some time to think. About myself, my family... How I protected them, to risk the Parker's family's happiness and trust. They've been miserable for years, and now... They deserve to know the truth. They deserve to move on. If I'm going to be

sentenced for perverting the course of justice, then
so be it. I'll hold my wrists out for them to slap the
cuffs on me. That's just the way it has to be, and I'll
apologise for my actions... But I will not apologise for
protecting my family."

"And what about your family now?"

Quigley looks at him with pursed lips.

"What do you think will become of your
family now?" he repeats, "do you think they'll be
disappointed in you?"

He shrugs again.

"As long as they're alive... Healthy... Safe, then
that's all I can ask for."

They sit in silence for several seconds before
McNally asks him the dreaded question.

"Do you think he did it?"

"Taylor?"

McNally nods.

"I don't know..." Quigley winces as he looks
out of the window reminiscently, "but I wouldn't put
it past him."

Chapter Seventy-Two:

Waking with his tongue stuck to the roof of his mouth, Smyth yearns for the water by his bedside table, but doesn't have the energy to actually reach out and grab it. He can't even bring himself to open his eyes, the thundering headache weighing down on them. He should have stayed professional. Stayed alert. Tried to slip water in between rounds. Even have some soft drinks and pass them off as alcoholic. But the way the Bull's Horn was celebrating last night, he knows he would've found it hard to hide. Especially with Macka's judging gaze, scrutinising everyone in the room.

He couldn't find out what had happened that had left the pub to open its doors so late on a Saturday night, and by none other than Darrell Boyle himself. Of course, there were whispers, but they were shut down by a single glare from someone high up in the organisation. Instead, they all cheered and clinked their glasses together. Celebrating the fact that Billy Taylor, their enemy and biggest competition, was behind bars. They sang rebel songs and talked about what this meant for Derry, and Northern Irish politics. How their United Ireland dream was looking brighter and right within their grasp.

He groans again as he remembers the fire whiskey shots. His round. He needs to remember he isn't a spring chicken any longer. At the tender age of 44, it isn't easy to just hop out of bed in the afternoon and go about your day after a feed of drink the night before. But despite himself, he was genuinely enjoying the craic with them all. Some were good critters, with some bad views. They did have some valid points; they all just hid them amongst fearmongering and sectarian slurs. He believes if some of them broke away and created their own party, they wouldn't have trouble gathering support. He hates to think what would happen them if they did, though.

Managing to finally collapse out of bed, he drains the pint glass of water as he pads towards the sink, before refilling it once more. He gazes about at the kitchen in the house the police had given him for the entirety of his undercover investigation. Not bad, considering the location in the west of the city. He's sure the fresh lick of paint, luxurious decor and expensive furnishing will not up the price though, given the area, when he moves on and the police sell it. If anything, they probably lost money getting this ready for him.

Just as he pops some bread into the toaster, all he can stomach at the moment, he hears the front doorbell go. Who the hell could that be? He isn't even sure anyone knows where he lives. It wouldn't be the police, would it? They wouldn't risk the investigation, and his life, to land at his front door? Deciding to ignore it as he refills his glass, brushing it off as some campaigners or Jehovah's Witnesses, he squints against the hammering of a fist on the glass. Not today. Not when his head is this painful. Trudging through into the bedroom, he pulls on a pair of tracksuit bottoms, reaching for a t-shirt before thinking better of it. Around these parts, if someone lands at your door unexpectedly, you just greet them with whatever you're wearing. He has to act the hard lad. Topless is intimidating, even tattooless.

Looking in the mirror, he squares his shoulders back and juts out his chin, before marching down the hall towards the front door, where he can see the outline of someone standing through the distorted frosted glass.

Chapter Seventy-Three:

2016

_____

The silence is bitterly cold. Perhaps even colder than the wind roaring against the windows of his car. The heat is turned right up, but the old hunk of junk can barely splutter anything powerful enough to heat you. You'd be better just to blow in your hands to keep yourself warm. They stare at the vista of the city spread out in front of them where they're parked in the Top of the Hill Park. Usually teens can be seen coming here for dogging or to smoke a few joints. But they're doing nothing of the sort.

 The twinkle of the Christmas lights should give Danielle butterflies and anticipation of happy times. It's only days away, with wrapped and unopened gifts clogging up the backseat. But how can she be happy? It's her first Christmas without him. Six months he's been missing now. Who's going to cut the turkey? Hell, who's going to actually cook the turkey? They've soldiered on with Ma's blackened oven food for now, but they need a turkey on Christmas Day. They haven't discussed it as a family, perhaps they're just going to treat it as any other day? After all, Ma hasn't been dropping the oh-not-so-subtle hints on what she can get them from Santa. They all know what they really want. And Danielle knows what Chris wants.

"Why did you bother getting presents?" she laughs, folding her arms around her front, the seatbelt digging into her, "you know we aren't going to make it that far."

"Why do ye always say that? If ye think we have such an expiration date, then what's the point in us goin' forward? Surely, we're just wastin' each other's time."

"If that's how you feel," she turns her head away.

"That isn't how I feel at all," he reaches for her arm, but she pulls away from him, pressing herself against his passenger-side door, "but you've been givin' me nothin', D. I can't begin to understand how hard this has been for ye, but ye can't shut me out. Constantly tellin' me that I want to break up with ye. Puttin' words in my mouth. It isn't fair, Danni... What's really goin' on? Is it *ye* that doesn't want to be with me? You're just projectin' it onto me. Not wantin' to be the bad guy?"

"How dare you accuse me of something like that?" Danielle spits, "my father is dead and I haven't so much as-"

"Ye don't know that."

"Oh, grow up, Chris. Crunch on those eggshells you're pottering around. He's fucking dead, and he isn't coming back."

Silence falls once more.

"This isn't about your da," Chris picks his words carefully, "we've had problems before he... Went missin'."

"Then just fucking break up with me then."

Chris looks at her longingly, her hair tussled and spread across her wet face. He goes to push it behind her ear, and she just observes him, shaking slightly.

"Is that what ye really want?"

"Well, clearly it's what yo-"

"Danielle!"

She jolts at his aggressiveness.

"Is it?"

She bites the bottom of her lip before nodding sullenly. He lets out a deep sigh before reaching for the gear stick to put the car in reverse.

"No, wait."

She untangles herself from her coat and grabs hold of his hand. Ice cold. They look at each other for several seconds before she smiles at him with as much warmth as she can muster.

"Please... Can we just... Stay here a bit longer?"

Chris stares at her, before nodding and leaning back in his seat, their hands still resting on the gear stick. They both resume their attention to the windscreen, the lights winking and dancing across the River Foyle.

Chapter Seventy-Four:

2019

———

Slamming the car door shut, McNally looks up at his parents' bungalow in the Glen Crescent cul-de-sac of Portrush. So much has changed since he walked through that front door with his suitcase, ready for his new life in England the September he moved over for uni. Yet, the house looks the same, the street looks the same and the town basically looks the same.

The seaside town is known for its popularity during its summer months, Easter and renowned events like the North West 200, but lies dormant in other months. Perfect for pensioners like his parents who only want a bit of peace and quiet. Luckily, even with the excitement going on in the other months, they're far enough from the town centre and beaches to avoid attraction.

Pottering through into the back garden, intent on surprising them, he sneaks forward as he sees the back door has been left open. The house is so small it can get very hot in the summer months. Scraping plates and muttering can be heard petering through it, so he gets on his haunches and slides over. As he stands, he looks in the kitchen window and pulls a funny face to a whoop of cheers.

"Liam! Ya boy ye, what are you doing here?"

McNally steps through into the kitchen to be embraced by his dad, who gives a gummy grin before leading him over to the kitchen table. The exterior of the house might look the same, but after McNally's parents retired, his mum got to work on home improvements, forcing his dad to get off his arse. They redecorated the whole interior and even knocked the wall separating the kitchen and the dining room down to make one giant space.

This is where he sits now, getting Yorkshire puddings and beef thrown onto his plate as his mother hustles and bustles with the cooker, despite his protests. He looks across the table and smiles at his sister, Lindsay. He's glad he's made the detour up here after talking with Quigley. It might've been out of the way and it might just be for a short stay, but all Quigley said about family made him realise how much he neglected his own. The drive helped him digest what he was told, but he's still confused and doesn't know how to move forward. He'd tried giving Dawson a call for some advice, but he wasn't answering his phone. Surely, a good home cooked meal should clear his head.

"How are you, son?" his dad beams at him once more, before scooping up a forkful of potatoes.

"Oh, same old, same old," he rolls his eyes, cutting into a slice of meat, "just working away."

"Are you on the Parker case?" his mum finally takes a seat beside him.

"I am, but I'm not discussing it. Sorry, you know I can't, but I also want to forget about it for a moment. Stressing me out slightly."

His mum taps him on the shoulder reassuringly as his dad nods, still diving his fork into his mash. Lindsay coughs and clinks the knife off her glass of milk for their attention.

"I was going to tell you both anyway," she spreads her gaze between her parents, before resting it on her brother in the middle, "so I might as well say now before you have to scoot off somewhere. Well... I'm pregnant!"

All knives and forks hit the plates as the momentary silence subsides with the screeching of chairs. She's pulled into a hug by both parents and McNally waits his turn, a huge grin on his face.

Lindsay and her husband, Sean, live in the neighbouring town of Coleraine, just under a ten-minute drive from their parents. Sean is also a copper within the PSNI, so McNally and Sean had clicked instantly, despite him marrying McNally's baby sister. McNally knows the couple were trying to get pregnant for some time, so the news brings tears to his eyes.

"Well done, Linds."

She smiles up at him and blinks back her own tears, before they all retake their seats and turn their attention to the next few months, food abandoned. This is what he needed. Despite living back in Northern Ireland for several weeks, he'd barely had a chance to make it up as often as he'd liked. He needs to try more, it's only up the road. It's simple things like having dinner with his family that go amiss in the loneliness of his own house. Only when McNally's phone goes half an hour later, to the groan of his family, does he realise that he still has a full plate. He excuses himself and steps outside, biting into a slab of beef he was able to pinch on the way out.

"Ferguson?"

"Sir, where are you?"

He looks around the back garden, before turning back around to see his mum pulling his sister in for another hug.

"I'll be back soon."

"Quick, sir. It's urgent. You're going to want to see this."

Chapter Seventy-Five:

"How's Dave?"

Georgia aims the question towards Chris, who stops tickling a squealing William long enough to look up at her.

"He's fine. Well... As fine as he can be, given the circumstances. I don't think he's in pain any longer. Obviously, he sends his condolences, but I don't think it's a good idea for him to come here. With everythin' that's happened... And I doubt we'll see much more of him anytime soon, to be honest. When I visited him in hospital, he wasn't too happy. Wanted rid of me. Think he's embarrassed more than anythin'. Had to lie and text me whilst I sat in the chair beside him. It was sort of heart-breakin' to be honest..."

Danielle moans sympathetically, grabbing hold of Chris's hand resting on his knee and tells him she completely understands. All the girls notice this and give each other awkward glances, pursed lips and raised brows. As William runs away, requesting for Uncle C to catch him, Georgia sighs before Chris pats her on the shoulder, stating that it's *'no bother.'* As he thunders off after a laughing William, Travis turns to join in the conversation with Ritchie and Jase on the next sofa and the girls collect their heads together, Danielle eyeing them suspiciously before leaning forward.

"So, Danni... What's the craic with you and Chris?" Georgia gives her a condescending look.

Danielle blushes, retreating her head again, observing Ritchie, but he's lost in a story, his hands flying about rapidly.

"I don't know..."

"You seem to be getting closer," Steph comments.

"We are... And we kissed earlier today."

Katie and Abbie *'whoop'* girlishly, before all of them laugh, Danielle hushing them whilst still keeping one eye on her brother.

"We're just taking things slow... I mean, I'll probably be going back to Newcastle in a few weeks... Days, maybe. Do I really want a long-distance relationship? And what if nothing has changed? I mean, it's been nice having him around again... It's familiar-"

"What about the guy you work with over at uni though?" Steph narrows her eyes.

"Who?" Abbie gasps, "you kept that quiet, you wee slag."

Danielle gasps and mocks fanning her face, another explosion of laughter coming from them, making the boys look over charily.

"It was just a couple of dates... Nothing happened," she licks her lips, "anyway, let's be quiet about this. Ritchie and I are only starting to get on good terms again, let's not ruin it."

Everyone nods as the doorbell goes, Ritchie jumping up, shouting that he'll get it. Crossing the hall, he opens the door and his mouth falls open. There, standing on their welcome mat, gleefully leering up at him, is Darrell Boyle.

"Hi, son."

He goes to move forward, but Ritchie doesn't flinch. He just continues to stand there, hatred in his eyes and his face turning into a snarl.

"What the fuck do you want?"

"Now, now. Is that any way to treat a guest?" he chuckles.

"You're no guest of ours."

"Well, I'm just here to pay my respects. I'm sure your father wouldn't approve of you acting this way..."

"You're not getting through this door."

"Honey, who's-"

Nuala steps out of the kitchen now, an apron wrapped around her front. Seeing the widow, Boyle's eyes shine brighter and his toothy smile spreads wider.

"So sorry for your loss, Mrs Parker."

Nuala marches over and slaps him across the face, her hands still wet from doing the dishes.

"Ma, no!"

Ritchie grabs his mum before she does any more damage. Boyle has already taken a few steps backwards, stunned at her reaction, raising a hand to his cheek, which is already reddening.

"Get the fuck off my property!" Nuala screeches, before reaching for the door and slamming it in his rodent-like face.

Chapter Seventy-Six:

As Ferguson continues to struggle to speed up the steep Lawrence Hill, McNally shakes his head as he rewatches the CCTV footage on his phone. How can they be so conceited? In broad daylight too. He observes the car slamming the brakes at the very peak of the Foyle Bridge, making the car following too closely behind them to swerve into the right lane to avoid a collision. Three men with their faces obstructed by masks and scarves clamber out before pulling a topless man from the boot. The man writhes around aimlessly before the men place him on top of the railings and push him off as if they were unrolling a carpet.

He rewinds the man disappearing from view several times. From way up there, the bridge's highest point, it would be like hitting cement when you reach the water. The Foyle Search and Rescue are out patrolling now regardless. The tech team had been able to highlight and sharpen the image, but McNally knew who it was right away. Smyth, or his recently revealed real name Kevin Doherty, had plummeted to his death. Of course, they'd checked the number plate, the vehicle reported stolen that morning, and had trouble tracking the car as it disappeared into the republic. Presumably to be burnt out in a field.

A stab of guilt overtakes McNally as he looks up to another set of traffic lights, Ferguson cursing beside him in the driver's seat. Was it his fault for showing up at the Bull's Horn last night? Did he make it too obvious? The last communication the PSNI heard back from Doherty was that rumours circulating why the bar had been closed were quickly stamped out, and it was now an unspoken agreement, but they ran riot in the bar celebrating the incarceration of Taylor. Maybe the presence of two detectives rather than the standard uniforms who would be deployed to a similar scene was the changing point?

Either way, they had fucked up. Big time. As if struggling to hold onto the remnants, they decided they'd pay the bar a visit. They know it's worthless, they'll be spat out of there. But they need to try something. The constant threat of violence towards the social drinkers is becoming infuriating. They're obviously bound far tighter than just *'drinking buddies.'*

"Ready, boss?"

McNally nods his head as they round the corner to the pub, but stop suddenly, confused. They're met with the similar shutters that the drinkers were greeted with yesterday, but no protests going on outside. Is it a lock in? This early? It isn't even five o'clock yet. Stepping out of the car, the door slams echo around the hungover cobbles as they trudge up to the door. Leaning their heads against the black wood, they're surprised to hear silence. What the hell is going on?

Chapter Seventy-Seven:

"That bastard. That fuckin' bastard!"

Nuala howls as she's escorted into the living room and plonked down on the sofa, the group of friends dispersing to let her through. Granny arrives in with tea loaded with sugar.

"For the shock," she winks at Danielle as she presses the mug against her daughter's lips.

Nuala drinks hungrily, barely coming up for air, the semi-boiling water not deterring her from finishing the mug. When it's empty, Granny hobbles out to make more as Nuala breaks into a new rant.

"I can't believe Darrell Boyle the fucking terrorist knows where I live now."

"Ma, he probably always knew," Danielle grabs hold of her shaking hands, "he came to annoy and upset you, don't let it affect you like this. You're letting him win."

Nuala stops her crying suddenly and gazes in front of her. They all turn to see Boyle still standing in the garden, looking in at them through the window with a big smile on his face, despite the red hand mark on his cheek.

"Fuck off!" Nuala throws Danielle off her as she stands, marching over to the window and hammering on it, much to the delight of Boyle, "just fuck off already, you fucking murdering scumbag!"

The girls manage to grab hold of Nuala and pull her away, back towards the sofa, whilst the boys fight their way to the front door, just after Chris pulls the curtains across the window, Boyle's smirk vanishing from sight.

"How could he do this to us?" Nuala looks into Danielle's face as she tries to calm her down, "him and his party... They've tormented so many families. And yet he can still show his face at your father's wake. Oh, God. What if he comes to the funeral tomorrow? I won't be able to cope... Oh, no..."

"He... He won't, Ma," Danielle splutters unconvincingly, not even able to reassure herself, "he wouldn't dare. With all those onlookers? And the police? He'd be stupid..."

"The police? The police! Dermott, where's Dermott?" she jolts upright again, hammering through into the kitchen, the girls following at a safe distance.

Danielle is the last to vacate the living room, and watches as Jimmy, Travis, Jase and Chris climb back through the front door. She leans her head into Chris's chest, who soothes her with a hand through her hair.

"He took off once he seen us comin'. Had a car outside on the road ready for him."

Danielle thanks him, before jutting her head towards the kitchen, where she hears her mother's hysterical cries once more. She moans, looking up to Michelle descending the stairs, an earphone in one ear.

"What's going on?"

She sighs once more. Where is Ritchie? She needs his help. She smiles towards that Cathal fella who has just left the kitchen, seemingly eager to find out what has happened. No doubt for his next story. Hearing hushed voices coming from the dining room, she reaches for the door handle and yanks it open. Stepping through, she gasps aloud. They might've jerked their heads towards her upon her entrance, but she seen what they were doing. Ritchie's sitting on Granny's blow up mattress, and hovering over him, hands still pressed against his cheeks, is her best friend. Steph.

Chapter Seventy-Eight:

The ringing of McNally's phone penetrates the awkward silence of the car.

"O'Connor?"

"Sir. We've just been to Boyle's... No one's home."

Cursing, McNally thanks him as he hangs up, signing off to keep him updated. Ferguson shakes his head as they continue to look at the abandoned pub.

"He must have another anniversary, so it couldn't possibly be orchestrated by him," Ferguson attempts to inject a bit of humour into the conversation.

Luckily, it works. Despite himself and the situation, McNally manages a snort and looks over at him with a shaking head.

"You're right. I wonder where in the world he is now celebrating Christ knows what. Never gets his hands dirty, that one."

They chuckle and stare out of the windscreen. They're stuck on where to go. Who could be behind this? Where is Boyle? And where are the members of Ardóimid? This isn't normal.

"So, what came of you and Niamh last night then, sir? If you don't mind me asking."

Ferguson breaks his train of thought as McNally looks over at his DS, a small smirk prominent on his face.

"Well, actually... After we left yours, we went to that bar down the street. Can't remember what it's even called now. Was a nice wee joint. All the guys flirted away with her."

Ferguson laughs audibly.

"I'd say that alright."

"But it seems she only flirted back to get served quicker."

Ferguson continues to laugh.

"I bet."

"Well, at the end of the night I got her number."

"That it? Pfft, you must be one of the lucky ones."

"Well, I might've gotten a quick kiss too."

Ferguson rolls his eyes and smiles, the crinkles by his eyes prominent.

"That's our Niamh, alright. Surprised you're not tied up in her basement now."

They share a laugh once more.

"Is she really that bad?" McNally grows concerned.

"Awk, naw," Ferguson shuffles around in his seat to get more comfortable, "it's just because we've been married for so long, and she's still single. We make her out to be this *Playboy* bunny... But she's had her fair share of boyfriends... Not to put you off."

McNally nods. He was expecting this. You can't date someone around the same age as you without the baggage of divorce, kids or a history. He realises he's been feeling a mixture of guilt for Doherty, and partly feeling responsible for Jane and Ferguson's fight. After all, if he hadn't proposed going, maybe they wouldn't have rowed. And maybe Doherty would still be alive...

"I'm sorry about last night, Ferguson."

"You're sorry, sir? ... If anything it should be-"

"You don't have to apologise. I crossed a line..."

They fall silent again. McNally turns to him with a smile.

"Are you two alright now?"

"Oh, aye," he shrugs, "she just had a bit too much to drink... It hasn't been easy for her, or for us... This job, I mean. But she knew what she signed up for. But..."

He sighs, rubbing his hands off the steering wheel, seemingly deep in thought.

"A few months back... Well, we received some bad news. Jane found out she had breast cancer. She's fine-" he holds up a hand as McNally goes to apologise, "she got the lump removed and thankfully things have progressed well without the need for chemo or anything. But it kind of... Put things into prospective, if anything... We barely made time for each other. Well, no... That isn't fair. *I* didn't make time for *her.* The stresses of the job, I mean... Well, I don't need to tell you."

He looks over to McNally with a smile on his face whilst McNally just nods along.

"Is that why you stepped down from the DI role?"

Ferguson blushes and looks at his lap before nodding, seemingly embarrassed and not knowing that McNally knew that. They're saved by the trill of McNally's phone again.

"It's Fleming," McNally informs his sergeant, before answering. "Hello?"

"Sir... We've found them."

Chapter Seventy-Nine:

Fighting her way through the hordes of people in the kitchen, Danielle manages to reach the back door and escape outside. For some fresh air. And away from people. Away from *them.*

"Danni?"

Anger sears through her again as she turns. Chris, Ritchie and Steph have followed her through into the garden, Chris making sure to close the door behind them.

"Fuck off!"

She rounds the empty conservatory, seeking solace at the bottom of the garden, away from prying eyes of the kitchen and living room. Towards the back of the house where the only window facing her is that of the downstairs toilet.

"D, please, wait."

Rounding on Ritchie, Danielle just continues to seethe with anger.

"Don't you call me *'D.'* You have no fucking right to call me that. You have fucking ignored me for the better part of four years, Ritchie. And now, what? Huh? Because our da's body is found we supposedly have to be okay again? Civil to one another? No, fuck that. Let's have it out, eh? You haven't spoken to me in all these years because I kissed your friend."

She jabs her finger towards Chris, who looks away uncomfortably.

"One kiss and you blew your lid. Well, it wasn't just one kiss, wasn't it not? We were a couple for over a year, for fuck sake. That's plenty of time to get used to it. But, no. You fuckin' disown me. Act like he's never existed. Fuck off to Wales and forget about your friends here. Your family. And now, if all that isn't enough, you go and fucking kiss my best friend the night before we bury our da? And why? Because you saw me and Chris getting closer again? For fuck sake, Ritchie, grow the fuck up. You're 22-years-old. I'm not going to have you use my best friend for some sick mind game you're playing."

"It isn't like that, Danni," Steph steps forward, her hands raised as if Danielle is brandishing an explosive weapon.

"Oh, it isn't? It's not? Well what the fuck is it like, then? Huh? 'Cause all I see is a pathetic little boy trying to get one up on his sister."

"*I* came onto *him*, Danni."

Danielle stares at Steph open mouthed. Is she seriously hearing this? And the night before her own father's funeral? This is unbelievable. This is... Just... Wrong.

"We didn't want you to find out this way. It started last night... I was comforting him and we... Well... We found each other," she extends her hand and Ritchie takes it wistfully.

"And what was that? There now?" Danielle points towards the house. "Let's have a quick shag on your granny's fucking bed whilst your own mother is out having a panic attack in the living room, is that it?"

Ritchie and Steph shake their heads as Danielle starts to pace back and forth in the corner of the garden, all three of them facing her and blocking her every turn.

"No, Danielle, that's not what happened," Ritchie goes to step forward, before seeing his sister's face and thinking better of it.

"He was upset," Steph pleads with her, "we all were. Seeing your mum like that especially. She's usually so strong. I was trying to calm him down."

"What? By sticking your tongue down his throat? I'm sure that worked nicely," Danielle growls.

Steph looks away embarrassedly.

"D, why don't we go a walk? Calm down, and we can come back and talk then?" Chris inches forward.

"Oh, fuck off with your knight in shining armour crap," Steph rolls her eyes, letting go of Ritchie's hand as it falls limply to his side. "Get out of her hole."

"Look, D... We're on the same team here," Chris presses both fists into his chest, before throwing them towards Ritchie's direction, "we just want what's best for ye. No fightin', nothin'... Let's just-"

"No, Danni. Do *not* go anywhere with him," Steph shakes her head once more, attempting to step forward, but Danielle has no more garden left to retreat, *"we* want what's best for you. He's proved himself in the past, Danni. He's proved he can't be trusted. You've-"

"Fuck off!"

"-known me since we were in primary school together, Danielle. C'mon, please... Let's talk. I'm so sorry for hurting you, it wasn't my intention."

"Then what the fuck was your intention?" Chris laughs, throwing his arms out by his side, ignoring Ritchie's glare, "oh, let's get off with my best friend's brother at their dad's fuckin' wake? What kind of person does somethin' like that?"

"Oh, fuck off. Like you're so perfect? What kind of person fucks me all week and then comes crawling back to Danielle only days later?"

Steph slaps her hand to her mouth. All eyes are on her now. Ritchie looks alarmed. Chris's eyes are huge, in shock. Danielle just continues to stare at her, a look of confusion on her face before she turns to Chris, fresh tears rolling down her cheeks.

"Is... Is..."

She shakes her head, staring at Chris as he looks at his feet.

"Is that true?"

Chapter Eighty:

When they had pulled up outside the Crown, it had taken McNally and Ferguson several seconds to react. They could only stare out of the windows shocked. The scene that greeted them wasn't a pretty one. It was like they had been transported back in time. To the height of the Troubles. Graffiti covered the pub's side wall facing the car park, thick green letters spelt out *'hun bastards,' 'Jack scum'* and *'Taylor = murderer.'* The car park also boasted some cars on fire, and the pub had one single broken window. Littered on the street were rows of police land rovers. The majority with their back doors opened as people were getting ushered inside. Other figures were fleeing in all directions from the police. Some still intent on finishing the job they had come here to do. McNally had spied one with a petrol bomb in his hands, the flames licking the bottle as he had gone to lob it into one of the pub's windows, before a uniformed officer had tackled him to the ground.

The Jacks had been collected around the pub in a line, protecting their sanctuary. Roaring obscenities and throwing glasses half full of stout towards the members of Ardóimid and the police who were ultimately trying to protect them. A few launched themselves forward. One uniformed officer was even struggling to take on a member of each community. A temporary alliance against who they believed to be the real criminals. McNally was just about to step out to give her a hand before a bulky officer weighed in, forcing himself onto the member of the Jacks, and he'd been handcuffed within seconds.

It's hard to believe that all that had happened, when now, only ten minutes later, the scene is quiet. Everyone has either dispersed, been arrested or the non-violent are slurring their way through biased statements. McNally shakes his head at the mess as he re-joins Ferguson in the car.

"This is our fault, Ferguson."

"Sir?"

"Arresting Taylor. We should have kept a closer eye on Ardóimid. That's what the meeting was about last night. An opportunity to attack the opposition when their ringleader is away. And Doherty? That was a distraction too. To deter us away from the Jacks. Have us parked outside the Bull's Horn like a couple of fools."

McNally sighs and brushes his hand down his face. Ferguson goes to retrieve his mobile as he hears his message tone go off. Alarmed, he looks up at his boss with a shaking head.

"What is it now, Ferguson?"

"Darrell Boyle has just landed at the Parker's house. Saying he wants to pay his respects to Aaron Parker."

McNally snorts as he unbuttons a top button of his shirt.

"Nothing to do with having an alibi for when this mess was happening?"

"They rejected entry, sir. He had to be escorted off the premises by the boy and his friends."

"Some balls, I'll give him that."

They hear a knock on the window, and McNally pushes down the electronic button. Haunching down, Fleming squints in at them.

"You're never going to believe this."

McNally chuckles and shrugs.

"The way the past few days have been going... Try me."

"We have a confession for Aaron Parker's murder."

Chapter Eighty-One:

"I... I wanted to tell ye."

Danielle laughs out loud, turning her head. She can't even look at him. Of course. Just her luck. Just when she's stupid enough to think that things are kind of going her way... This bombshell hits. Her best friend... Shagging her brother and her ex-boyfriend... Fantastic.

"You sick wee bastard," Ritchie shakes his head at Chris.

"Both of you go. Now!"

Danielle points towards the house, glaring between Steph and Chris.

"Danni... Please..." the former attempts to step forward once more.

"Fuck off!"

Hurt etched across her face, Steph turns and gives Ritchie a pat on the shoulder before climbing up the garden.

"You too, Chris," Danielle blubbers.

"No, I'm not goin'."

"Just fuck off now, will ya?" Ritchie narrows his eyes at him.

"Can you leave us alone, please?"

"Like fuck I am."

"Ritch... Just, please... Will ye?"

Ritchie eyes his old friend, but still holds his ground, his arms folded.

"Please, Chris," Danielle shakes her head.

"I wanted to tell ye, D. I really did. That's why I asked for ye to go that drive with me today. I wanted to tell ye then, but ye started goin' on about how happy ye were and... And I just chickened out... I couldn't do it. And there's somethin' else."

He steps forward towards her and Ritchie intercepts. He marches up to Chris and lands a hand on his chest, pushing him gently.

"Just fuck off now, mate. I think you've done enough damage for one day."

"Danielle, we have t-"

"Out, now. I mean it."

"That night when-"

"I said fucking go, man."

Danielle turns to see the two boys interlocked. It looks like they're hugging until one falls to the ground, dragging the other with him.

They scramble about the grass, grunting and badly aiming their fists towards one another.

"Tell her!"

"No!"

"Then I will."

"Naw you won't."

"Tell me what?"

They look up from their wrestling match to see Danielle leering over them.

"Now isn't the time. You've heard enough already," Ritchie climbs to his feet.

"No, now is the perfect time, Ritchie. Tell her what really happened that night."

"What night?"

"Chris, I'm warning you, fuck off. Now."

"Danielle, we know what happ-"

Ritchie turns around and clenches his fist, launching it right at Chris's nose. Blood squirts out in all directions as he falls backwards onto the grass once more.

"Ritchie, for God's sake."

Danielle goes to console Chris, before remembering recent revelations. She watches him fumble himself up, leaning his head back to stop the bleeding.

"Danielle," he says nasally, trying to look at her through the streaming blood, "it's about the night your da went missing."

"What about it?" she orders, before turning to Ritchie, who is staring at his shoes, "Ritchie? What about it?"

Ritchie sighs, looking between them both, disgust etched over his face. Finally, he nods and leans on the brick wall separating their garden. He resumes his attention to Danielle before opening his mouth to speak.

****

I'm well aware how late it is. The chance of getting home to surprise my family before they've gone to bed is long gone. But how could I resist? A £9.99 flight? It's nearly as cheap as the taxi fare I'd paid to get me to the airport. So, deciding to finish my coursework early, I booked on, knowing that the middle of the night flight was the reason for it being so cheap. But, so what? It'll be nice to see their faces. Surprise them in the morning at breakfast. Ma will be so shocked. And it is Father's Day after all. We can go for lunch or something. Play happy families.

Renting a car from outside the terminal building, I barrel into the Fiesta and head for home. Singing along to the radio, tapping my fingers off the steering wheel. Luckily, at this time of night, the journey to Derry is smooth. Very little cars meet me on either side of the motorway or road directly after it. Basically, a long stretch of road with a few roundabouts. That's what links the two biggest cities in the country. Of course, a longer motorway would be more favourable. Or better railway links. Despite my home having to be demolished for the chance of the former. I put that thought out of my head. I'm excited for a whole summer back home. Catch up with old friends. Of course, I'd have to see my sister and her boyfriend, Chris. They'll no doubt be at the same parties, like they've always been. But what kind of friend gets off with your sister? I haven't spoken to them in almost a year. Still refuse to now, the thought making my blood boil. It's sick.

When I'm a few miles from the house, I narrow my eyes at the figure staggering along the right-hand side of the road. I would normally just presume it to be a drunk, or a homeless person, but they primarily congregate in the city centre, and even at that they're few and far between. And this one is too smartly dressed. Slowing down, I roll down my window and come to a halt once I recognise who it is. What the hell could he be doing away out here at this time of night?

"Da?"

The figure stops once he hears my voice and registers the car. I open the car door so the light above my head illuminates my face.

"Ritchie?"

"What are you doing?"

He marches across the road and hops into the passenger seat, eyes in front. The smell of drink instantly hits my nostrils. Great. He isn't exactly the kindest when he's sober, but having a drink still doesn't explain how he could've ended up this far from home.

"Da? Are you okay? What happ-"

"Just fucking drive, Ritchie!"

Shaking my head, I pull back onto the road. We continue in silence for a few more moments before I can't help myself.

"Are you okay?"

"Never better."

"I don't believe you somehow."

"How will I sleep at night?"

I bite my tongue. I can't continue this fight. Not with drink in him. We've never really seen eye to eye, but nothing like this has happened before. Usually it's stupid arguments, made worse by his drinking and my teenage years. The stress of his job. My hormones taking over. I'll wait until morning, maybe he'll be a bit more cooperative then.

"And don't you dare tell your mother or sisters about this."

It's like he's read my mind.

"Da, what's going on? Why are you way out here by yourself in the pitch black?"

"It's none of your fucking business, so watch yourself."

We sit in silence again, my fingers clenching against the steering wheel.

"What the hell are you doing back, anyway? Been kicked out of university, no doubt."

"What? No, I actually came back to surprise you all. Good thing I did too, or you still wouldn't be home by the time I was supposed to arrive. We'd be filing you as a missing person."

I chuckle, trying to make a joke out of it. Make him open up.

"Why the fuck would you wish that?"

My smile drops as I look over at him.

"I don't want that, but Jesus Christ, Da, you were way out there in the sticks. Anything could've happened."

"Nothing will happen."

"You don't know that. Drunk driver. Murderer. Could've fallen down a ditch and hit your head. Why didn't you call a taxi, or phone for help?"

"Lost my phone."

"Well, that was smart," I mutter, shaking my head.

"What was that?"

"How did you lose your phone? Where even were you?"

Silence once more. I can feel my anger burning inside of me. He's always had a problem with me. My sisters are his little girls. His pride and joys. Yet, me? He's always looked at me with such disappointment. As if I was a mistake. The black sheep of the family. Problem child.

"What's your issue with me, seriously?"

He doesn't answer, just continues to look out of the window. I hammer on the brakes, making him jolt forward, almost banging his head off the windscreen.

"Fuck sake, Richard, you could've-"

"You should be wearing a seatbelt. Honestly, Da. Who's the parent and who's the child here? Now, tell me. What the fuck is your problem with me? What have I ever done to you?"

One of my earliest memories is bringing in a painting and he didn't even bother to look at it, just continued on his phone. He placed it on the countertop, and then threw it in the bin when he thought I wasn't looking. I want to get this out. Now.

"What, Da? What?"

He sighs, shaking his head in revulsion before looking away once more.

"Just take me home, Ritch... It's been a long night. I just want my bed."

"Why? What's happened? Why won't you just fucking talk to me?"

He still doesn't budge. Exhaling frustratedly, I punch the steering wheel, making it pomp the horn promptly, before taking off my seatbelt and leaning back in the chair.

"I'm not leaving here until you talk to me. What the hell is wrong, Da?"

He laughs bitterly, bringing his hand to his mouth in annoyance. We sit like that for several minutes, before he yawns and reaches for the door handle. Falling out, he slams the door and continues his journey up the road. I stare at his retreating back, shaking my head, before trudging after him. Forgetting the keys in the ignition, just wanting to get answers from my father. I follow him, the headlights behind me. Making my shadow looming after him look huge. We must be about a quarter of a mile from the house now. He races on, not looking back. Is he limping? Or is it just my eyes playing tricks on me, following him in the moonlight?

"Da? Slow down. Fucking answer me, what has happened? What's going on?"

I hurry after him. He might be closing in on his fifties, but the bull of a man still thunders on, not wavering for a second. It takes me several moments to catch up with him.

"Da? Dad! Please, talk to me. You're fucking scaring me."

It's like I don't even exist. Like he can't hear me. As we round the corner on the Glenshane Road, our driveway in sight, I reach for his arm, and he swivels away from me. I grab it with both hands, urging him to slow down. He just drags me along, my feet skirting across the pavement. I give one tug and he makes a swipe for me, making me lose balance and fall onto the grass embanking the surrounding field. He towers over me, looking ominous in the dark, and I think he's going to offer his hand, to help me up, but he just continues to stare down at me. I make out the silhouette of his balding head and his clenched fists.

Perching on my elbows, I'm determined not to succumb to his violent advances. Not to become the person I was before. Scared to even look at him. In case something I said would encourage him. For years, it was like this. Blaming cuts, bruises and even a broken hand on Gaelic injuries. When in fact, it was always him. Twisting my arm. Throwing me against a wall. Waiting until the house was empty, before unleashing his tyranny out on me. For something I said. Something I did. Or nothing in particular.

His punching bag. His rag doll. But I'm not going to stand for it any longer. I'm an adult now. I've just completed my first year at university. I haven't had to live in fear. Sleep with one eye open. I'm a man, just like him, and I want us to talk it out like a pair of them. We're old enough and ugly enough now. I want him to treat me like one. Show me as much respect as I deserve. We're going to have it out. Whether he likes it or not.

But just as I go to open my mouth, I hear the approach of a car engine, coming from Drumahoe towards us. I turn my head to see headlights, but before I know it, Da is on top of me. He wrestles me back to the ground and wraps an arm around my face. I struggle to breathe, battering him with my hands before he pins them to the ground by rolling over on top of me. All I see is darkness. I scream, but the attempts are muffled by his jacket. Continuing to struggle, I hear him breathing in my ear. Feel his body tense. What the fuck is wrong with him?

Moments later, he relaxes and climbs back on his feet. I struggle for air, turning around to see the yellow sign of a taxi company returning back towards the town. Why was he so scared of a taxi? What the hell is going on? I watch as he marches towards home, before hobbling after him. My head light from the lack of oxygen, but adrenaline buzzing through my veins. What the fuck was that? Did he try to kill me? Had to stop himself? And why now? What is his problem? Is he a psychopath? He's seriously starting to freak me out. I need to know where he was. If someone turns up missing in the morning, would I really have the balls to turn him in? You see it on the news and films and TV shows. Distraught and bereaved family members begging for someone to come forward. To let the police know if a member of your family is acting strange. Or if you have reason to believe they are guilty. Right now, all the warning signs are sounding in my brain. Sending off alarms.

As I reach the house, I see him ascending the garden. I shout after him. He turns and marches over, grabbing me and dragging me over to the garage. His hand covering my mouth, he slams me against the back of it. Hidden away from the house and the busy Glenshane Road. I can feel the pebble-dashed wall scraping my back through my t-shirt. I see his eyes, wide and frantic looking, jolting between both of my own. The small slits of moonlight breaking through from the surrounding trees. I'm genuinely scared. More scared than I've ever been. Who knows what he's capable of? Right here, right now, I'm completely at his mercy.

"You tell no one about tonight? You hear me? Go back up, get your car, bring it down and get to bed. You didn't see anyone and no one saw you. We'll be surprised to see you in the morning. As far as you know, I made it back from the charity night and went straight to bed. You'll do as you're told if you know what's good for you. Do you hear me? Not a word about this, to anyone."

"Da, what the fuck have you done?"

"Do as you're fucking told!"

He brings me away from the wall, just to smash me back onto it again seconds later. I cry out in pain, my feet stretching to meet the ground centimetres below me and my arms flying around either side of me. Trying to push myself away. Push him away. Or find something to help me. He starts going off into another rant, talking about how I don't know what's good for me, before my arm catches the side of something. Inching my head to the right, I see discarded items from the garage resting against the wall. A battered washing machine, a punctured bike and an old barbeque, with a half empty toolbox rested on it.

Seeing the hammer inside, I make a split-second decision. Just wanting him off me, scared for my safety, and my family's. I reach for it and swing it at his head. Looking to deflect him. Make him back off. Leave me alone. To finally tell me what's going on. But as I hear the sound the hammer makes when it connects with his skull, and as I fall to the ground with a thump, I look over at him lying sprawled out on the grass, and know there's no chance of him telling me anything ever again.

Chapter Eighty-Two:

She can't believe what she's hearing. She sits on the toilet with her arms around her head, as if that will stop the voices coming in from the tiny open window behind her from penetrating her skull. Stop her son's words from pouring in and over her. She had come to the downstairs toilet to finally calm herself down from her full-blown fury earlier. She'd sat, urging her beating heart to slow down, and that's when she had heard her two eldest in the garden, mere metres from her. And what her son had said has broken her heart. She knew that Aaron and Ritchie always had problems, she won't deny that. But she guesses that she just chose to ignore them. It wasn't Ritchie's fault. And it wasn't her fault. It was Aaron's jealousy. His controlling nature. She saw the way Aaron looked at Ritchie sometimes, but she never for a second thought that he would be violent towards him. Treat him any different from his girls.

They were married for two years the first time Billy Taylor entered her office. He seemed to take a shine to her, she won't deny Aaron's jealousy that, but she was only doing her job. Her stomach clenched as he requested all these leaflets and pamphlets with the Ulster Jack's slogan and logo on them. Especially when he found out her name was Nuala, that was a sure-fire giveaway that she was a catholic. But it didn't deter him from continuing to ask for everything he could think of plastered in the red, white and blue of the Union Jack. However, she stayed the professional and ordered him what he needed. And after finding out who he was, climbing the political ladder within the Jacks, she wasn't surprised to see what he had been ordering.

What did surprise her, however, was his insistency to speak with her directly every time he wanted to order more. Even calling back or returning to the office for her if he ever showed up on her days off. It was like he was obsessed, and the wedding ring she consistently tried to subtly show him at every given opportunity didn't seem to bother him. If anything, it made him more determined.

It wasn't long before Aaron became jealous. He was always like that growing up. When they started to go to night clubs and other boys would grab her ass or offer to buy her a drink. It would always end in fist fights and tears. But since they got engaged, he'd wised up considerably. Apart from a slight hiccup on their wedding day when his cousin got too drunk and kissed her on the cheek, he seemed to have settled down.

He pulled a strop when she told him, more to inform him of the politician's distasteful attitude, and stated she wasn't to see him again. She laughed, reiterating to him that she was just doing her job, but he wasn't having any of it. Things got worse, however. Taylor started showing up on their date nights, parking himself in front of Aaron, giving him a great view of his arse as he openly flirted with Nuala, who remained polite, but didn't offer anything more than one-word answers. The fights they would have after would be astronomical.

His insecurities got the better of him one night in the bar when Taylor had showed up, and he'd stormed off in a huff, leaving her to fend for herself. Taylor tried to kiss her that night, and Nuala had finally snapped. Slapping him across the face, she had informed him she was a happily married woman before leaving him ashen faced at the deserted table. Telling Aaron what had happened when she finally managed to get home, she expected him to be happy with her. To offer her sympathy. Say she did the right thing. To apologise. To finally give this charade up. But instead, she got accused of giving Taylor the wrong signals. Was she having an affair? She left the house in tears and slept at her parents' house that night, fearing for the future of her marriage. He had shown up that Sunday night, begging her forgiveness, but her father hadn't let him in, saying she had to make her own decisions.

Weeks later, when she agreed to meet with him to talk things out, he promised he would change. That she was everything to him. She gave him one last chance, saying to herself that if he showed any signs again that she would be out of there. She wasn't going to be accused of things she didn't do... But then, days later, she found out she was pregnant. A dark shadow passed over his eyes when she finally plucked up the courage to tell him, and for a second, she thought he was going to start accusing her again. He did a bad job of reassuring her that everything was alright, even cupping his hands around her stomach in a tight and uncomfortable grip for good measure. She walked on eggshells around him the entire pregnancy, expecting him to flip out at any moment and start brandishing her an adulterer, but it seemed he'd learned his lesson.

Even when Ritchie was born, and looked the absolute spit of Aaron as a child, he still didn't warm to him. He would do his fatherly duties, but wouldn't offer much outside of that. Shortly after, when Nuala became pregnant with Danielle, she noticed a difference in him. How much more excited he was, how he doted on her. And when Danielle, and ultimately Michelle, were born? Like a completely different man. She bit her tongue, wanting to keep the peace in front of the wains, but always resented him for having that chip on his shoulder when it came to Ritchie.

If she ever offered a slight concern, he stated that it was because they were girls. That's why he was openly more affectionate towards them. She couldn't argue with that, not without bringing in the whole Taylor dilemma again. An argument that had been buried 20 years ago. And when they'd see Taylor out and about every now and then, he would blank both of them. Refused to acknowledge that she had rejected him. Even when Aaron started going to the fancy political dos, he would be professional towards Aaron, but wouldn't so much as take a quick glance Nuala's way. She's sure if anyone noticed, they'd assume it was because of her religion. Because of this, and the fact that almost two decades had passed, she never felt like his initial attraction to her was a motive in the disappearance, and then death, of her husband. Who would be that petty? And it isn't like he's ever even tried to make contact with her since...

That surely should have given Aaron an eye-opening. But still, it didn't. How was it her fault that another man had flirted with her? And at that, be angry with her, not his own son. She had half a mind to go forward with a DNA test, but didn't entertain the idea. She knew she wasn't unfaithful, and wouldn't give him the satisfaction. They aren't on some midmorning reality TV show with four teeth between them. This was their life. Their family.

She thought she hid this from Ritchie. He'd never spoken to her about it. Why hadn't he? She remembers the broken hand well, wondering how he could cause that much damage during an indoor training session. But he insisted it was his own stupidity. Even laughed that he didn't have to do schoolwork now since he was right-handed. All this time, it was Aaron. God knows how many more times there were. What else was he keeping from her? From them? Bringing herself to stand, she decides to join them. Sort everything out. Ask Chris to go home and they could talk things out as a family. Tell Ritchie it isn't his fault that his father rejected him. He did nothing wrong. But just as she reaches for the door, she gasps. What did she just hear? He... He did what?

Chapter Eighty-Three:

2016

——

"Sshhh."

Danielle topples about, nearly knocking down the vase at the top of the stairs, but luckily Chris grabs her on time. Straightening her again by holding both of her shoulders, Chris leads her to her bedroom. He snaps on her light and positions her over the bed. Placing her on the mattress, he battles with her shoes. How does she wear these things? He closes one eye to see better as he fights with the buckles. When they're both off, he looks down at her snoring and shakes his head. Sliding her dress off over her head, he fishes a t-shirt from the chest of drawers and struggles her into it.

Plopping her onto the pillow, he turns her on her side before deciding he'll need a bucket. She's been sick a few times now already. Tottering down the stairs as quietly as he can, he tries manoeuvring himself around the kitchen in the dark, his phone to his ear. No taxis are answering. He was lucky he could jump in Dave's, who had ordered one well in advance. Just when he goes to open his mouth to give Danielle's address, the ringing stopping, he grunts impatiently when he realises that someone had hung up on him right away. Fuck, they're annoying. Finding a basin in the cupboard below the sink, he stands to return to Danielle's bedroom, only to see her dad making his way up towards him through the garden. He looks angry. Chris doesn't want to be hanging around to get on his wrong side.

Taking the basin back to the bedroom to position it strategically beside Danielle, he decides he'll walk home. After the fight this evening, he doesn't want to stay over as planned and the taxis are taking the piss. And he doesn't want to risk sitting downstairs with her annoyed dad. Kissing her on the head, irritated at himself for cracking up so easily, he turns off the light, pulls her door and makes his way back down the stairs. Closing the front door behind him, he wraps his jacket around him as the crisp night air cuts at his neck. That's when he hears murmurs coming from behind the garage. Who could that be? They're relatively secluded out here. Curiosity taking over, he pads around the corner.

He's met with the darkness of the shadows. Straining his eyes, he begins to see two figures. He steps forward and his mouth falls open. Danielle's da has Ritchie against the wall by the scruff of the neck, Ritchie's arms and legs flying around blindly. Her da's face is inches from Ritchie's, spitting words he still can't make out from this far away. Should he interrupt them? Cough to announce his presence? Or walk on like he'd seen nothing? Just as he's battling with himself, he sees Ritchie lift an object from beside him and swipe it towards his da's head. He gasps as they both fall to the ground. Several seconds pass before Ritchie starts breathing again, crawling forward to observe the mess he'd made.

"What the fuck have ye done?"

Chapter Eighty-Four:

2019

———

Backing away, Danielle hits the wall. Shaking her head. She can't be hearing this. This can't be real. Her brother and her boyfriend. In cahoots. All this time, they knew. When she cried herself to sleep. The whole family sick with worry. Thinking he'd left them. That he'd taken his own life. That he was somewhere alone and scared. And the whole time, they knew he was behind the garage. Dead.

"That's why you were so adamant for us not to move," realisation kicking in as she stares at Richie, who looks a lot greyer than ten minutes ago, "because you knew they would've found him?"

He nods, not even bringing himself to look her in the eye.

"And you?" she rounds on Chris, "you...
Helped?"

The two boys share a moment of alliance as
they finally look at each other.

"I didn't know what to do," Chris bites his
bottom lip to stop it trembling, "we just sort of stared
at him. Hopin' he'd move. That he'd gasp for a
breath. Neither of us wantin' to touch him. To
actually see if he'd stopped breathin'. After a while,
Ritchie checked. He was dead. We didn't know what
to do, honestly. Next thing I know, Ritchie has a
shovel in his hand. He grabs a foot and begs me to
take the other. He was so heavy; we could barely
move him. He was a big guy, like. Thoughts of takin'
him somewhere secluded abandoned, we decided to
just bury him there, beside the garage. The old
barbeque placed over his restin' place, so we'd know
where he was and to hide the recently upturned soil."

Danielle shakes her head once more,
clenching her eyes shut like that will stop the
memories flooding her brain. She remembers
packing away the garage before they moved months
ago. Seeing the old barbeque, deciding to throw it in
the skip. Asking Michelle for a hand on lifting it.
Treading on their father's corpse.

"We walked for miles through the fields with
the shovel and the hammer. We buried the hammer,
then threw the shovel away. It took us ages to get

434

home. We were drenched right through by the time we got into the kitchen... My head was up my hole, I just didn't know what to do. So, I just got into bed with ye, somehow wantin' to be close to ye. Protect ye."

The thought now turns Danielle's stomach, knowing she was lying in bed beside him when he was fresh from burying her father. Hiding all this from her. Even today when they kissed. She doesn't know him at all.

"The next mornin', I genuinely forgot what happened. I mean, I was so far gone. Seein' him lyin' dead... It was soberin'. But I must've just blocked it from my brain. But then when I got downstairs, it all came floodin' back. Seein' the detectives... That's why I boked."

"And you?" she glares towards Ritchie, awfully quiet despite the fact that he was the murderer here, "what did you do?"

"I went back to fetch the car and drove around all night. I drove around the whole country, basically. I was in Lisburn when Ma rang to tell me she had booked the flight home."

"So, that night when you *'arrived home'*" she air quotes, "you were even lying to us about that?"

She feels sick. Watching him nod, hiding his face embarrassedly. Who can lie about something like this? Turning back once more to Chris, she bites her bottom lip to stop herself blubbering, mustering all her courage.

"So... Whatever this was... This *thing* we've been doing... It was only to protect your own back? Don't come near me!" she almost squeals as he shakes his head and steps forward. "You only wanted to get back in contact with me to keep this a secret... Or to see how the investigation was going. Don't fuckin' lie to me."

"I'm not, D... Honestly, that isn't why. I mean, aye, a selfish part of me wanted to know... But it also made me realise that I'm still mad about ye... I wanted to protect ye."

She whimpers through his words, wanting them to go away. She looks over to her brother again, a look of revulsion on her face.

"How could you have been so stupid? I mean, you knew they were going to find his body?"

"I know, I know... I mean, I tried to get home on time... But, I..." he sighs again, "it was just hard. It's like something happened that night. Like a light just went off inside of my head. Everything went downhill. I went back to uni in the autumn and I just... Fell apart. Turned to drink, drugs, anything that anyone would give me. Anything to just take the pain away. I failed my second year. Not showing up for exams or handing in coursework. But I couldn't tell you all. I felt too ashamed, so I just... Kept pretending."

"That's why we couldn't go to your graduation this summer," she shakes her head, "and you said you were working."

His grave face darkens.

"I know, I took a photo in my friend's cap and gown, pretending it was a laugh, but I was going to send it to you all this winter... Pretend that I had actually graduated."

"So, what have you *really* been doing for almost three years?" Danielle blinks rapidly, realising she doesn't know her own brother either.

He shrugs.

"Bits and bobs. I could never really hold down a job. I arrived drugged-up or drunk, or just didn't show up at all. That's why I couldn't afford flights back to move the body once I knew work was starting on the house. And of course, I had to consider the rental car, petrol and a cheap Airbnb. The shitty jobs I was doing, they barely covered my rent. I got by with living on takeaways. And stealing from housemates. Be it drink, drugs or a pack of instant noodles.

"I managed to eventually get back at about two o'clock in the morning on Thursday. I was intent on moving the body then, especially after seeing all the machinery already. I knew they weren't going to be long finding him. But 12 hours later? I mean, come on. Give me a fuckin' break... Anyway, I landed from Belfast and came down to move him, but there were kids spray painting the house. Then, someone else landed and scared them off. I don't know who it was bu-"

"It was me."

The trio gasp and turn around to see Michelle standing back by the conservatory, deep in thought and staring at a plant. None of them had heard her approach them. How long had she been standing there?

"Michelle!" Danielle gasps, "what the hell are you talking about?"

"I tried to move him. I saw you two," she nods towards the boys, "that night. I was up getting a glass of water and I saw Chris walk around towards the garage. I was wondering what he was doing. I sneaked out the back door and looked around the side of the house... And I saw you two... Burying him."

Danielle shakes her head. No. This can't be happening. They all knew. They were all in on it.

"I couldn't remember where abouts specifically that you buried him, and obviously the barbeque was gone... I started making a bit of progress, but the builders arrived early. Really early. Like 5am early. So, I had to scatter before they saw me."

"I ran off because of you," Ritchie almost laughs, before realising what situation he's in, "if I had have known it was you... Maybe we could've avoided this."

"'Avoided this?'" Danielle almost screeches turning back towards her brother, before composing herself and whispering once more, *"'avoided this?'* What, so just continued to live a lie? Lie to us and to yourselves? And what the hell were you going to do with the body, eh? Just throw it in a skip with the barbeque?"

Michelle continues down the garden and slides into the place where Steph was only moments ago as the two boys share concerned glances before looking away.

"We didn't have a plan, D..." Chris shakes his head, "short of him bein' in the house after your da went missing-"

"Oh, don't give me that shit!"

"- we genuinely haven't spoken. I mean, we never had each other's numbers and there's no way for me to contact him as he has no social media. And I didn't know until there now that Michelle saw us. Did you?"

Ritchie shakes his head as he stares at his former friend. "I went to your house that night last week too. I was told you moved up the road, so I wanted to make contact with you... But obviously, being the middle of the night it isn't like I could exactly ring the doorbell."

"Wait..." Danielle physically grips her head to try and get her mind around this. Counting days on her fingers. "Thursday night, when I met you at the airport... You were here all this time?"

He nods.

"But why now?" Danielle almost laughs hysterically, "what took you all so long to try and move him? I mean, you had three years."

The boys stare at their feet and Michelle bites her lip.

"We were scared, Danni," Chris says, going to put a hand on her before she spits *'don't touch me,'* "well, I can only speak for myself... But I was scared of gettin' caught."

"But you didn't kill him?"

"I wanted to protect ye, as well as your family... And myself, selfishly. I wanted ye to just live in ignorance, because, like Ritchie, this secret has eaten me up for years. I haven't been the same since that night either."

"And do you two feel that way too?" Danielle turns to her siblings, "scared?"

They nod.

"I wanted to do it so many times that summer..." Ritchie glares into space, memories creeping back. "But I just couldn't. I had nightmares of seeing his corpse. His rotten flesh... Anytime I seen a fox or rat in the garden I just begged that they hadn't found him. I was half expecting to see his hand lying in the garden when I left the house every morning. After a while, being over there, and off my tits on what have you... It just became easier. Ignorance is bliss," he nods towards Chris, who smiles at him weakly, "I just pretended it never happened. But then, when you moved... Like I said, I couldn't find a way home, short of asking for help... And a part of me should've gone ahead and asked for it, but I didn't know how I could do it without sounding guilty... I just felt like if I did, everyone would know why. You would all be suspicious of me, especially how I've been the past few years... Wanting to be anywhere but here. I'm sure now you know why."

Danielle nods, tears still spilling down her cheeks.

"I tried everything, though," Ritchie shakes his head, "even threatening that wee reporter bastard in there now."

"You did what?"

"He was bringing the case back into the press. I just sent him a few messages about his sister. To try and put him off the scent... I don't know why I thought it would work. I was stupid... I..." his own eyes begin to fill with tears now, "oh my God. Can you imagine if someone did something like that to me? Targeting either of you two?" he motions his head towards his siblings. "I'm a monster. I killed my father, and... And I haven't been the same since. Maybe I do belong behind bars," he winces, shaking his head. "Whenever he came to talk to us and you were all going on about how amazing Da was... I just couldn't hack it... No one knew the real him."

They all continue to stand in silence for several more moments, the odd chirping of a bird the only thing breaking the barrier.

"I know now... Looking back... After hearing about how the Jacks were threatening us... It was to protect me. He didn't want me to come to any harm... That's why he had me on the ground, scared in case it was one of them, coming to hurt us... And that's why he wouldn't tell me where he was... He just wanted me to be safe."

Danielle looks over to her brother, who is crying freely now. What the hell is she going to do? She can't tear this family apart any more than it already has been...

"This family has been through enough," Danielle states, more to herself than to the others, still not able to bring herself to look at any of them, "we don't need you in prison to make matters worse..."

"So, you... You're not going to tell anyone?" Ritchie narrows his eyes at her as Chris looks up expectantly.

"No... It seems the police are getting somewhere with the Jacks... We'll see how it plays out. But!" she snarls, holding up a hand to stop him coming towards her, arms outstretched, "this in no way condones what you've done. What either of you have done," she points towards Chris, who nods.

She glares at her sister, not knowing what to say, but Michelle looks down guiltily. It seems she doesn't even have to say anything to her. The burden she's had to bear the past few years... She can't imagine it. Turning back to her brother, she tries to be somewhat sympathetic, despite her blood boiling.

"What happened between you and Da... It was awful, but there were means and ways... I won't be telling anyone; I don't want to upset Ma any further... But I think what you're doing... Staying away from this family... It's a good thing. I'd continue as normal. After the funeral, of course."

"But, D... I have nothing to go back to."

"That's not my problem. I'll be getting the first flight back to uni this week and I'll be forgetting that any of this happened."

"It's easier said than done," Chris shakes his head, crossing over to her, "we all know now. All four of us. We should stick together. Form a bubble of some-"

"No!" Danielle spits, "this is the way it has to be. We sweep it under the carpet. It's never talked about again, you hear me?"

The group stare at each other, the unspoken agreement forming between them. When the other three have nodded, Danielle gives a curt one in reply, before turning and marching towards the house. As she rounds the conservatory, she almost walks into Dermott standing at the back door, fag in hand. Her face drops and she feels her face redden. How long has he been there? How much has he heard? They never heard the back door go. How loud were they talking? What is he going to do? But she's confused to see him smiling at her, before stepping back to let her through the back door, raising the cigarette to his lips once the smoke he'd recently blown out obstructs him from view.

Chapter Eighty-Five:

"I did it."

McNally and Ferguson sit at one end of the table, staring into his face. Looking for signs of insincerity. Signs of weakness. Chinks in the chain. But everything that he said has added up.

"So, why now?" Ferguson sits forward once more, interlocking his fingers, "why have you suddenly changed your story?"

"I'm tired of running," he looks the detective in the eye, his body shaking slightly, his foot incessantly tapping on the ground, "I don't want to waste government time and money only to be banged up in a few weeks or months when it all comes back to me. I don't want to live in fear, also," Victor Sargent sighs. "Throwing Taylor to the wolves... I just want to own up to my own crime and hopefully the Jacks will leave me alone. Too little too late, probably, but as long as I can live without constantly checking over my shoulder... I'm happy with that."

"And why Parker? What significance did he have?"

Sargent shrugs.

"He disrespected me. He disrespected us all. Including Taylor... I just saw red... Waited around until Taylor kicked him out... Then I bludgeoned him in the head. That'll show him for disrespecting us... After, I buried him behind his garage, no one would look for him there... I mean, until the house was getting demolished for that new road... But he'd be worm food by then. I thought there'd be no evidence. I was cocky... Too cocky. But last night opened my eyes. It shows I have no control. Last night was a warning. Confess... Don't land us in it... It's taken all my courage, but I'm ready for the truth to come out. Hopefully the family will get a bit of peace..."

The detectives continue to stare at him, mesmerised. A part of them believes that he's only doing it to protect his own back. Maybe he's safer inside? Not constantly on the run. But he knew too much. How could he possibly know about his injuries? And that Taylor dropped him off somewhere off the Glenshane Road? They turn to one another and sigh, before reading Sargent his rights. As they ask him if he understands, he just crosses his arms on the table and buries his head in them, howling.

Ten minutes later, they're in the car crossing the Foyle Bridge, still unable to speak. Heading to the Parker's house to give them the update. After three years, Parker has been brought home. He'll be buried tomorrow and now, tonight, despite all the sectarian and political violence that occurred, they have the person who murdered him behind bars. They will be able to sleep soundly tonight.

Chapter Eighty-Six:

Tossing his keys on the coffee table in the living room, Cathal sighs, respects paid at a wake that died pretty quickly. The vast majority of guests vanishing questionably. He steps through into the kitchen to find Orla bent over the sink, her attention on the back garden.

"Alright, Orl?"

He fetches a glass from the cupboard and the milk from the fridge. Pouring himself a slither before bed, he frowns when he looks over to Orla once more as he raises the glass to his lips. What's going on? She's acting strange. And is she... Yes, she is. She's shaking.

"Orl? Orla?"

He reaches over to touch her back reassuringly, but she shrinks away from him, finally turning her body to face him. Her eyes are frenzied,

and he can smell vodka from her short bursts of
breath.

"Orla... What's going on? Are you okay?"

His heart's in his throat. Has something
happened? Did someone come after her? Follow her
home? He reaches out and she steps back again,
banging into the washing machine.

"Don't touch me!" she spits.

He has her cornered, and he can see she
knows that. Her attention dodges from left to right,
trying to find an escape route, before landing back
on him, pleading. Stepping back and away from her,
he holds both hands up, palms facing forward in a
form of surrender.

"Orla, are you okay? What's happened?"

"Is... Is it... Is it true?"

"Is what true? Orla, you're starting to scare
me."

"*Me?* Scare *you?* You must be joking," she
gives a manic laugh, "you tell me the truth right now,
Cathal, or I swear to fuck."

"What? The truth about what, Orla? I have no
idea what you're talking about."

"Oh, you fucking do," she flails an arm behind
her.

His face drops. Was it just for effect, or did
she motion towards the shed?

"Just... Calm down, and tell me, Orla... What's bothering you?"

He directs a hand towards the chair beside her, which she perks onto. He takes the one farthest away.

"Where were you tonight?"

"Anna's," she mutters, "we were having a few drinks with girls from work, then some of her other friends landed. Whenever I got introduced to one of them... I can't even remember her name now... All I know is she went all quiet. Wouldn't look me in the eye. I wondered what I'd done, but thought better than to ask. After a few more drinks, I was just after coming out of the toilet, and the girl was waiting outside. I went to walk past her, thinking she was waiting to use it... But she grabbed me. Pulled me into a bedroom. She sat me down and asked to talk. She told me there were rumours... That... That her auntie had been murdered. And that Dad killed her."

Cathal stares at the kitten coaster, unable to bring himself to say anything. How can he talk to his sister about something like this?

"And it made me think of Mum... And your mum... It's so similar. Like her auntie, she said she just went missing. One day she was here, the next sh-"

"I don't want you hanging around with girls like that. Putting stupid thoughts like that inside your he-"

"But they aren't stupid thoughts, are they? She recognised my name, my *surname,* and she knew right away who I was. I've noticed it before. Subtle looks from other people... It's because of him. What did he do, Cathal? Please, just tell me the truth."

Cathal blows out, rubbing his knuckle against his temple aggressively. He has to protect her. He can't have her finding out what he knows.

"Orla, you know as well as I do... It's all balls. It's just rumours. Because he up and left. You know around these parts people do it all the time. Sure, there are rumours about them running around with the wrong people. Or getting into trouble with Ardóimid. Or drugs. Or money... There are endless amount of opti-"

"But, Dad, Cathal? Why did Dad leave?"

They stare at each other solemnly for several seconds before Cathal clears his throat and looks down at his picked nails.

"I don't know."

The three words hang in the air before Orla stands and walks out. Ten minutes later, Cathal finally brings himself to follow her, intent on going to bed, before he walks out to see a bag waiting by the front door. He follows the scrambling noises coming from Orla's room, and looks in to see her bottom half hanging out from under her bed. He observes her for several more seconds, until she slides back out with an armful of shoes, none of which even match. Mascara lines streak down her face, and she avoids his stare as she drops the collection into another bag.

"Orla... What are you doing?"

She tenses, but doesn't answer him. After grabbing a handful of underwear from her top drawer and shoving them in the same bag, she hitches it up and pushes past him.

"I'll get the rest later," she groans as she picks up the second bag by the door.

"What are you doing? Where are you going?"

"I don't know... I'll stay at a friend's... I'll figure something out."

"Orla, don't leave. You don't have t-"

"No, I do, Cathal," she finally turns to him, eyes glistening, her body in the plastic archway as she opens the door, "I'm not staying here a moment longer whilst you shut me out. When you finally feel like you can tell me what's been bothering you for the past few years, then call me. But until then, I'm sick of being trapped in this house, with his ghost around every corner."

She stops and observes him, but he just continues to stare at the skirting board to her left.

"Have a nice life," she tuts, before turning and closing the door with a click behind her, leaving him in complete silence.

Chapter Eighty-Seven:

"It's over."

Michelle and Nuala gasp, almost squealing aloud, as they turn to hug each other, fresh tears streaming down their eyes. Danielle and Ritchie, however, stare straight in front. Towards their father's coffin. Deep in thought. Finally, Ritchie turns towards his sisters, as his mother makes a big performance of going to fetch tea for DI McNally and DS Ferguson, but neither of them will even glance his way. Danielle coughs and thanks the detectives, wiping a crocodile tear from her right eye. That's when McNally's phone goes. Excusing himself, he steps out into the front garden, a triumphant smile creeping over his face when he sees it's Dawson.

"Sorry it took me so long to get back to you, son. We were at the beach all day and my phone was back in the flat."

McNally shakes his head and chuckles. Oh, how the other half live.

"No problem, sir... I mean, Donald... Dawson? Where in the world have you ended up now?"

"We still have to agree on what to call one another by the sounds of things," Dawson chuckles, "we've ended up in Torremolinos, you're bound to have heard of there."

"That one I have heard of," he smirks, "but what happened to *'off the beaten track?'*"

"Oh, give us a break, McNally, we're taking a holiday from all that," he can hear the smile in his former DI's voice.

"Your life's a holiday, sir."

They share a laugh once more before Dawson asks to be caught up in McNally's investigation. Like Quigley earlier, he sits and listens attentively as McNally does laps of the front yard.

"And what's going to happen to Quigley?" Dawson asks once McNally has finished.

"I don't know," McNally physically shrugs, "I can't imagine anything good."

"Might be different to English policing over there," Dawson's tinny voice rings out over the handset, "but I'd say he might get a hefty fine. And disgraced internally within the police. And that's a best-case scenario. The worst is being dragged through the courts and prison on obstruction charges."

McNally nods, staring out onto the quiet main road, wishing he could've saved Quigley from himself.

"And Sargent?"

"What about him, sir?"

"Do you believe him?"

"I have no reason not to, sir. He's given sufficient evidence, evidence that wasn't available for the general public. How else would he know how he was killed, and by what weapon?"

"Hmmm," Dawson moves the phone around.

"Sir?"

"So you don't think he's maybe doing this just to get the underground organisation off his back?"

"Well... In a way, yes, but not in the way you think... He's obviously guilty, and that's why the Jacks tried to go after him. They didn't want Taylor taking the blame for his crime."

Dawson doesn't sound convinced.

"Well, I'm sure time will tell... Until then, let's see if he pleads guilty in court."

"Yes, sir."

McNally frowns. Is he doubting him?

"And anyway, what about the woman?"

McNally's initial annoyance is lifted as he smiles, remembering the text he'd sent Niamh just a half hour ago.

"We're going out for dinner on Wednesday night."

Dawson whistles down the phone.

"Romeo, Romeo."

"Fuck off," McNally laughs, before turning and seeing the family through the living room window, looking at each other defeatedly. "Look, sir, I have to go. The investigation may be over, but there's still a few pieces to be picked up."

"Of course, stay in touch, son. And good job, you're making a great asset over there."

Chapter Eighty-Eight:

Pulling at the wrinkled white shirt, trying to tuck it into his straining trousers, Ritchie looks at himself in the mirror. The muffin top leaking over his belt. The black tie he'd picked from Primark only days ago. The dark rings under his eyes. Today's the day. The day they bury his father. He never thought he'd see it. He believed if there was a day that he'd be behind bars. Unable to attend.

But when the two detectives arrived last night, giving them the news that Victor Sargent had confessed to their father's murder, everything seemed to stop. Go in slow motion. Is it possible... They did it? Got away with killing someone? With hiding and obstructing evidence? You'd think he'd be happy, but somehow... He feels worse. The thought of hard single mattresses and iron locks dispersed. Instead, replaced with freedom. But at a cost. Freedom, but feeling like this forever. Feeling this way... Will he ever feel better? He always thought confessing would lift the weight, but, if anything, he feels hollower.

"Ritchie, c'mon, we're going to be late."

He nods towards his reflection, trying not to look himself in the eyes, before crossing the landing and descending the stairs. He's met with his mum and sisters at the bottom, looking up at him with sombre faces. Granny sticks her arthritic fingers through the spindles and starts brushing hairs and fluff off his bum, muttering about how handsome he looks. The doorbell goes then, and McNally and Ferguson march into the already cramped hall through the open door, shortly followed by Dermott.

"Everyone is looking well," McNally's eyes shine as he looks around at them all. "I'm so sorry to delay the inevitable, I'm sure it's been a long time coming. But I'm afraid we have some more news..."

The family stare at them, transfixed. Their black suits making them look no different to the rest of the mourners, but somehow more elite with this new information they have hanging over their heads.

"Victor Sargent has been officially charged for the murder of your father, and we're reassured that he will plead guilty in court."

Danielle feels Ritchie's eyes glaring into the side of her head, but still she ignores him. She won't give away anything. Especially around the detectives. It's too dangerous.

"Thank you for letting us know," Nuala nods, before clipping over to the front door in her kitten heels, "the bastard has taken enough away from us, so we won't let him take away bidding Aaron farewell. Care to join us?"

The detectives nod as they're all led out to the hearse, Nuala standing at the door, ready to close it behind her and her children, before she stops Ritchie, who is avoiding her eye. She turns his head to make him look at her and smiles sweetly, tears collecting once more. Does she know? He narrows his eyes, as if being able to telepathically ask her, before she gives a subtle nod and pulls him in for a hug. What's going on? She drags herself away and wipes her nose with a hankie, grabbing his hand and trying to slog him out. But he can't move. It's like he's cemented to the spot.

He starts shaking uncontrollably, unable to breathe. His mum turns around, concerned, before reaching for him before he falls to the ground. Lying on the wooden floor in the hall, he tries desperately to catch his breath, ignoring his mum's pleading and screaming. He's aware of more people around him, overwhelming him, spilling in from outside. He needs to get up. He needs to go to his own father's funeral. He needs to act like he's in control.

But every fibre of his being is screaming at him to get out. Run. Don't look back. Get away from these people who could easily convict him. They roll him over and he looks up at the light beating down on him from the skylight at the top of the stairs. Ignoring the faces sliding in and out of view, he focuses on the light as the darkness creeps in.

Epilogue:

Pulling up outside Steph's house, I slam the door and hurry in from the rain. Wiping my feet on the door mat, I shout out that I'm home, but she must still be at work. I check my watch; she'll be running late. Climbing the stairs, I strip off and hop into the shower, feeling the water crash over me. Only then do I allow my thoughts to overtake me.

What was I thinking? Visiting his grave... How would that make me feel any better? I didn't even attend his funeral. I couldn't bring myself to. I sat at home with DS Ferguson, who brought me too-sweet-tea and toast lathered in jam. Saying he's funny with funerals too. That he laughed at his grandad's dead body lying in the coffin when he was 16 years old. Trying to console me. Not having a clue what my main reasoning for missing his funeral was.

Everyone came back and tiptoed on eggshells around me. Even my friends were funny, staring at me like I was going to burst into flames at any moment. My sisters wouldn't meet my eye. Neither would my mother. She bustled about, draining herself out by serving tea and biscuits, before Dermott forced her to take a seat beside Cathal, who was actually a nice guy. Sparking my guilt even more.

When I could finally bring myself to stand, I got up and packed a bag whilst I listened to the idle chatter downstairs. Sneaking out the back door, I marched around the side of the house, wondering what to do. I couldn't go back to Cardiff. I had missed my flight back, and didn't have the money to either buy a new one or even afford my rent over there. As I rounded the street, I saw a familiar face peering out of a VW Beetle. Rolling down the window, Steph peeked her head out and smiled at me.

She took me home that night. We cried and clung to each other. I didn't tell her everything that happened. How could I? I used her... I still am, six months later. But I've made a better life for myself. She made me see a counsellor, got me set up with a job in her father's business and has been letting me live here rent free. Her daddy bought her the house, so all she pays is bills. I try to buy the groceries as much as I can to show I'm grateful, but nothing I can do will ever be able to repay her for turning my life around.

Taylor was ultimately released without charge, despite unlawful imprisonment of Da. It seems with everything that went on outside the Crown, they were too afraid to take things further. Worried at the prospect of another civil war outbreak. Sargent, however, never made it to plead guilty in court. He died in police custody; that's all the media could tell us. Of course, rumours circulated that he was attacked in jail by another inmate, but you don't know who to believe. I haven't been able to speak to Dermott to find out whether any of it is true. I still don't know why the man pleaded guilty. It seems a life in prison seemed more favourable to a life hiding from the Jacks. I'm guessing one of them finally got to him anyway. The guilt I'll feel that an innocent man died whilst being inside for my crime will eat at me for the rest of my life.

I've still not spoken with my family since that night. They know... And Ma must've definitely overheard, and Danielle thinks that Dermott did too. But if he did, then why didn't he turn us in? Loyalties with us? Softness in his old age or retirement? We're not sure, but we didn't even discuss it. Just a wary look between us that night. Even after finding out that Sargent had confessed... She just wouldn't acknowledge it. Like she was able to wipe the slate clean.

None of them have attempted contact with me. Nor me with them. I think it's just the way it has to be. Maybe years down the line... Something could turn us around. But until then, we're better off without one another. I already ripped the family apart once before; I might as well take myself out of the equation too.

Under Construction

Bradd Chambers

Bradd Chambers grew up on the outskirts of Derry~Londonderry in Northern Ireland. From a young age, he started reading and writing stories. He exceeded in English at school, and went on to obtain an NCTJ Diploma in Journalism at his local college, before graduating with a 2:1 in the same subject from Liverpool John Moores University. He has studied Creative Writing for years at colleges around the UK. He currently writes for several online magazines. Bradd's debut novel *'Someone Else's Life'* was released in June 2017, with the prequel novella, *'Our Jilly,'* following in November of the same year. *'In Too Deep,'* a book centring on suicide and mental health in his hometown was released in February 2019. *'Daddy's Little Girl'* followed almost a year later. He is currently thriving on bringing Liam McNally back onto the scene, with a few standalones also in the pipeline.

"Thank you so much for taking the time to read my stories and helping to make my dream of becoming an author possible. If you enjoyed 'Under Construction,' *or any other of my books, please don't forget to spread the word through word of mouth and/or social media. Also, a review on Amazon or Goodreads goes an awful long way, especially for Indie authors like myself who a lot of people haven't heard of."*

@braddchambers

Printed in Poland
by Amazon Fulfillment
Poland Sp. z o.o., Wrocław